I0691226

Hesitant Desire

The Desire Series book 5

BARBARA DONLON BRADLEY

HESITANT DESIRE
Copyright © 2023 by Barbara Donlon Bradley

ISBN: 979-8-88653-207-4

Published by Satin Romance
An Imprint of Melange Books, LLC
White Bear Lake, MN 55110
www.satinromance.com

Names, characters, and incidents depicted in this book are products of the
author's imagination or are used fictitiously. Any resemblance to actual
events, locales, organizations, or persons, living or dead, is entirely
coincidental and beyond the intent of the author or the publisher. No part
of this book may be reproduced or transmitted in any form or by any
means, electronic or mechanical, including photocopying, recording, or by
any information storage and retrieval system, without permission in
writing from the publisher except for the use of brief quotations in a book
review or scholarly journal.

Published in the United States of America.

Cover Design by Ashley Redbird Designs

To my readers,

This story came out of the characters' desire to let you see a different side of them. It steps away from my overall plot, but I hope you enjoy it as much as I enjoyed writing it.

Barbara Donlon Bradley

WHO'S WHO IN THE SERIES

Although each book is a stand-alone book, there are returning characters and I felt a little of their history might come in handy.

Heather – One of the main characters of the series, was raised on earth and a member of Earth's military. In the first book she was assigned to guard Storm, ambassador of Vespia. She ended up mating with Storm and they have three children. The twins, who will be named a year after their birth, and Samantha who was genetically aged. When Heather and Storm mated a protective devise in her back started to break down, allowing her true abilities to develop. Heather learned she was genetically engineered after the devise was gone and certain abilities appeared. As her mind started to expand, she learned she could read thoughts. Heather and Storm have a special bond that allows them to speak to each other mentally. She can also speak to her children the same way.

Storm – One of the main characters of the series. He's the ambassador of Vespia he's also the heir apparent of his planet and head of planetary security. Although the thought of Heather protecting him was laughable, he found her intriguing. Vespians are over seven feet tall and even though Heather is tall at six-foot three Storm towers over her and makes her look petite. After Storm mated with Heather, he gained the ability to shape-shift. He is overly protective of Heather and their children.

Admiral Barrister – Heather's commander and friend. He was the one person who was there when she was young and watched over her as she grew and started working for the UCE, short for the United Countries of Earth. Heather's nickname for the admiral is Bear.

Kuarto – His story was book two. He is Heather's brother. Although Heather is genetically engineered, she was placed in the womb of one of the pregnant Vespian women and grew in that woman's womb. He didn't know he had a sister until her mind reached out to him. Like Heather Kuarto was removed from Vespia at a young age and raised by another race. He is a galaxy famous doctor who was hiding from those who wanted to exploit his talent until Storm and Heather went looking for him.

Fridon – he is being trained by Storm to be his second in command. The first time we meet Fridon is in book one. He is the soldier that is shot during the exercise where the android tries to kidnap Heather. He does show up in other books, but you really get to know him in this book.

Micali – this book is the first time you meet her.

ONE

Heather had a few minutes before she needed to get to council chambers for the afternoon and was taking advantage to play with her children.

"There is a communiqué from Admiral Barrister."

"Thank you, Cim." After picking up her daughter and putting her in the play area that Storm had created for the twins, she went for her son. Once she had them settled, she returned to the living room. "Go ahead and put Bear on the main screen."

"Good morning, Commander."

"How are you, Admiral?" He was awfully formal. Why did he call her commander?

"We need your help."

"You don't mess around, do you, sir." Great, another assignment. She had tried to leave security several times, but Earth wouldn't take her resignation. She sat on the couch.

"Time is of the essence." He looked off-screen for a moment and nodded before he focused back on her. "The daughter of the ambassador from Basuya has been kidnapped and only your expertise will work."

"You know Vespian protocol, sir. You have to ask the ambassador before you can even approach me."

"I know that, and he has given his permission as long as he gets to accompany you."

She smiled. Her mate always sought to protect her. "What do you need?"

"The ambassador and his family were learning about Aruka."

"Oh, no thank you." She didn't want to hear anything else. The last time she had been on that planet she came close to spending the rest of her life as a slave and swore she would never go back.

"You are an officer of Earth's military. You don't get to refuse."

"Yes, sir. Sorry, sir." From his tone, she knew better than to say anything else.

Bear steepled his fingers as he chose his next words. "Heather, you know the native language, have more personal knowledge of their society's dos and don'ts, and firsthand knowledge of the land. I don't have anyone else I can send, and we must get her back as quickly as we can."

"Permission to speak freely, sir?"

"Granted."

"Let me guess." Heather pinched her nose. Anger filled her as she realized she couldn't say no. "You're trying to sign a treaty with them and getting the daughter back will make sure that happens."

"When can you leave?" He didn't answer her question, so she had to be right.

"How come I seem to be the one you turn to when you need to make sure treaties are getting signed all of the sudden?" She muttered the words to herself but knew Bear heard her. Heather sighed as the data stream on the young woman she was to find filled the screen. "What do you know?"

"Not a lot right now. I have included your old file as well as everything you need for this mission. Storm has the same file."

"Oh, great." Now her mate would learn about one of her not so great missions. The only good thing about it was he could say no after he read what happened to her.

"I have explained to Storm that I need you to leave as soon as possible. She has been missing three days."

"Three days?" Her eyes widened. A couple of hours were all a kidnapper needed on that planet. Three days would leave them with a very cold trail to follow. She stood, knowing every minute she wasted could mean failure in finding the girl. "I'll send a message when we're on our way."

She ended the communiqué and walked into the play-room to look at the twins. Their naming ceremony was just a few days away. Would the council allow them to postpone it? "You know I love you two very much."

"Yes, mama." Her son toddled over and hugged her leg.

"I need to go help someone's little girl make it back home." She leaned down to pick him up. "Goodness, you're getting heavy."

"I help."

"And you will. You need to take care of your sister and listen to your uncle and aunt. No more grabbing his nose." She touched his with gentle fingers.

Her son's bottom lips poked out.

"He wants to protect your sister as much as you do. That is why he goes to her first. You need to let him know you want to be picked up first and he'll realize he's favoring your sister without knowing it." Heather stooped to pick up her daughter as well when the doors opened.

"You really do like trying to get yourself into trouble. You know they are too big for you to pick them up like that anymore, yet I catch you continuing to try." He took their son out of her arms so she could pick up her daughter. He then offered her his hand so she could stand without too much of a problem. "Old habits die hard, don't they?"

"Read the file already I see." She brushed a few hairs out of her face, waiting for him to chastise her.

"You're still my heart."

"Yeah." She never wanted to think about that assignment again, yet here it was, rearing its ugly head. "I knew you'd be happy to see how bad that got before I was able to turn it around."

"I now see why Bear feels you are the best." He headed toward the doors and waited outside for her to join him. "Anyone else would have ended up dead. Including me. You did what you had to do to get the job done."

"I lost control."

"Why do you say that?"

"I was a woman. When I first arrived the people who pretended to buy me wanted to brand me which I fought. Then I broke the number one rule and fought with a man." Did he read the whole file? She had made mistake after mistake on that planet and had never forgotten about it. Heather moved down the hall, holding her daughter close. "Have you spoken to the council?"

"Informally. I spoke to my mother who contacted the rest of the council, and they understand. The decision is ours."

"Great." She had hoped someone would say no, but so far nothing was going to stop her from reliving something she'd rather leave in the past. "You know I don't want to do this."

"But you won't leave that girl to be trapped on that world."

He knew her too well. The thought of what the girl would go through if she didn't try to bring her home drove her to face her demons. She walked into the medlab with Storm on her heels. "Kuarto."

"Heather? They're not sick. I just saw them, so why are you here?" His voice held an annoyed tone. He had complained before that she worried too much about the health of the twins.

"I know, and I promise I didn't bring them here for another check-up. I need a favor. Can you and Toki babysit for a few days?" She placed her daughter in the crib he had set up for the twins. "Earth's government has asked us to go on a mission and we need to leave immediately."

"What about the naming ceremony?" His frown showed his confusion.

"Storm has spoken to his mother, and she understands. The one thing we need to do is formally approach the council and ask permission, but we already know they're going to say yes. Can you ask Toki if she could postpone it for a few days? We'd really appreciate it." She touched her daughter on the head, not wanting to leave her or their son, but she knew she had to do this.

"Then Storm is going with you." Kuarto looked at Storm for answers before he reached for their son.

"Yes." Storm patted his son on the head as he settled in his mate's brother's arms. "So we're relying on you and Toki to care for these two until we get back."

"That won't be a problem. You know that." He kissed their son on the head before he set him down next to his sister. "Can I help you with anything?"

"We're going to need some physical alterations to fit into Arukan society," said Heather. She fought hard to keep her anger and frustration inside. She knew she was focusing on the task at hand instead of her brother's curiosity, but if she wasn't careful, she just might lose the tight hold she had on her emotions.

"Arukan? Have you been there?" He grabbed his scanner plus his pad and walked to the computer to pull up a three-dimensional image of Heather and Storm.

"I have." She kept her features under tight control, trying not to show how the memory of the place made her feel.

"So you know how women are treated there."

All she could do was nod.

"Anyone else going with you two?" Kuarto looked at Heather for a moment before he started to alter their images to get the desired look for the race there. He never missed a thing, and she wondered what he suspected. He didn't ask her anything else as he used his pad, the screen, and their images to get what he wanted.

"Fridon will be coming as well." Heather couldn't keep the flatness out of her voice.

Kuarto nodded and loaded his image as well. "You realize you're all a little tall for this race."

"Yes." Heather hated this. The last time she was on this planet her height had been one of the reasons she was so coveted. That and her hair. No one on the planet has such light hair. Then there was the length. The shortness of it made them think she had been punished by her master and then sent away because whatever she had done had been so bad, he never wanted to see her again. It made her a target for many reasons and now she had to go back and face that reality again. "We'll have to work around that."

"And women are second-class citizens with no power?" He watched her face as he brought up the subject again.

"I am all too aware of my status there." She refused to rise to the bait as she watched him make the changes. Her fair skin turned golden with the sparkle the people from the planet had. They all looked like they had glitter on them from the way their skin sparkled in all types of light. "Can you make that stick?"

"Let me guess, the last time you went there you went just as you are."

"Earth doctors couldn't change my skin tone and hair color. My chip didn't allow it."

"Well, we have the ancient computer who knows your DNA so we should be able to make the proper changes." Kuarto circled her image, bobbing her ears so they came to a point like the people from the planet. Then he changed her hair color. "One down, two to go." Now that he had made the changes to her image all he had to do was press a button for Storm's and Fridon's images to switch. In an instant they all looked like the natives.

"I'm going down to the main compound to work on our outfits." Heather headed out the door. Kuarto had what he needed to get them physically ready, now it was her turn to make sure their clothing fit as well.

———

"She seems very upset about this," Kuarto commented as he continued to work on their images, perfecting their looks. "Can I assume the last time she was there it didn't go well for her?"

"Not the way she wanted, but she still had a successful mission." Storm pointed to the images. "How long before you're done?"

"I should have a chip to implant in about fifteen minutes."

"Good. I'm going to see what I can do to calm my mate." Storm strode out of the medlab and headed to the ancient complex. Using his implant, he contacted Fridon and made him aware of the mission and let him know he had to visit the medlab to get the changes necessary for the mission to be a success. When he entered the lab, he saw another three-dimensional image of the three of them all lined up as Heather worked on the outfits. His and Fridon's outfits were pretty nondescript. Tunics and flowing pants. Typical for an arid planet like the one they were going to. "My heart?"

She turned to look at him. "I hate this, Storm. Women have no power. They aren't allowed to speak to men unless spoken to. They can't own any property. Most women are the slaves of the family. There for breeding and doing all the work."

"The men don't do any of the work?"

"None of the labor. That is left to the women." She pressed a button and worked on the intricate details of the garments. "The admiral has set up our identities already. You are a man of wealth and power. I am your most prized possession."

"That much is true." He stepped up to her and touched her cheek. "You will not be alone on this mission."

"I know, but it's the memories that get the best of me." She pressed her face into his hand.

"Do you wish to talk about it?" He could feel her distress over this mission, but nothing else. She had locked everything else deep inside.

"No." She gave him a smile, but he could see the sadness in her eyes. "Maybe when this mission is over I will, but right now I'm not ready. It's something I had tried to forget. I need to come to terms before I can tell you anything."

"What are you doing now?" He turned back toward the images, knowing it was time to change the subject.

"Making sure our garments are ready. Men of power have a brand or mark that adorns their clothing. It is also on all their possessions." She tapped her pad. "What would you like as a brand?"

"How about this?" He lifted her hair and gently brushed her mark. "No one can deny that you are mine if it is on my clothes."

Her smile was more genuine. "It also might keep them from branding me with your mark if I already have one." She put the pattern on his and Fridon's garment. Once she was happy with the image, she made several other outfits so they would have the proper garments to change to when they had to.

Storm watched as she brought up her image. Her Vespian gown disappeared and was replaced with an outfit he swore was appropriate only for the bedroom. "That is what you must wear?"

She nodded.

"My heart, my eyes will be glowing the whole time we're on that planet." The two-piece dress left a lot of skin exposed. The bejeweled top had demicups that he was sure wouldn't contain Heather's breasts for long and the skirt sat so low on her hips he wondered how it stayed up.

She gave him a fleeting smile then worked on the image, putting the mark on her outfit as well. There was a band at the top of the skirt about six inches wide made out of the same thin material as his and Fridon's clothes, then a border of it on the bottom. Everything in between was a thin transparent material. There was also a thin strip of cloth that held his mark halfway down her upper arm, but he didn't see any other straps that would keep her top on.

"Can I see you in that?" If she had that on all the time, he wasn't sure he could keep his hands to himself.

"Storm." She didn't want to have that awful outfit on before she had to.

"My heart, if just this image is making my desire for you

skyrocket, then I need to see what the real thing is going to do. I need to be able to control myself."

That got a laugh out of her. "You have never tried before."

"I can't help that your luscious body calls to me, begging for my touch." He grinned as he pulled her into his embrace.

"I know your one-track mind and there is a lot to do. I need to show you how to use my chain."

"You'll have my undivided attention in that." He looked at the image once again. "I know you see the outfit as degrading. What better way to wipe that feeling from you then to have me worship your body while wearing it."

"So you think it will empower me?"

"Has in the past." His need for her was getting stronger by the second. "One wonderful memory to burn away the others."

She closed her eyes for a moment, probably talking to the ancient computer. Her dress disappeared to be replaced with the outfit she hated so much.

She took his breath away. His hands had to touch her. They gently followed the edge of the small top, causing goosebumps to rise where his fingers had been. Sliding along the edge of the skirt, his touch caused her to take a sharp intake of breath. It was one of her more sensitive spots. He noticed a small gold chain around her waist. A long length of it fell to the floor.

"What is this?" He picked it up. The lightweight material didn't look like it would take much abuse.

"My chain."

"Excuse me?" He heard the flatness of her voice. It angered her. Another thing she resented. His libido needed to wait so he could find out why.

"Like a pet, I have a leach that you control."

He was starting to understand why she hated this so

much. To treat women in such a way went against his beliefs as well. "And you must wear it?"

"And you need to know how to use it to control me."

"I have never been able to do that," he joked as he continued to slide his hands over her soft skin. Time to defuse the strong anger she felt.

"Storm." She stopped him then placed the end of the chain in his hands. "It's all in the flick of the wrist." She made a few movements to show him what she was talking about. "My place is behind you as we walk. If you wish to stop, you drop your hand to signal me." She showed him what she meant. She went through several other movements.

"And what if I wish to show you affection?"

"I don't know." She looked sad. "I never saw any of the men show affection to their women. But I do know some of the commands for different sexual poses."

"Perhaps I need to make a few of my own commands." He started drawing the chain to him, so she had to step closer. "Like when I want to kiss you, I'll just drag you to my side." He lowered his mouth to hers, drawing her tongue out to dance with his. Tension flowed out of her.

He knew he needed to tread lightly with her. She needed to be in control the whole time. With a thought he produced their favorite chair. Another thought removed his clothes. Breaking the kiss, he stepped back and waited.

She stared at him.

"You tell me what you want."

Heather hesitated for a moment then shook her head as if she was shaking the last of the bad memories away. "Climb on the chair."

He didn't waste any time.

"And put it in our favorite position."

"We have several of those, my heart. Any particular one?"

"Hmmm." She placed her hands on her hips and gave him a sultry smile. "I'll let you pick that."

One click of a button and he had the chair in a position she recognized. He watched as she sashayed toward him, the sway of her hips hypnotizing him. "You are so beautiful."

"You are biased." She climbed up on the chair and placed her feet on the railings on each side.

"I am." He smiled up at her. This was one of the few times when she was taller than him. Her long skirt brushed against his thighs as she looked down at him. "But it doesn't make my statement any less true."

"You are so good for me." She got down on her knees. "I'm going to need a little help. My skirt is too big so I can't help guide you."

He helped center her and closed his eyes as her tight sheath slid down his length. The heat of her body as it surrounded him fired his desire. His hands had a mind of their own as they skimmed across her hips and stomach, moving up to her breasts. They felt their way around the bra top, trying to find the closure. "How does this come off?"

"There are releases on each side, but I want to warn you..."

The weight of the top smacked him in the stomach, drawing a woof out of him. He held out the heavy thing. "How does this thing stay up?"

"I don't know, but it seems to defy gravity." She braced her hands against his stomach. "The skirt is the same way. It doesn't move off the hips even though it looks like it could."

He dropped the top onto the floor so he could focus on her. He gently cupped her breasts, playing with her nipples as she set the pace. She arched into his hands while she slid up and down his shaft. Knowing her body as well as he knew his own, he knew what aroused her, what brought her to the edge and what pushed her over. He rubbed his knuckles against the peaks before his hands continued to caress her velvet skin. The tips of his fingers skirted the edge of the waistband of the skirt, dipping in and brushing the edge of her mound, taking her breath away.

Her muscles tightened against him, and she started riding him harder. Storm moved his hands to her legs, finding their way under the full skirt, feather-like touches working their way up the back of her calf, the inside of her thigh, until his fingers reached their target and slipped into her folds. Time to bring her to the edge. She reacted to his touch. Her head dropped back as her breath came out in little pants.

"My heart." He watched her face, keeping his hand between them, working her softly, slowly bringing her closer and closer. Gently he wrapped his hand around her neck, drawing her down until he could feel her breasts against his chest, allowing his lips to make contact with her mark. His lips tugged lightly on the soft tissue, and she shattered in his arms.

"That is what you do to me while you wear that outfit." His voice was a whisper as she floated along through her climax. She was quiet for a few moments, waiting for her body to return from her release. Then her eyes opened, and she gave him a satisfied smile.

"My heart." She touched his face. "You are so good for my ego."

———

Proper protocol said she needed to go to the council and explain what Earth wanted from her. As a member of the council and the mate of the future leader, anything that took her off planet, or away from the council, had to be cleared. They gave their approval quickly. Storm had gone with her and stayed to clear his joining her on this mission as well.

She went back to the outfits. The fashions hadn't changed that much since she was there last, but she made sure she made the subtle changes, so they didn't look dated. Her outfits were the last thing she worked on. The low hip and tiny top exposed so much. The last time she had to wear it brought attention to her in a way she didn't want, and she had fought it all the way. Yet after her mate's reaction to the outfit and the tenderness he showed her, she knew he was right. Knowing Storm would be there and how it aroused him gave her the confidence she needed to do this.

Next, she focused on the information Bear sent. There was a lot of data. Hopefully, she'd find what she needed to pick up a trail to follow.

———

Heather strode into the medlab, a cloak over her mission outfit. She didn't want to be gawked at until it was necessary. Storm and Fridon were already there, wearing their costumes, their chips in place. Seeing Storm with pointed ears brought a smile to her face. "Good work, Kuarto. Hope you can work the same magic with me."

"I'm going to put the first one in your hairline." He gestured for her to lift her hair off the back of her neck, and he inserted the chip. Pressing a few keys on his pad he worked with her hair color. "Your hair won't be as dark as the race that you're imitating but it won't be the white blonde you normally have either. More like a golden brown."

Heather turned and looked at the mirror Kuarto had.

Her hair was now a light brown with gold highlights. "Wow. I look so different."

"Now for the skin tone." He pulled aside the cloak and inserted the next chip against her right pelvic bone. "Depending on how this works I might need to put a second one in."

"Whatever it takes." She looked at Storm who seemed to be frowning. "What is the matter?"

"I'm not sure I like that hair color on you." His eyes widened when her fair skin darkened to a golden honey color. "You look so different, yet exotic."

"Kuarto, you are amazing. What about my eyes?"

"I've tried several times, but I can't alter their color. I can give you contacts."

"They don't work either. My eyes have always been too sensitive for them. At least I'll fit in a little better this time." She lifted her feet. "Need to do something about this though."

"Right." Kuarto handed her two jewels to decorate her feet. "I've been working on that. Attach those to the juncture next to the big toe and press it."

"I'm not sure I understand," Storm said.

"I'm not allowed to wear any footwear. The women there are used to it and can walk in the sand and hard rocks, but my feet are too tender for that." She bent down and placed the jewels on her feet. Pressing each one, she felt something cover everything up to her ankles. Heather looked up at Kuarto and grinned.

"It's a force field. About the only thing I thought would work since if you left any kind of shoe print behind there would be questions. I made you four. Each coordinating with the color outfit you might wear."

"Thanks." She turned to Storm and Fridon. "Ready?"

"Yes." Storm took her arm and headed to their transport.

"Although I'm not sure I like this place we're going. What else are you not allowed to do?"

"There is a lot." She let out a sigh. "I'm not allowed to eat with you. In fact, I can't eat until you and Fridon are done. If there is any food left over then I get to eat. If you attend any meals, you have to abide by this. I can't sit with you at any of the major functions unless I am to feed you."

They reached the ship. Heather waited as Storm lowered the gangplank.

"I can't ride any of the animals either. I must walk everywhere."

"That is ridiculous."

"I know, but it's their law." She took her seat and helped Storm prepare for liftoff. "I gave you the list. Did you read it?"

"I didn't get to the walking everywhere." Once the ship was out of orbit, he programmed the coordinates and set the autopilot on. "But if you are my most prized possession then why can't I set the rules for you?"

"You can. To a point. An example is like riding the horse. If I'm pleasuring you then I'm allowed, but that is only when we're alone. Men don't degrade themselves by letting their lust get to them while they are with other men."

"And how long must we be there?"

"We find the girl and get out as fast as possible."

———

Storm stepped onto the tarmac first. The heat was the first thing that hit him. He waited for Fridon and Heather to exit before he sealed the ship and sent it back into orbit. The computer would be his eyes and ears to make sure they were under surveillance while on the planet.

Their translators had been adjusted for the language on

the planet, but since the people here didn't use translators there would be a language gap until they could learn to speak it. Heather was the only one who was fluent, and she wasn't allowed to talk to men. He wasn't sure how this would work.

Their first stop was the embassy to check in. Heather had donned the hood on her cloak so no one would be able to see what gender was under the garment. She had kept the cloak on since she came into the medlab earlier. He was happy because he knew he'd be aroused the moment he saw her in the outfit. Storm strode in the door with Fridon on his heels. His mate came in last, already in character.

"May I help you?" The young man behind the desk didn't look up from the task he was doing.

"Yes." Storm's deep voice filled the room. "We have an appointment with the admiral."

"And your name?" He looked up then to find Storm glaring at him. Storm recognized the man. He was Bear's second. Heather called him an assistant. "Oh, ambass...ador? Um, he's been waiting for you." The doors to their right swung open.

Storm walked in the door, not happy with the situation. "Why are you making my..." He stopped his rant when he noticed Bear wasn't alone.

"Storm?" Bear laughed. The same fake one Heather had been known to use from time to time. He looked at Storm's ears and grinned. "Like the ears. Thank you for coming. I'd like to introduce you to the parents of the young woman taken."

He gave them a stiff nod.

"I must say you do look the part. So does Fridon." He looked at the garbed figure. "Heather? Can I assume you do too?"

"Yes, sir." She lowered the hood so the admiral could see her face.

"Wow. Then let's get down to it." He had been sitting with the girl's parents. Standing, he walked to his desk and picked up a small remote. "This is the young woman in question. She was in the garden of the home they were using here, off the embassy grounds. She was by herself when they heard her scream. By the time anyone made it outside, there was no sign of her. We did get this from the surveillance equipment."

An image filled the screen of the young girl, maybe sixteen, being grabbed by men in nondescript clothes.

Heather stared at the screen for a moment. "Can you play that again?"

She watched it several times before she sat next to the parents. "Was your daughter speaking to any of the local boys?"

"One or two," the father replied. "You can't be saying that she was taken by one of them."

"These people don't think the way most do. Women are like an object you would trade or sell here. Someone could have seen your daughter as a potential present to a son of a wealthy family coming of age. Especially if he showed an interest in her. They could have taken her to gain favor with a wealthy family." She saw the stricken look on the mother's face. "I know this isn't what you want to hear, but it is the truth. I'm very good at my job, but I need all the information I can get to bring her home safely."

"There was one boy who kept calling on her," the mother responded.

Heather smiled. "Tell me everything."

———

"Heather, I was about ready to read you the riot act when you started talking to the parents the way you did, but you got the information we needed," Bear snapped at her.

"I'm sorry I had to do that, sir, but I knew it was the only way to make them think about anyone she might have talked to. Now we have three leads instead of a very cold trail." She stood, pulling the cape in front of her to keep her outfit concealed. "As you said, time is of the essence, and I want to make sure that girl comes home."

"Understood, Commander, but next time you better let me in on what you want to do beforehand, or I'll court-martial you."

"Considering my position in Earth's military is all on paper since they refused to retire me, your threat really doesn't have that much weight." She stood in a relaxed military stance. "You need me more than I need you, sir."

"Storm, I do believe you created a monster here." He sat back in his chair and laughed. This time, it sounded real. His relaxed state surprised Storm. Was Heather that good?

"You had a hand in her development as well." Storm wrapped an arm around her waist. "We need to talk seriously. No harm can come to my mate. I will kill the man who looks at her wrong."

"Which is why you are going with her. You will keep her safe. Too many things went wrong the last time. That can't happen again." Bear ran his fingers through his hair. "How much of the language do you know?"

"Heather has been teaching us, but the intricate levels of the language makes it difficult to learn very quickly. I know the most important sentences at all levels." He grinned. "I know the word 'mine', 'do not touch' and 'the woman speaks for me'. My mate also taught me a few swear words just in case I need them."

"And your translator?"

"The language has been loaded so I'll know everything spoken. Then the nuances of the language will download every night, and Heather will help us practice what is downloaded when we're traveling. We should be fluent quickly."

"I don't want to put you in this situation again, Heather. But as you told the parents, you are very good at your job. No harm meant, Storm, but if I could have, I would have put Heather and Skye together. They both have a knack at finding the people in jeopardy."

"Could Skye protect her better than me?" He still didn't like the man. It didn't matter if he was his daughter's mate.

"I didn't say that." Bear looked at Heather for a moment before focusing on Storm. "I guess that is still a sore subject for you. I have registered you two in the system. I need to load something to prove Heather is your property."

"Her mark." Storm pointed to his clothing. "She bears it as well."

Heather released the cord holding the cloak against her body and she dropped it so Bear could see her outfit and the proof of her mark on her clothes.

"Damn, Heather, I see working with Vespian security has done some wonderful things for you. You're no longer that skinny woman I knew. Your muscles never had such definition."

Her hand splayed across her abdomen. It took Storm's hands to pull hers away. "She has what you call a hard body, yes?"

"Yes, and that makes her more desirable to the men who will see her. Be warned, Storm. Your mate will turn a lot of heads." He stood. "The sooner you get started the sooner you're done."

Heather nodded. "If we have all the information available, we should get going."

Bear nodded.

She picked up her cape and handed Storm her leash.

"Wait." Bear looked at the chain and frowned. "How cherished a piece of property is she to you, Storm?"

"What kind of question is that?"

"The chain is too long."

"Admiral, I don't mean any disrespect, but many men like the chain long so they can wrap it around their own waist when in a crowd so their possession doesn't wander off. It is where they hold the leach that matters, and Storm has learned about that."

Bear checked his screen before he spoke. "Sorry, I had the wrong data."

"It's okay, Bear, but when you live it, you never forget." She took a deep breath and looked at Storm. "Let's go."

Storm nodded. He wasn't sure if he wanted to allow Heather to be put into danger once again, but they had promised. Making sure he had a good grip on her chain, he headed out the doors of Bear's office. They walked out of the embassy into the crowded street. The heat hit him first then the noise level. His sensitive ears had found it hard to ignore.

Heather stayed behind him, her distance based on the thin chain he held. Fridon had gone on ahead of them to secure the animals they would need for traveling. Once they were away from the town, he would breathe easier. He also hoped Heather would relax out of the confines of the city and the rules.

"You sell?" some young boy asked him, pointing to Heather.

"No." Storm wasn't sure if it was the right dialect, but he didn't care.

"How much?"

"You sell?"

"I buy."

Now he had three wanting to know if he'd be willing to part with his mate. Were they crazy? A growl escaped him. "No."

He took another two steps and there were two more about to ask him about Heather. Storm turned around, grabbed Heather by the waist and threw her over his shoulder. As he walked, he glared at anyone who started to approach him. He could hear his mate's laughter in his head.

This isn't funny, my heart. Why would they think I'd be willing to part with you?

I am property to them, and everyone has a price. The fact that you want to keep me close shows them I have value and they will try to see why. You don't even give them a chance to make an offer. That has their curiosity. What have I done to make you not want to sell me?

He shook his head. Fridon was only a few feet away with their animals. Along with two animals saddled for him and Fridon to ride, they also had several pack animals carrying tents and items they would need if they stopped for the night away from any town. And if this was the way all the men were going to behave around his mate, he didn't plan on stopping at too many of them.

Storm was stopped once again by someone wanting to buy his mate.

Ask him secudo demaliasent.

Storm repeated the words.

"I will offer thirty million secons and my master's current favorite." The young man looked at him with a hopeful smile.

Tell him senmareio efactinga.

What does that mean?

You'll think about it.

Heather.

It is only to give them something to think about. Make them believe you might sell for the right price.

How much is thirty million secons?

About the same in old earth dollars. Vespia doesn't have anything that I can show that would equal. Just be happy that it is a lot of money. They're not trying to insult you.

He caught up with Fridon, reluctantly set her on her feet and mounted his animal. "What is this?"

"They call them frulas. Like earth's horse." Fridon climbed on his mount as well. "They move about fifty clips an hour. If you are ready, we can head out."

"Who packed the animals?" asked Heather, her voice low. Storm could sense the touch of fear racing through her.

"They were like this when I arrived."

"Bear must have gotten them ready for us." Heather's shoulders relaxed as she walked to the animals and added the packs she had carried from the embassy. "Remember, Fridon, you are in training to learn Storm's trade. You're not to do any of the labor."

"I remember, Heather. As much as I disagree with it, I would never do anything to put you in danger."

"I'm sorry, Fridon." She kept her eyes downcast. "The crowd has me worrying about everything. The sooner we're out of here the happier I'll be."

"Then let's go, but make sure Heather can keep up." Storm looked at the surrounding crowd. He didn't like having all these strangers near his mate, knowing how easily they took the girl. "My mate will not be forced to run to keep pace with us. The moment we're out of sight I want her up on my mount."

"Yes, sir."

Fridon set an easy stride for the animals. Once they were

out of the view of the town, Storm circled back and offered his hand to Heather.

"Storm, I can't."

"You said the rules could be bent as long as it profited me. I want you up here. I don't care if you have to straddle me and give me pleasure the entire time, I will not allow my mate to walk when I am riding. So you either get up here or I will climb down off this animal and walk beside you." He reached for her again. "Your choice."

"I saw that spark enter your eyes when you said I could pleasure you the whole time." She took his hand and allowed him to pull her into his lap. Once she settled in the saddle with him, she worked herself around until she faced him. "Now we get to see how much torture you can take before your libido gets the best of you."

"My heart, when it comes to you, I have no control." He wrapped his arms around her, his hands sliding up and down her back.

"That isn't true, or we'd never get any work done." She wrapped her legs around him, pulling her body against his.

"You haven't read my mind enough, then. It is all I think about." His lips brushed against her mark. Too bad Fridon was with them, or he would show her just how much just being near her had him constantly wanting her.

TWO

"I know all about the one-track mind. I doubt you are any different from any other man." She adjusted herself until she was comfortable and stable on the animal. "And I know how much you enjoy sex."

Having her pressed up against him had him wishing they were in their rooms on Vespia. He'd have her moaning in minutes. "I find it interesting that you seem to enjoy how upset their attitude is making me."

"Your anger boosts my ego. I feel precious and special because you care so much." She touched his face. "These people don't know the joys of having someone that close. Nothing matters but what they can gain. They don't know love, joy, trust. I have all that with you."

"You are my mate." He rested his fingers against her mark. "No one shall disrespect that." He could feel only the thin barrier of his pants between them. "There is nothing under that strip of cloth about your hips that covers you?"

"No." She smiled at him, noting the glow in his eyes getting brighter. "Easy access for the men."

Fridon had been riding beside Storm, but when Heather

had joined her mate on the animal, he dropped back to give them privacy. Knowing Heather as well as he did, Fridon knew she was shy when it came to intimacy. He always showed proper respect to the mate of the future leader, and she was grateful he understood her little quirks.

"He is a very good man, Storm." A gentle breeze had Heather's hair dancing in front of her face.

"I know, but he's still very new at this." He helped her brush her hair out of the way. "The mission where he was wounded was his very first one. He has years of training ahead. You think I'm rough on him, but he understands and is proud to be training as my second."

"I know that. That's why he puts up with you."

"And I with him." Storm held a section of her hair out of her face. "So now that you have my undivided attention and Fridon has given us some privacy, what would you like to do?"

"We could talk."

"Okay, you can talk, and I will do my best to distract you." He lowered his head so his lips could cover her mark.

"Don't you always?" Her head tilted to give him better access.

Fridon caught up close enough for him to warn them they were about to have company. Heather quickly released her jeweled bra and threw it to him.

"Put that on the pummel of your saddle. They will know what it means." She pulled her skirt up so there wasn't any material trapped between them, then wrapped her arms around Storm's neck. "We have to make this look good, or you are going to wish you had let me walk."

"I don't understand some of these Earth phrases you use. You are stunning when you climax. You remember your picture? These men will see why I don't want to part with you." Storm touched her face, seeing the fear in her eyes.

26

He caught her mouth with his, his tongue delving and searching for hers. Her body was tense. As their tongues danced together, he felt her relax against him. In order for him to feel her skin against his, he had to break the kiss and pull his shirt off. Knowing Fridon was behind them, he dropped it on the ground. That should warn them to tread lightly when approaching them.

His lips left hers and they worked their way down to her mark. A sigh escaped her. Storm slid his fingers into her folds, massaging and teasing her, heightening her arousal. He didn't care about the rules. Heather needed to forget for a few moments. She sucked in her breath as he caressed her, her desire so strong now she didn't care who was watching them.

"Storm, I need you." She looked over his shoulder to see the approaching riders. Sadness filled her eyes. "But they are almost here."

"I don't care, you're my heart and I want to take that sadness out of your eyes." He touched her face, knowing her shyness and fear kept her from asking for what she needed. The other men had to be very close since they chose to ignore the signs of their intimacy. "So you want me to 'make it look good?'"

At her nod, he lifted her up. Anyone watching would think he was lifting her so he could enter her. The animals of the other men came a little too close, causing his animal to dance to the right. Still holding Heather up, he turned his animal to face them. He moved her off the saddle and dropped her to the ground. "Why are you so stupid to interrupt me at such a moment?"

Heather stood with her back to the men. Keeping her voice soft, she translated his words so they could understand what he said.

He heard them grumble something about how she

deserved to be beaten for speaking to them, and he charged at them. "The woman speaks for me!"

Having a huge man standing in the saddle, no shirt, all muscle, bearing down on them had them scattering. Storm gave them a satisfied smile. That should teach them to respect his desires. He knew Fridon had tried to warn them. Heather had worked with him as well and taught him what she felt he needed to know. "Explain to them that I will kill them if they make one more derogatory remark about you."

"My master takes offense that you question my value to him."

"Why doesn't he speak?" asked one of the men.

"We are from a long way, and he is still learning the dialect here. He can understand you."

"Every word?" The same man looked at him. Storm nodded. The translator gave him the men's words as well as Heather's.

"My father wishes to invite you to visit his home."

"Tell them no. Not after that." He wished she would look at him, but she was very good about staying in character.

We should ask what family he belongs to.

When Heather remained silent, the other men looked at each other. "My father is one of the richest men in the area."

Storm crossed his arms over his chest. He wasn't impressed.

"My master wants to know the name of your house. He is very particular with who he breaks any fast with."

Storm watched as the young man bristled.

"I belong to the house Cheteckan."

He recognized the name. It was one of the families that had a son coming of age. The young man in front of him was probably the boy in question. "Tell him yes, but I have some ground rules."

He's not the one to speak to. His father has last say. To even mention your demands to the boy will make you look weak.

"This is so stupid!" Anger lanced his words, making Heather cringe. He knew it was an act, but seeing it upset him.

"My master wishes to speak to your sire before he will stay, but he has decided to follow you." Her shoulders hunched as if the anger he felt was directed at her.

Fridon came up to them, handing Storm his shirt before dropping Heather's top in the dirt beside her. She slipped it back on and stepped behind Storm's mount. He led the three of them, following the young man back to his place.

Did you have to cringe? Storm was grateful for their mindlink. It saved them earlier.

Sorry, but it worked. They took my word and are leading us to the Cheteckan house. Now we can see if the girl is there. You realize we'll be here for several days, and I will be put with the women.

Not if I can help it. I am beginning to understand why this place frightens you. You could disappear while standing in a crowded room of women because no one would say a word or lift a hand to help you.

But if I don't go and spend some time with the women I can't ask about the girl. We need to see if she is there.

I don't like it, Heather.

The wealthier families are very honorable. They will do their damnedest to try to trade or buy what they consider valuable. Stealing is below them.

But the girl was stolen.

Yes, but it doesn't mean the boy's father ordered it. It could have been one of the lower families who kidnapped her and plan to offer her as a gift, hoping to gain favor with the higher family. We need to start with the wealthier families because she is the perfect gift.

You don't think she could have already been sold? Storm looked at their escorts.

No. She's been gone long enough that she could already be in the household and is being prepared for the boy, but I don't think that is the case. Each of the boys coming of age haven't had their banquets yet. Bear checked all the families once I got the mother to talk.

It took about a half an hour before they reached the large home. Storm was surprised to find the father out there to greet them.

He studied Storm and Fridon, not really paying much attention to Heather. Storm's height and shoulder width overshadowed any man there. His son stepped up and whispered to him before looking back at them once again. The young finished speaking and moved off.

"So you are our guest from Vespia."

Storm couldn't help but grin. He had wondered if anyone paid attention to the transport he had landed in the spacefield. So this man had contacts that informed him of the comings and goings of off-world visitors.

"And you don't speak the language yet can understand everything I say. Some sort of translator?" He now looked at Heather.

Storm nodded.

"And the female knows the language. Can I assume she is someone trained to help you blend in?"

"Yes. You don't seem to be surprised about any of this." Heather translated for him.

"I have family working at several of the embassies as well as the spacefield. It does come in handy at times. Have you come to study our planet? See if we are a planet you wish to sign a treaty with?"

"Maybe." He wasn't about to give out any information that would jeopardize their mission.

"I'm honored you have gone so far to fit in with our society." He gestured for Storm to follow him. He signaled another to take Fridon with him. "Many just show up and try to force their way of life on us. This is how we have lived for thousands of years. As backward as our world seems to the rest of you, we like it and don't plan on changing too much. We have no desire to go to space. But trade, who doesn't like to trade."

"And my man?"

"He has gone to ready your room for you." He looked back at Heather for a moment. "I will send the woman to you when it is time."

"She stays with me."

"No harm will come to her. I will guarantee that, but to keep her away from the other women will make her scorned by them."

"I don't care. She is under my protection."

"Which is why you never put your tunic back on." He gestured to his bare chest.

"I was rudely interrupted and wanted to make sure your son understood just what he interrupted."

"He got the message, but all you have done is pique his curiosity. He wants to know what makes her so special."

"Look at her."

"She is quite beautiful. Very exotic with her violet eyes and lighter hair. Very few of our women have that."

"And mine. I warn you now that if anyone tries to touch her, they will have to deal with me."

"I will spread the word that she is off limits." One of the men approached them. Behind him was one of the women. "Everything is ready."

"I must send your female with the others. She will be returned to you."

He didn't want to let her go, but knew he had to respect

31

their rules. It would give Heather a chance to find out if the young woman they were looking for was there. She could talk to the women, maybe get some answers. "I will hold you to that."

Heather was brought to the area where the women were kept when they weren't serving the men. As the door closed behind her, she found her way blocked.

"You don't belong here." The woman speaking had her arms crossed over her chest in a menacing manner as she kept Heather from taking another step.

"My master is a guest of yours." She looked at the woman who questioned her. Here she had to stand her ground. Most women didn't like a stranger joining. What if the new woman became the favorite?

"You belong to the big one?"

"Yes." Heather smiled. That probably made all the women happy. She was sure they were afraid of Storm because of his size.

The woman walked around her, studying her physique. "You have born him children."

"Two." Heather wasn't quite sure how she knew this. Everyone kept telling her she didn't look like she had given birth.

"Males?"

"One of each."

"Ha. Good. These men need to understand what it is like to have daughters." She stopped so she could look in Heather's eyes. "What about his servant?"

"I only care for my master."

"Ah. My name is Usatha. Come with me." She started walking, expecting Heather to follow. It was like dealing with Storm at times. "You will help him get ready for the meal this evening. I will instruct you on how my master wants this meal to happen."

Heather knew she had passed the interrogation. She hoped she could keep up with the instructions so she didn't show her lack of training and draw unwanted focus.

———

Storm paced the floor of the lavish room they gave him. The walls were gold and covered with unique tapestries. The floors were a hard wood covered with thick beautiful carpets of all different sizes and pillows of all shapes and sizes about the room for reclining. He did notice a lack of hard furniture, but he didn't care. He wanted Heather.

The doors to his room opened and a parade of women filed in. Not what he wanted. Ten of them pulled a few carpets aside to expose a wooden cover, which they lifted to reveal a large tub. Ten more came in carrying large urns filled with hot water. The steam from the liquid filled the room as they filled the tub up. One more woman came in carrying big fluffy cloths for drying. She set them on a pile of pillows near the tub. Once they were done, they all filed out the way they had come in. The last woman came in carrying a tray filled with bottles. The angle of the tray kept her face from him, and she wore a nondescript cloth over her outfit so he couldn't see any distinguishing marks. She sat the tray down just as the doors closed and turned around to face him.

"Heather." His heart leaped in his chest to know his mate was untouched and now standing in front of him. He closed the space between them and took her into his arms. He captured her lips with his, taking her breath away with the intensity.

She was the one who broke the kiss and stepped back. "I am here to prepare you for your bath, Master."

Why would she call him master unless there were listening devices? But she used the local language so she wanted to be heard. She gave him a smile and pointed to the doors. Shadows blocked the light that streamed in under them. The ladies were eavesdropping.

He saw the spark of mischief in her eyes. Wondering what she was up to, he went along. "Good."

She picked up one of the vials, sniffed the fragrance and poured it into the hot water. Heather then stepped up to him and ran her fingers along the waistband of his trousers. "Shall I undress you, Master?"

"Please."

Her warm hands slid inside his trousers, giving him a caress, before she released the ties that held them up.

"You are overdressed." His eyes had to be glowing with his desire for her.

"Of course, Master." She touched his face gently before pulling the cloth off her, then she released the top, allowing it to drop to the floor. Heather made sure it hit an exposed piece of the hardwood floor, making a loud bang as it landed. A giggle floated into the room followed by a bunch of shushes.

He grabbed her by the hips and pulled her close. "How many?" he mouthed.

"I don't know." Her words were soft so the ladies who could be listening wouldn't hear. "Why?"

"I think it's time for us to send them on their way, unless you want them listening while we're intimate." She didn't have to answer. Storm backed her up against the doors to his room, slamming his hand against it before he pinned her against the cool wood. He smiled when he heard them scurrying away. "That should have cleared them out."

"I hope so." She wrapped her arms around his neck. "That sounded like it could have hurt if it had really been me."

"It was just for effect, although now that I have you here, I am serious about the intimacy part." He started to nibble on her throat, inching his way to her mark.

"I have no doubt about that, but the water will get cold in the meantime, plus there are the oils they had me bring in. We could utilize them."

"On each other? The last time we tried that we didn't leave our rooms for days." He pulled her off the door and headed to the tub with her wrapped round him.

"We did enjoy it." She started to slide her legs down his body, but he grabbed her thighs to stop their descent.

"I'm just warning you we might not get out of here for this all-important meal."

"I have a feeling they'll drag us out naked to be sure we make it, but I'm willing to take a chance to earn your forgiveness from earlier."

"My heart, I know you were portraying the proper behavior of a woman here."

"But it upset you. I wanted to show those men you could control me with just your voice, but all it did was make you angry. That wasn't my goal."

"Control you? My heart. I strive to get you to lose control." He stepped down into the water, lowering them as he went to his knees. "Just like you try to find ways to get me to do the same thing."

"Very true." She reached for the vial she used earlier and poured the oil into her hands. "Oil? It's supposed to cleanse as it is rubbed into your skin."

The deep masculine aroma filled the air as she started to massage the oils into his shoulders. Heather slid off his lap and knelt in front of him, allowing her hands to work their way across the dips and plains of his muscles.

The feel of her hands on his arms and chest made him want to touch her the same way. Instead of putting the oil into his hands as she did, he poured it on her body, up near her collarbone, and watched as it eased its way down. His hands slid through the thick liquid, spreading it over her breasts, then down to her abdomen. With a grin, he lifted her up to the lip of the tub and sat her there so he could spread the oil between her folds. She squirmed under his touch.

Storm slipped two fingers inside her as he put his mouth to her breast, waiting for the most wonderful sound of her moaning in pleasure.

———

Between the heat of his mouth and the pressure of his fingers, Heather found it hard to breathe. Her heart pounded in her chest.

"This oil has a nice taste to it." He nuzzled her breast before lifting her once again. He centered himself and entered her.

Feeling him fill her so deeply drew a moan out of her.

"There it is, and early too. It gives me high hopes that I just might get a scream this time." He spoke softly, his lips close to her ears. "Let's see how lucky I am."

His words caused her body to clench against his shaft. The muscles under her hands jumped at the sensation.

"We definitely won't get to the dinner then. When you have a goal, you work at it until you get what you want," she said, her voice barely a whisper.

"I do, don't I?" He leaned her back a little before he

started to rock into her. The angle was perfect for him to hit the spot that caused her most powerful orgasms.

She gripped his arms as need swirled through her. Each time he drove into her, muscles tightened. The faster he moved, the quicker her muscles clenched then relaxed until her whole body quaked in his arms. It started low in her abdomen, the force overpowered her, and she screamed as the orgasm grabbed her and flung her out of her body.

Storm continued to pound into her as aftershocks filled her. All of a sudden, she felt another orgasm take over, this one just as powerful but she couldn't scream, she couldn't do anything but feel, like she was having an out of body experience as she floated along in the waves of the climax that still had a hold of her.

"Oh, my heart, that was beautiful." Storm pulled her up and wrapped his arms around her as her body acted bone-less. "And that second orgasm was mine."

"Wow." She touched his face. "Our mindlink is so deep it felt like mine and it would have made me scream again but I didn't have the energy for the second one."

He kissed her forehead as he held her close.

A hesitant knock shattered the moment.

"Must be time to get ready." He helped her up out of the tub so they could dress. He chose the deep purple tunic and trousers, and Heather put on her matching skirt and bra.

This time she attached a sheer material to the bottom of the bra and to one hip in the deep purple with her mark emblazoned on it. Storm gave her a curious look.

"More formal attire." She checked the fastenings once again before she was ready to leave. "Some of the special dinners require that I cover my hair as well. One of the reasons I need to mingle with the women. They will direct me properly."

Heather opened the door for Storm, then took her place once he exited the room. Fridon was waiting for him.

"Where is your room?"

"Next to yours. They think I'm your servant so expected that I'd have to be close to fulfill any need you might have." Fridon looked at Storm. He lowered his voice. "The walls are pretty thin here."

"Heard the scream?" Storm kept his voice low too but knew Heather still heard him.

"I think everyone in the building did."

Storm chuckled. He knew Heather would fight any sound she made the rest of their time there now that she knew she could be heard.

Not funny.

My heart. Why does it bother you that these people know I give you such pleasure?

That's not it. It's the snide comments and little jokes that could be poked at me that bother me.

Who would do that to you? I will speak to them. They reached the banquet area and Busandio's favorite stood off to the side, waiting for Heather. She gestured for Heather to follow her. As much as he wanted to keep her at his side, he knew he had to give her permission so they showed normal behavior.

Heather went off with the woman, but with his sensitive ears they were still close enough for Storm to hear.

"Does he beat you?"

"What?" He could hear the confusion in Heather's voice. "No."

"But you screamed. My master was getting ready to knock on the door when he heard it."

"Oh. That. That wasn't a scream of pain." He could feel Heather's embarrassment over having to explain her scream.

"Oh." The woman looked at her as what she implied sunk in. "Oh! He brings you that much pleasure? You will have to tell me how he does it. I have never screamed like that before."

"Yes, he always makes sure I am quite satisfied." Storm knew Heather found discussing her intimacy with him disconcerting when it came to strangers, yet she stood proud, looking the woman in the eye. "Is there anything I need to be aware of?"

"No. This evening is a quiet family gathering. Tomorrow is the big gathering to celebrate my son's coming of age. There will be several things I will need to train you on for that."

Heather nodded. "You have done your master proud, then."

"Yes." She gestured for Heather to rejoin Storm.

Heather took her place behind Storm. He was happy to have her close once again. The place he had been given was covered with pillows for him to recline against. A small table was placed in front of the cushions. His mate sat on the ground with nothing to protect her from the hard dirt.

The leader of the household sat opposite of Storm. There were about twelve men attending, spreading out in a half circle.

"I realized after you had been shown to your room, I hadn't introduced myself. Nor had you." He smiled. "But I have heard that Vespians aren't known for using names when speaking to people."

"That is true." Storm answered when he could. Heather took over when the answers became very complicated.

"I am Busandio. This is my family." He started naming off his brothers and two nephews who had come of age. "My son will be joining us tomorrow when he comes of age."

39

"You must be very proud." That would mean if the boy was getting the girl, it would be tomorrow if someone wanted to offer her as a gift. He wished they didn't need to stay. "May I ask what your gift is?"

"I will be giving him his own land. A small section from mine." He nodded to the women off to the right and they started filing in with plates laden with fruits and nuts. "But he will be able to build on it and make our holdings larger."

Women, who had been behind each of the men stood and went to the table. Out of his peripheral vision, he saw Heather mimicking their movements. After she filled his plate with what she knew he liked, she knelt in front of him and picked some of the smaller fruits to offer to him.

"You haven't told me your name yet."

"I am Storm." Heather gave him a look. Using a fake name didn't sit well with him, and he doubted this man knew of him. *It will be fine.*

"You are the Storm who is the ambassador to Earth? Who married the human Heather Drexel?"

You sure about that? He knows who we are now.

"Yes."

"I don't want her to do any more work."

"Excuse me?" Storm stood, not sure what was going on. If this man planned on trying to harm his mate he would defend her.

"I will explain later, but I am allowed to show honor to one woman during these types of dinners. Your woman will be treated as one of my family members. She may sit beside you and will be fed like you are, unless you don't want that. As her owner, you have final say."

He didn't know how to respond to that.

Tell him the truth, you wish me to be honored, but don't want anyone else to feed you.

"She deserves to be honored, but this female is very

special to me. I will not dishonor her by keeping her from her duties."

"Of course." He gestured for one of the women to bring her a cushion.

Heather knelt on her knees to feed Storm one of the small fruits she had set on the plate in front of him. She tried very hard to be quick and succinct with her movements, but he captured her fingers with his mouth, sucking the juices of the fruit from her fingers before he released them.

She kept her eyes downcast because that was what she was supposed to do, but he could tell by the way she was breathing she was affected.

Each time she fed him he did the same thing. He knew some of the other men were attracted to her and he needed them to understand she wasn't for sale. This was the only way he knew how.

More food came out. Storm smiled. If Heather had to hand feed him everything, things were going to get very hot very fast.

You are being evil.

There are too many men who are looking at you like they want you. I'm only marking my territory.

She moved her hair out of the way so her mark was visible. Several of the men did notice the mark on her throat matched the pattern on their clothing. They murmured amongst themselves before they stopped paying attention to her. *Better?*

Much. Although he enjoyed teasing her when she couldn't return the favor, it was affecting him just as badly. He eased off, although he still teased her from time to time. There was drinking and jokes told afterward but it wasn't long before the meal was over.

Busandio's family said goodnight and headed back to their homes. Storm hoped he would be allowed to go back to his room as well. As he stood to say his good night, Busandio stopped him.

"I wish to speak to you a little more now that we have some privacy."

He nodded, although he wanted to say no so badly.

"Please sit." He gestured to a seat closer to his. "I wish to speak to you without being overheard."

Storm moved closer, with Heather behind him. Her fear flooded him. Sometimes the mindlink caused problems when her emotions overpowered it.

Busandio tilted his head as he studied Heather. "She doesn't look like the same woman. Heather was tall, thin, very fair and had very light hair. The height is still there but she has filled out nicely and her skin and hair looks like any one of us."

"How do you know so much about Heather?" He knew better than to deny it. The man knew too much.

"I have done my homework. Being your mate has done wonders for her." He looked at Storm. "That is the right word, correct?"

"Yes, and it is the reason I will never sell her."

"I don't want to buy her." He sat back. "But I wish to repay a debt. If it hadn't been for your mate, I wouldn't have all of this."

"I'm not sure I understand."

"Heather Drexel came here to rescue someone's daughter years ago but got caught up in a terrible misunderstanding. She saw my mother being beaten and interfered. After causing a lot of damage to property and men, something unheard of and against our laws, she helped my mother to her feet and hurried her on her way." He looked at Heather. "If you hadn't done that I would have died. My mother was getting medicine for me. The man who beat her was a rival of my father and knew if his heir died, he would have to sell to the highest bidder. Instead, my mother was able to give me the medicine I needed, and the man lost everything."

Heather looked at the ground. Storm could see it was hard for her to hear this.

"By the time my father found out what happened, she had been rescued by her people. We heard Heather had taken sixty lashes before they could get her to safety. Lashes meant for my mother and would have meant my death."

Storm turned to look at Heather. She hadn't mentioned the beating and he hadn't read about it in her files. She looked up at him, silently begging him to not ask any more questions about what happened. The haunted look in her eyes angered Storm.

"How can you treat your women so badly? They bear your children. Without the women you men wouldn't be here." He turned back to Busandio. "And can she please come and sit with me? I'm getting tired of having to turn to see her face."

"Of course." He gestured for Heather to move up beside her mate. "Ambassador, not all of our women are treated so badly."

Storm wrapped an arm around Heather when she settled beside him.

"My favorite will always be that. I have many women, but none of them join me in my bed except my favorite. Most of my women are bedmates of some of my most trusted men." Busandio watched them with interest as Heather leaned into him. "I have saved others from men who I know would have mistreated them. We do have laws to protect women from brutal men. They are healthy and happy with me. Most of our men treat their women the same way. But just like anywhere else we have a few who have a cruel streak and they take it out on the women. Heather met one of the crueler ones on her last visit."

"On my planet anyone who mistreats another is punished. We don't allow it so it doesn't happen." Having her lean against him reminded him of the game they played during the meal. He had an arm around her and splayed that hand across Heather's stomach. He wanted to touch her intimately and this was the only way he could satisfy his desire until he could get them back into his room. The teasing he did backfired and the need he felt for her was strong.

"My father wished he could have made up for what she endured since he was too late to stop it." He stood. "I have a gift for you both, if you will allow me to give them to you."

"The best gift you could give me is to allow me to retire for the evening." He kept his hands on her, brushing his fingers against her mark. "With my mate."

"Of course. I will let the guards and my favorite know she will be with you instead of in the women's quarters, but I do wish to show my respect for what your mate did all those years ago. Giving things to a woman must be done a certain way." He watched them with curiosity. "Perhaps I can stop by your room later."

"Understand I might not answer." He looked at Heather, hoping they would be allowed to retire soon. "I plan on being a little occupied for a while."

"Then I will come quickly with the item I wish to give to Heather."

"Very quick." He kept his arm around Heather as they stood. One of Busandio's guards led them back to his room. She did try to step away from him a few times, but he wouldn't let her. Why was she behaving this way? "You don't have to be somewhere else, do you?"

"No, my heart, but I am trying to keep my distance while we're around others. Remember what I explained earlier?" Her voice was soft.

"About men not lowering themselves to their baser needs in front of other men?" He looked at the guard leading them. Good thing he couldn't speak Vespian. "That includes servants?"

"Any man." She hesitated for a moment. "You also need to know most women are sent to the main sleeping hall once they are no longer wanted in their master's bedchamber."

The guard opened the door for them and allowed Storm to bring Heather into the room with him.

"You will be needed all night long." He pulled her close. "But that has always been the case."

"We'll need to make the bed."

"We don't need sheets."

"Storm, if you look closely, you'll notice all you have there is a frame. We have to add pillows to make it comfortable."

He crowded her back against the wall. "I don't need a bed."

"I know." She touched his face. "But sooner or later you will need to rest and the way it is now will be too uncomfortable."

He looked at the large frame she pointed to. "It doesn't look that bad."

"I promise I will make it very comfortable for us." She smiled as she stepped out of his embrace. "And it will only take a second."

"It has already taken too long." He crossed his arms over his chest.

She laughed as she started working on the bed. She placed a long flat pillow in the center of the bed followed by two more, one on each side. Then she started placing pillows of every size and shape on the bed.

He was enjoying watching as she bent over the bed, giving him a wonderful view of her derriere. A soft rap against the door dragged his attention from her efforts. He walked to the door and whipped it open.

"I'm sorry. Am I interrupting?" Busandio had a shocked look on his face.

"No." Storm knew his eyes must be glowing for Busandio to react the way he was. He had startled many people since it started. With a strained smile he opened the door more so the man could step in. His gaze went back to Heather and the bed.

"I have brought my gift for Heather."

That caught her attention. She climbed off the bed and walked to stand next to Storm.

He handed the small pouch to Storm who opened it and allowed whatever was inside to spill into his hand. A long silver chain fell into his palm. "And what is this?"

"You add it to the chain Heather wears. It shows she's also protected by my house. Anyone stupid enough to ignore your chain wouldn't be able to ignore both."

Before he could ask the man if he thought he couldn't keep his mate safe, Heather touched his arm and thanked their guest. She took the chain from Storm and wove it into her other one. They actually looked nice together. The moment she was done she went back to making the bed.

"Well, I shall see you at the first meal. Then I will give you your gift."

"In the morning, then." Storm wanted to tell him that he didn't need another man to protect his mate but could feel her urging him to just say thank you. He closed the door and turned to face her. "What is so important about that chain?"

"It shows you have power so I'm a privileged piece of property. If someone were to take me, they would have to face you and Busandio's house. It should make them think twice before they mess with your property." She undid the top of her outfit and let it drop to the floor. "The bed is ready."

"And you?" He walked up to her and cupped a breast.

"Always." She worked on pulling his tunic off, but his height was a hindrance. "I can't believe as tall as I am by Earth standards, I feel so petite next to you."

"I like your height." Storm grabbed the hem of the shirt and pulled it off. "It has never caused a problem with our sex life."

"Thank goodness." She worked on the ties holding his trousers up and smiled as they slipped down his legs to pool at his feet.

His fingers worked on the fastenings on her skirt, happy when it fluttered to the floor. He wrapped his arms around her and lifted her up to carry her the few feet to the bed. Storm lowered her onto the bed, then joined her. Pillows were everywhere. "You sure we need all these pillows?"

"Yes." There was a sparkle in her eyes. "I thought we could place a few right where we need them."

"Really?" He climbed on the bed, then up her body. "The plans I have for you don't include pillows. Just you and me."

"I promise it will be worth your while." She moved further onto the bed, slipping out of the gentle hold he had on her.

"And where are you going?" He kept a hold of her thigh as she moved and climbed back up her body once more.

"Just getting more comfortable." The pillows she talked about lifted her hips and legs. He could tell by the angle that these pillows would do what their chair did.

"You have been thinking about that scream, haven't you? You wish to have that happen again?" He pressed his lips against her throat.

"Actually, I was thinking about us. I was taught how to

use the pillows for different sexual positions the last time I was here. Having you here with me lets us see just how well they work."

"You never tried them before?" He touched her face, placing his finger under her chin so she would continue to look at him. Heather had told him very little of the life she led before she met him. The only time he learned anything was like this when she had to tell him.

"No." She looked up at him. "The position the government created for me was more of a servant, so I was never seen as anything else. I was invisible as long as I did what was expected of me. But the pillows always made me curious."

"Are they designed specifically for sex?" His hands skimmed across her shoulders and down to her breasts. He needed to taste her skin.

"Certain ones are." She arched against him when she felt the heat of his mouth on a breast. "A couple of them are what my hips and legs are on."

"Hmmm." Storm continued to focus on her instead of answering. The hum though made Heather giggle. He had to lift his head and glare at her.

"I'm sorry but you hummed. You know that makes me laugh."

"You know how I feel about you laughing at me." He moved his body back up hers so he had her pinned to the bed.

"I'm not laughing at you." The sparkle hadn't left her eyes. "You know what makes me laugh and what makes me sigh."

"So you're saying it was my fault?" He started to nibble on her throat. His lips found her mark, pulling the sensitive tissue into his mouth, and he felt her body melt under him.

"Of course not, but you did hum and that did make me laugh." Her voice came out like a sigh.

"Oh, now you're complacent. I will remember that." Joy filled him as she tilted her head so he could easily access her mark.

"Like I said you know what makes me laugh and what makes me sigh."

"I also know what makes you scream." He shifted his weight so he could enter her. Her eyes fluttered shut as her body adjusted to him filling her. "Shall I strive to bring you to such heights once again?"

"Now what kind of question is that? You know I would love that, but you also know that I don't scream that often and you already got one out of me." She shifted her legs to wrap around his waist. "I don't want you to be disappointed if it doesn't happen again."

"I am never disappointed with our intimacy." He pulled out and drove back into her to prove his point. He felt the slight shudder from her. "But it won't stop me from striving to get more from you. Your screams are like music to me."

Her cheeks turned a beautiful shade of red at his words, but she never broke eye contact as they worked to reach the heights of ecstasy they had when they were intimate. Her body accepted him over and over. The blush didn't fade until she felt her first wave of release.

"My heart." He could feel her getting closer. A pillow close by caught his attention. He knew because of their mindlink that she wanted him to place it under her back when she arched up against him again.

"Wow," she said softly.

She had always been quiet when they were intimate, but once she was focused on her release, she became silent. A single word like that told him she was close, and it was going to be powerful.

"Shall I get my scream again?"

Her muscles clamped down on him. "Storm."

He knew she couldn't talk to him now. She was at the point when she was only feeling. Each time he filled her, he felt her shake and her sheath tightened around him. Her breath started to come out in short little pants. His was too. The grip she had on him was exquisite, but it always was. Being able to feel what she was experiencing heightened what he felt. He picked up the pace, drawing a moan from her.

She clenched against him one last time before her world shattered. It was like she was freefalling while in his arms. He was so close too. Her muscles spasmed against him and he skyrocketed toward where she floated in her release. Joy danced in his veins.

Heather let out a pent-up breath.

He gave her a quick kiss. "Holding your breath affects your orgasm."

"Can't help it." She touched his face as she looked up at him. "You always take my breath away."

He disengaged himself from her and pulled her into his arms. She curled up against him.

"What did you think of the pillows?"

"They did add a nice touch." He pressed his lips against her neck. "But you know I don't need anything but you."

THREE

He heard someone at the door the next morning. Storm inched away from Heather, hoping to not wake her. Pulling the door open, he found his host there.

The man's eyes strayed to their bed, making Storm turn and look. Heather's eyes were shut, yet she had turned from her earlier position and pulled the pillows around her. They covered all of the right places, but her right shoulder, hip and very shapely leg could be seen from where they stood. She looked alluring, sexy and he found it highly arousing. A quick glance told him his host felt the same way.

Storm didn't like anyone ogling his mate. He turned back and growled at the man. "Why do you disturb me?"

"Oh." He brought his gaze back to Storm. "Your gift. It is ready."

"Can it not wait for us to break our fast?"

"Of course, but I thought early in the morning would be best, considering the type of gift it is."

"Fine. Let me dress." He closed the door and turned to find Heather looking at him.

"You did very well there. I'm glad the nightly downloads are working. Fridon should be at the same level as you are." She propped herself up on one elbow. "Only a few of the words were in the wrong dialect."

"He's lucky I didn't just thrash him." He crossed to the bed and ran his fingers down her thigh. "Too bad I need you to join me to answer when I can't or I'd leave you there and ravage you when I come back."

"You can still ravage me when we return." She stood and reached for her skirt.

"I hope to, but these people like to keep you busy." He walked up to her and wrapped his arms around her before she could reach for her top. "But maybe we can steal a moment or two somewhere along the line."

"Just remember the walls are thin here. I don't think we should use one as a prop. Wouldn't want to go crashing through because you got a little overzealous."

He laughed. "Get dressed before we don't make it out of here."

———

They stepped out into the hot arid day. The single sun of the planet filled a good section of the sky. Storm found the closeness of the sun uncomfortable. He didn't know how Heather handled it, considering she wore so little. He hadn't noticed her burn from the exposure but as fair as she was she should fry easily.

The change in the pigmentation helps keep me from burning. The computer also put in a special protection to make sure my skin doesn't get damaged.

Eavesdropping?

Sometimes you just broadcast your thoughts. Especially when you're worried about me.

They were led to a large corral. Inside it were several of the pack animals they were using. Another animal caught Storm's eye. "Is that an Earth horse?"

"Yes. I have five stallions and five mares. Been inter-breeding them to make our frulas stronger." He grinned as one of the animals approached. "I wish to give you one."

"You're trading early," stated a new voice.

"It is a gift, not a trade." Busandio's smile faded as he turned toward the man who spoke.

"What did he do to earn such a prize?" The man turned to look at Storm. His sharp eyes took in the cut of his clothes. Storm also saw his gaze flick toward Heather. "I have tried to get you to part with one of those animals for months and you refuse me."

"You are early." Busandio ignored his comment.

"My nephew becomes a man today."

"Storm, this is my favorite's brother, Undar. He is a very resourceful trader."

"Why, thank you." He gave him a mock bow.

"I didn't say honest." He glared at Undar. He then gave Storm an apologetic look. "Perhaps we could finish this later?"

"Don't stop what you're doing because of me." Undar gripped his collar. "I shall go find my nephew."

Busandio waited until he was gone. "I am sorry. I wouldn't let him near my home if he wasn't family. He has ended up with items that he shouldn't have been able to get his hands on. He has always been able to prove he got it legally when questioned, but I don't trust him."

"Perhaps we should wait, then?" Storm wondered just how bad he could be if his own family didn't trust him. His thoughts went to his mate and how he could keep her safe.

"No. I will not let that man ruin this. I brought out all the frulhorses. You may pick whichever one you wish."

"May I walk among them?" He needed to be sure the animal took to him. That fact that he could shift was something these animals should be able to pick up on. Some accept it but not all.

"Of course." Busandio opened the fence so Storm could step in.

He wandered through the animals, looking at those who would look him back in the eyes. It didn't take long before one of the mares started to nuzzle him. A grin spread across his features when Heather mentally commented about the sex of the animal.

"Very good choice. She's one of my favorites."

"I can choose another."

"She chose you." He opened the gate for Storm once again. "And I will honor that."

"Is there anything else needing my attention right now?"

"The first meal of the day will be served in about an hour. Your favorite and servant will be required to help with some of the preparations for this evening's festivities, but you have until first meal before they will be collected."

"Fridon isn't a servant. I am training him as my equal."

"Oh." He paused for a moment. "Then I will make my head servant aware. I will see you at the morning meal. Then you'll be free until the feast to honor my son."

Storm fought a frown. What was he supposed to do all day with Heather away helping the women?

———

The dinner was a major affair. Once again, he and Heather were dressed in the same colors, and she used another slip of material to attach to her top and hip that converted her outfit to a more formal one.

"Where did you hide these things?" He touched the see-through material then brushed his fingers against her stomach.

"They don't take up much space. They were in the satchel on the back of the frulas."

"And what would happen if I hid it on you?" He wrapped one arm around her and pulled her close.

"You don't have to hide my clothes to get me naked, my heart." She touched his face. "I'm not wearing that much anyway."

"I know, and it's all I can think of." A quick knock made him frown. "I miss home, where no one would dare interrupt us when that door is closed."

"The perks of being the future leader of Vespia." She followed him to the door.

"You think we'd be interrupted if we were standard citizens?"

"If we were regular citizens, we wouldn't have to worry about someone interrupting us. But then again, we'd have other obligations that would interfere." She grinned. "Face it, Storm, you would have sex every minute of every day if you could."

"With you as my partner? Of course." He gave her a quick but heated kiss. "Time to go before they knock the door down."

———

Once again, he sat on pillows with Heather sitting behind him. What he found interesting was that the merchant he had met earlier was the only male without someone to serve him.

"I see how you treat family." The man was rude, too.

"The last time you were here, you beat one of my women so badly she was unable to work for a week. I warned you then I would never allow my women to take care of you again." He looked at his favorite before turning his attention back to her brother. "I was serious."

"Then it is a good thing I brought my own."

"You brought your own and didn't have her help the other women prepare for this meal?" Anger rolled off him as he stood.

Why is he so angry?

Because it is proper to lend your property to your host for big parties like this. Every one of us here worked to bring this together. It is rude and says you think you are better than everyone else.

Storm found it fascinating. No wonder why Heather wanted to go and work with these women. She knew what they would think about them if she had refused.

Covered from head to foot in the same type of hooded cloak Heather wore when they first arrived on the planet, a young woman shuffled forward. The merchant stood and pulled the cover off the young woman.

She stood there shaking. Storm wondered what she was afraid of. Then he noticed the ugly blotches on the part of her arm that was exposed, as well as the one on her cheek. The man beat her.

Anger filled him. How could a man beat a woman? He straightened so he could stand and found Heather's hand on his arm. One look from her made him stay seated instead of getting up to thrash the man.

Storm looked around and noticed a lot of the other men looked just as angry as he felt. With a nod from Busandio all the women stood and headed out of the room, taking the young woman with them.

———

Heather waited for Busandio's favorite to approach the young woman.

"He did this to you?" She pointed to the bruises and swelling.

The young girl couldn't look any of them in the eye as she nodded.

"My owner will teach him a proper lesson if you wish," Heather commented.

"No need. We have our ways." Usatha picked up a small jar near where she stood. "This will smell bad for a few moments but will heal you quickly."

The girl nodded and waited as the woman spread a thick salve on her bruises.

"Do you have any more?"

She nodded once again. It took her a few seconds to reveal her inner thighs. Several women sucked in their breath. Ugly purple bruises marred her skin.

Busandio's favorite's lips thinned. She signaled another woman to her side. "Help her if she needs it."

Once they stepped to a quiet corner to apply the salve, the woman spoke to the rest of the women. "We shall add something special to my brother's favorite sauce. I will signal Busandio so he knows what we have done and pass it onto the rest of the men, but we mustn't let our newest guest in on our little surprise."

The two women came back to join them.

"You should feel the salve working in a moment or two, and your bruises will fade by the morning." She gestured for her to go out. "You should rejoin him before he gets angry and tries to strike you again."

Heather followed next. Keeping her eyes downcast, she rejoined Storm, taking her place behind him. The rest of the women did the same, all waiting for Busandio's favorite to enter. She carried a large tray with a large bowl.

"My favorite prepared her brother's favorite sauce," announced Busandio.

Usatha sat the tray down with the rest of the food then spooned out enough bowls for all the men. Heather stood with the rest of the women and carried the small bowl back to the low table Storm reclined next to.

When the meal resumed, she took her place beside him so she could serve his meal. As she prepared his plate, she cast a glance at Busandio's favorite. She never saw any signals but none of the men asked for the sauce from the women serving them.

What happened?

He abuses her. She has these hideous bruises on the inside of her thighs. Please don't react. I will explain more later. Just don't ask for the sauce. Something has been put into it.

Storm watched as Undar slathered his food with the sauce Heather warned him about. The man should have just drunk it outright with the amount he had on his plate. He stuffed his face, nodding as he enjoyed his food. It didn't take long before his eating slowed. His brow broke out in a sweat, and then his face went from a sparkly tan to a sickly brown.

He stood, looked around for something, and then dashed out of the tent.

"That should teach him not to beat women," said Busandio. He sat back and laughed. His favorite nodded to two serving girls who gathered the small bowls with the sauce and removed them. "He won't be ill for too long, but he will break out in hives in a few hours and that will be painful."

"Do you think he will learn from this?" asked Storm.

"Doubt it, but one can hope."

They continued to eat, waiting for Undar to return. The women were clearing the plates when he did. His color still off, but he held his head high and tried to keep his stomach from revolting again.

The women remained, standing by their owners until Busandio gave the signal for them to leave. One by one the women filed out.

Storm touched her arm as he looked up at her. Heather placed her hand on his. *It's okay.*

"It is time for my son to receive his gifts. The women are not allowed to be here for that," Busandio explained. "You will see her in your chambers."

Storm let go, but not before he gave her a heated gaze that held promise.

———

Storm noticed the merchant watching his mate leave with the rest of the women. Knowing what he did to the young woman in his care had Storm wanting to growl. "Why do you stare at my property?"

"She is very beautiful."

"And mine." He didn't like the gleam in the man's eye.

"Have you—"

"No. She isn't for sale." He glared at Undar. The one that always worked.

"Not even for—"

"Never. Ask again and I will make you wish you hadn't."

Busandio did his best to defuse the moment by having his male servants bring out the gifts brought by guests, but Storm spent the rest of the night glaring at Undar.

———

Storm finally walked into his room. The time with the men was long and tedious. He didn't understand why he had to be there, but nodded and smiled at the appropriate times, hoping they would release him quickly. He also kept his attention on Undar. The man hadn't given up after the first time. He had cornered him as they left and offered to buy Heather from him again. It took him grabbing the man by the throat and shoving him up against the wall for Undar to understand just how serious he was about not selling her.

He needed to feel the joy he always did when he was in Heather's arms.

Heather wasn't waiting for him as he had hoped, but she was there, curled on her side, surrounded by pillows and sound asleep, her skimpy outfit lying on the floor. He loved that garment, even though she hated it. Storm couldn't help himself, seeing her in it gave him a constant hard-on. Every time she moved, he kept watching, hoping something would escape. All that exposed flesh begged for his touch. He had a hard time keeping his hands to himself.

She made a soft sound as she shifted on the pillows. Heather faced the door so he knew she was aware he had returned. Her training would have brought her to her feet instantly if anyone else had come in.

He shed his clothes and climbed into bed with her, placing soft wet kisses on any part of her body showing as he climbed up her length.

"I wondered when you'd stop staring at me and join me." She turned to face him.

"Can't help it. This is my favorite playground, and it is beautiful to look at." He trailed a finger down her arm. "Seeing you in that revealing garment all day long spikes my need for you. Then to have you lying here, naked and waiting for me just shoves it over the edge."

"Storm." She looked up at him as she opened herself for him.

"I know you hate what that garment represents but seeing you in it is very arousing. I keep waiting for something to slip. The anticipation of seeing more of your beautiful body is arousing. Having you at my beck and call is causing these wonderful fantasies. My mind keeps imagining what I might be able to talk you into." He entered her. Her body closed around him, causing a delicious friction. "You feel so good."

"What sort of fantasies?" She wrapped her legs around him.

"Having you straddle me in that outfit." He paused as he felt her muscles tighten against him. "Feel your body accept me in."

"But we have already done that."

"Ah, but we'd be in a crowd of people, and they aren't aware of what we're doing." He slid out and then back in. "It would be your position to feed me, and no one would question it."

"Storm." She shifted her hips.

"The fantasy excites you." He brushed hair away from her face. "What happened to my shy mate? The one who wanted to change in the bathroom when we were first bonded."

"You corrupted me." She slid a leg down one of his. "You have showed me there is nothing wrong with the way I look. Maybe you worshiped my body too much and it's all gone to my head."

"It is all truth." He felt her shake a little when he stroked her just the right way. "You just never had anyone show you just how exquisite you are. And that worked in my favor because now you're mine."

She stopped moving and touched his face. "Someone is coming."

"They wouldn't dare interrupt us."

"We're not home, and most women don't spend the night with their owners."

"If they are stupid enough to try, they will face me." He slid out and back in.

Loud banging filled the air. Before Storm could move the door opened and the head guard from the women's quarters entered. Heather had her legs wrapped intimately around Storm's hips. She turned her face away from the door. The man dropped his gaze the moment he realized what he interrupted.

"What?" Storm growled.

"I am sorry, sir. I had been told to retrieve her." He bowed as he backed out the door. "I'll be back to retrieve her later."

"No. She stays with me. I might have need for her later."

"Of course, sir." The man stepped out. Storm's keen hearing heard him speak to another man. "I dare not disturb him again."

"My heart, search and tell me who is out there." Storm touched her face gently. He was asking her to do something she didn't like to do.

Her face showed disgust before she spoke. "That merchant."

"I will kill him."

"Forget about him." She touched his face again. "It's just you and me right now."

Part of him wanted to go after the man and thrash him, but he couldn't leave Heather. The look on her face showed something he hadn't seen in a long time. Fear. He had to erase that. Storm started to move inside her again, each stroke perfectly timed and aimed. She was the one who needed to forget, not him. She sucked in her breath, and he knew he was close to his goal.

"I made you scream the last time." He continued the pace, watching as her face flushed.

"I know you wish it every time, but it doesn't always happen."

"How about a moan, then?" He hit just the right spot and she arched against him.

Her muscles contracted around him as he pulled out and drove back in. She shook in his arms when he hit the right spot again. The grip she had on him had him moving faster. Building the friction between them.

"So close," she said, her voice soft.

He could feel it in his mind. She was on the edge. Her body gave off a slight tremor. Storm ground his hips against hers and felt her release flow over her. She whispered his name as she reached the height of her orgasm.

"My heart." He pumped into her two more times and climaxed as well. Storm touched her face. "You bring me such joy."

"I feel the same way."

He shifted his body and wrapped her in his embrace. "Rest. I know you worked hard today."

She snuggled against him. "Meanwhile, you're going to come up with a way to get back at that merchant, aren't you?"

"You know me too well." He kissed her, a slow bone melting one he knew made her thoughts shatter. "Did you see her?"

"No. The son did get several women as gifts, but none of them were our target."

"At least we know we can eliminate Busandio as a possible owner." He pressed a kiss to her forehead. "Now relax. You know you'll only get a few hours before I wake you again."

———

Storm strode into the main hall and confronted his host. He had waited until mealtime to be sure the merchant was there as well. Heather followed behind him like she was supposed to.

"Your brother through ownership decided he knew what was best in your house and talked one of your guards to barging into my room to try to extract my property last night. It was an inopportune time and I'm not pleased."

"What?" The merchant looked at Busandio. "That wasn't me."

"It was. I have already spoken to the guard." Storm walked up to him, using his height and size to intimidate him. "After I told you that she is my property and not for sale."

"All my guards know she is to stay with you at night. All night. They wouldn't dare disturb you." Busandio stood. "Which guard was it? I will make sure he is punished for his indiscretion."

"Someone who didn't know better and will never listen to anything this dog has to say again. I just feel you needed to know about his interference." Storm sat in the place they had given him. Heather sat behind him, waiting until she would feed him. "I do wish to thank you for your kindness, but it is time for me to see more of your world."

"Oh, but the celebration isn't over." Busandio gestured to two of his guards. "If you're leaving because of my brother, I will send him away right now."

"Sending him away might not fix the problem. You said yourself he is resourceful." Storm didn't want to keep

Heather there another day. He couldn't keep an eye on her the whole time and with this merchant trying to separate them he feared for her safety.

"It will make it harder for him to try anything." The look on his face said he really didn't want Storm to leave. "And I will wave your property having to work with the women."

"I don't want special treatment, but I don't trust him." Storm pointed to the merchant. There had to be a reason Busandio didn't want them to leave. He had shown them honor when he learned their true identity, and now they knew the girl wasn't here. Storm wanted to trust the man. If they were going to stay, there had to be a few conditions. "I wish access to her whenever I have need. To be sure he doesn't try to make off with my property."

"I will post three guards with her. They are the only men allowed in with the women."

Oh, Heather wasn't going to like that, but he needed to keep her safe.

———

Storm.

You heard the man. It is the only way since you don't want to seem better than the other women, and I can't keep you at my side. This way, I know you're protected.

I can protect myself.

Not here. Women aren't allowed to raise a hand to men.

She didn't say anything else, but he knew she wasn't happy. Once the meal was finished, Heather stood with the rest of the women.

"Where are you going?" Storm stood as Heather started to leave. Addressing her directly wasn't normal, but there was no law against it.

She looked at him, concern etched on her face. She hated

being the center of attention and he wasn't helping anything.

"Come here." He waited for her to come close enough he could take her into his embrace. Having her upset with him didn't sit well, and he wanted to wipe that frown off her face. He claimed her lips, his tongue delving into the recesses of her mouth. Their tongues danced together. Storm tightened his hold on her as he allowed his desire for her to take over. When he finally broke the kiss, he wished they were in his room.

Heather looked up at him. Her frustration with him and the situation they were in was gone, replaced by sexual frustration. The smile she gave him spoke volumes.

———

"He truly cares for you," Busandio's favorite stated once they were out of earshot of the men.

"I know." Heather felt such joy that he wanted to do that in front of all those men. It wasn't against any rules, and Storm never hid his passion for her, but it just wasn't done, and he had been trying to do his best to fit in.

The other women stared at her in wonder. Usatha shooed them to get to work cleaning up while she continued to talk to Heather. "Busandio says you aren't considered his property. You are his mate?"

"Each planet has a different name for a life partner. On Earth it is husband or wife. Here it is favorite." Heather had noticed how Busandio treated her. Maybe there was hope for this planet after all. She worked beside the woman, making sure she was thorough as she helped clean up.

She looked around to see the guards were all at the edge of the room. None had stepped inside the female area. Storm wasn't going to be happy.

"That might be, but I worry I am only his sex partner at times. He can have any of these women if he wanted, and some of them are quite beautiful." She kept her voice low. "Like you."

"True, but does he? He shares information with you. Information that he wouldn't share with anyone else. You are the only one who has born him children. That means something." Heather had been right earlier. She had feared he had found a new favorite.

"You think so?" Her voice sounded hopeful. "I am getting older."

"I have found that male and female, no matter what planet they are from, all want the same thing, someone who will share their life with them without judging." She studied the woman. "We all want love."

"True." She was quiet for a moment. "He has always shown me favor when dealing with the other women. I know you don't understand our ways, but I was raised this way. Having someone like Busandio to care for me is what I want. I couldn't ask for a better owner."

"You want to be his property?"

"You sound surprised." She looked at Heather.

"Storm doesn't own me."

"Do you control the relationship?"

"No. Vespians are very dominant." She liked the way he tried to dominate her when they were intimate.

"So, you let him make all the decisions?"

"Well, yes, but he would never do anything that would upset me." Heather could see where this conversation was going.

"I see." She stacked the empty baskets that had held the bread that Heather had gathered and put them in one large box. "Busandio does the same for us. Each time he makes a decision for one of the women here he always takes their feelings into consideration."

"You can only go to him when he calls you."

"And you can be with your mate any time?"

"Yes, unless he's working or I'm working."

"So not any time." She folded a few of the cloths they had used to cover the bread.

"I get to do anything I want."

"But would you if you knew your man wouldn't like it?" She set down the pile of linens. "Our worlds aren't that different. My society might seem strange to you because of the distinct line between men and women, but my goal is to keep him happy. You can't tell me yours isn't the same."

―――――

Storm found sitting there staring at the rest of the men boring. They had already started drinking, but he learned last night their alcohol didn't affect him. At home, he would either be working his men out or being intimate with Heather.

He had to get out.

As the men got deeper into their cups, they paid less attention to him, which gave him an opportunity to escape. He thought about going to his room, but he would be just as bored there. That big bed just made him want Heather with him.

He followed the hallways until he was out in the sunlight. It felt good against his skin. Since he was near the corrals, he decided to check on their animals, including the one Busandio had given him. She was a beauty. He couldn't help but notice the stallion that stayed near. When she approached Storm, he started stomping and snorting.

"It sounds like he isn't happy you picked me." Storm

rubbed her nose. "I might have to leave you here, so he won't try to challenge me."

"He is very fond of her." Busandio stepped up beside Storm. "I am sorry if you find our gathering boring."

"I didn't mean to be rude but needed a little fresh air." He turned toward Busandio. "I'm not used to being so inactive."

"You realize other leaders might not understand your behavior." He rubbed the nose of the animal.

"I do and I wouldn't have left, but since you know who I am, I didn't see any harm in coming out here. I would never do anything to cause harm to Heather." He shook his head. "You do have some very strange rules. The ones designed to protect your women seem to harm them as well. Not allowing them to speak for themselves."

"It might seem like that, but most men do cherish their women. If a woman can't speak to a man, she can't inadvertently insult him and run the risk of being beaten."

"By men like that merchant."

"Yes." He sighed. "You must have abusive men on your planet as well."

"No, we're a highly aggressive race. If a man were to try, he'd find a battle on his hands from the woman, but I have heard there are abusive men on other planets." He rubbed the animal's nose again. "It is one of the reasons I wanted to leave. My mate has a tendency to draw danger to her and with him here I felt it would be safer if I took her away."

"I thought that might be the reason, but I have heard that the man she shamed is nearby and he is dangerous. Although you have altered her looks so she blends in a little better, her violet eyes will give her away. No one here has them." He paused for a moment. "It is best if you stay within the safety of my walls until I'm sure he is gone. My favorite's brother has dealings with the man from time to time."

"And you assume that is why he is here?"

"Yes." He sighed. "Undar is a greedy man, and I fear he let his friend know of her presence the moment he saw her."

"But you're not sure."

"I have had one of my guards following him since he arrived, and he did go and speak to the man. I just don't know what they talked about. But I feel you are safer here until he moves on."

———

Undar stood close by, listening to everything they said. He thought the big man's property looked familiar. When he heard the name Heather, he was sure. That was an off-worlder name and her eyes. No one had such a color. This could make him a lot of money. All he had to do was tell the right person. Busandio had been wrong when he said he thought he had told Lewmard she was here, but he would correct that as soon as he could.

———

"Your owner has requested his bath."

Heather looked up at the young woman who spoke. "This early?" She stood. Storm had been aroused when he ended the kiss earlier, but he had kissed her like that before and they were able to function until they could get back to their rooms. The sex was great after bone-melting kisses like that one. Especially if those kisses had time to work on her and Storm as they did their jobs. But these women wouldn't understand if she wanted to make him wait because they would never make their owners do that.

"Did he say when?"

The young girl shook her head.

Okay. *My heart?*

Are you done this early?

I was told you wished your bath.

I have been talking to Busandio. I'm still out by the corral.

I will join you since it seems someone wants me to leave this room.

Be careful, my heart. It is probably that merchant again.

She headed to the main doors and walked down several corridors to step outside.

"Where are you going?"

Heather dropped her gaze and shrank back. One of the guards blocked her way. "My owner has asked for me."

"We shall see." He grabbed her by the wrist and brought her out to the stables. He slowed when he approached Busandio and Storm. He waited until they acknowledged him. "I found her outside the women's quarters."

"That is because I asked her to join me." Storm stepped up and grabbed the guard's hand, squeezing until he let go of her. "It is time for her to draw my bath."

The guard nodded and went back to his post.

"I don't remember you asking for her." Busandio watched as Storm pulled Heather into his embrace.

"I was told Storm had asked for me."

"Where is your brother through ownership?"

"He left several hours ago and isn't due back until after the sun sets."

So it couldn't be him unless he doubled back. Heather leaned against Storm for strength. Without him here she couldn't do this assignment.

"Doesn't mean a thing," Storm growled. "He could have gotten someone else to do this for him. What happened to the three guards?"

"They are probably still at the main entrance. Please understand that this type of thing doesn't happen here. They felt she was safe with a room full of women."

"Yet here she is without those guards. I want my man guarding her at all times. What does he have to do to be able guard her in the female section?"

"It's never been done. These men are groomed for this position."

They're eunuchs, Storm.

Fridon will not go for that.

"Heather doesn't want special treatment, but if you won't allow my man to be with her when I'm not then she will be at my side all the time. I don't care what your friends and family will think. Her safety is my priority."

"I will have one of my guards explain what he needs to do."

———

Heather did feel better with Fridon there. She didn't feel as trapped as she had earlier. Doing her best to ignore him, she continued to help the ladies, after she made Usatha aware of the young woman who tried to separate her from everyone else. They found out the woman was only following what she was told, but they needed to know who gave her the message. The young woman had been near a window when she heard his command.

Heather picked up a pile of cloths and carried them over to where they would be hung.

"This is beneath you," Fridon said softly so no one else would hear, and spoke in Vespian so he wouldn't be understood if he was heard. "You're the mate of our next ruler. I should be doing that for you."

She could only smile. Setting down the pile, she found

several of the cloths snagged on her top. A sigh escaped her as she carefully unhooked them. Not too many of the fragile materials were badly damaged.

"Why didn't you take your covers off?" asked Usatha.

"They come off?"

Busandio's favorite took her arm and pulled her away from the rest of the women. "You didn't know that?"

"I was a servant the last time I was here."

"Ah." She pressed a button on her top next to the juncture where the two cups met. The top opened and then unhinged. "We aren't allowed to remove them when in public or around men who aren't our masters, but here we are, and of course in the privacy of your owner's quarters."

"Is there anything else I need to know?"

"The gauze also comes off if that is desired. The skirt hooks in the front and back for riding or work where your skirt could get in the way."

"We're not allowed to ride," Heather reminded her.

"Yet, that was how my son found you, wasn't it?"

She had no answer for that.

———

"Did you find out which guard told the girl to have Heather go to our room?" Storm asked. He stood with Busandio at the corral where they felt it would be safe to talk.

"No. She only heard the voice through an open window. I have had her listen to every male voice here and she didn't recognize any of them." Busandio frowned. "I don't know how the intruder got within the walls surrounding my home without someone detecting him. I thought you would be safe here, my friend, but I'm not so sure now."

"Then we should leave now." Storm turned to head back to the house.

"After I made such a big deal in front of the rest of my guests? They would know you're running." He put a hand on Storm's arm. "Stay, make them think you didn't catch on. When you leave tomorrow, I will make sure you leave with a flourish. No one in their right mind would try to follow you."

———

He was true to his word. Everyone came out to say goodbye. Busandio also made a big deal of the frulhorse he had given Storm. The meek horse followed the rest of Storm's animals out of the corral, each laden down with provisions for them to make the trek to the next city.

"You have done too much." Storm looked at the heavy burdens the four animals had. Busandio had made sure they had plenty of provisions. Along with the items Bear had prepared for them, more packs had been added to their pack animals, plus the frulas he and Fridon would ride had several bags tied to the saddles, but at least there was room for them to ride comfortably.

The stallion attracted to Storm's newly acquired mare, started to rear in the corral when it realized she wasn't there. He stomped and whinnied his displeasure, shaking its head as it clawed at the air. Charging the gates, he jumped over the six-foot fence, then ran to where she stood.

Storm laughed as he brushed his fingers down his muzzle. He looked at Heather. "I know how you feel."

"I was afraid of this. He doesn't want to be separated from her."

"Then I shall leave the mare here. You can care for her for me."

"No." Busandio shook his head. "She is a gift. I want you to have her. But it looks like I shall also have to give you the stallion as well. As you can see, he doesn't want to be separated from her."

"Then let me pay you."

"You already have." He smiled. "Let my women redistribute the provisions and you can be on your way."

What could he say to that?

FOUR

The moment they were out of sight of the place Storm slid off his horse.

"Is there a problem?" asked Heather, who walked beside his animal.

"Is it against the laws here for me to walk with you?"

"No." She smiled. "You can do whatever you want."

"I don't understand their rules. If women are considered valuable property, then why can't they ride?"

"It has something to do with several women traveling to help one of the houses prepare for a coming-of-age event years ago. The owner only sent three men with them. The men were killed, and the women were all stolen from him. Without his women, he lost everything. The men felt a woman riding without proper escort was too dangerous and because the ratio of women to male servants is so high to protect the women they banned them from riding. Stupid rule if you ask me."

Storm wrapped his arm around her waist. "It does have a few perks."

She looked up and saw the desire glowing in his eyes. "You've found quite a few of these rules to your liking. There was the outfit, me having to straddle you in order to ride, the bath, feeding you, shall I go on?"

"It's why my eyes glow all the time. I am constantly in need of you."

"I'm going to scout around and look for a good place to camp for the evening." Fridon then urged his steed forward.

"Poor thing." She watched Fridon ride away. Heather knew he didn't want to stay due to the way they were talking. "He's really out of his element here."

"I think all of us are, my heart."

Heather had to agree. She sure didn't feel comfortable and wished they were back on Vespia.

"I'll be happy when we find this girl and can go home."

"Me too."

They walked along in silence.

Fridon rode up to them several hours later. "I have found a place to camp, but I also doubled back and found we're being followed."

"By whom?" Storm frowned.

"That merchant."

———

They stopped at the spot Fridon recommended, and as Heather put the tent up, Storm waited for their guest.

"His presence doesn't surprise me," commented Storm. He stood outside the huge tent with Fridon while Heather worked to get the interior set up. "He has a fascination with my mate that I don't like."

"You could tell him to move on if he tries to camp here with us." Fridon looked at the tent and sighed.

Storm knew Fridon felt the same way he did. Heather shouldn't be forced to do everything. It took a lot of willpower not to go in there and help her. "There is an old Earth saying that I like. Keep your friends close and your enemies closer. If he is here, then I know he can't be plotting something to take her from me."

"Here he comes." Fridon pointed to the figures they could just make out on the horizon.

Storm crossed his arms over his chest and waited. The pose was meant to intimidate, and it worked every time.

"Ah, sir." Undar pulled his animals to a stop, a gross little smile on his face. The young woman in tow dropped to her knees, but it was from exhaustion instead of respect. "I had hoped to catch up with you."

"It looks like you pushed to find us." Storm noticed the ugly blotches covering the man's face. A gift from consuming all that sauce the women treated. The way he scratched his arms and stomach gave Storm the impression he was covered from head to foot with them. He smiled. The women did a good job making him miserable for what he did to his property. Even though he was still treating her badly. The poor thing was having trouble catching her breath. "Your animals and property are laboring to breathe."

"They have had to keep a quicker pace in the past." He patted his animal as he slid off his frulas. "They can handle it."

Storm didn't agree. If he wasn't careful, he would kill them all. He just stared at the man, waiting for him to make the next move.

"It is good I found you." He scratched his leg. "The more tents here the safer everyone is."

"And who says you can camp with us?" Storm glared at the man.

"I, ah, well."

"You show me no respect as due my station. I want you out of my sight." Storm turned on his heel and pulled the flap up to enter the tent.

"I mean no disrespect."

Storm smiled as the man's words stopped him. He turned back to him and waited. Wondering how much back peddling Undar was willing to do.

"I had thought my brother explained how dangerous it was to travel alone."

"You think I can't protect my property?" Storm asked, disgust lacing his voice. "As I said I want you out of my sight."

"I am sorry. I have offended you without meaning to. I hope you will extend your hospitality to me and allow me to share your fire." He dropped his gaze to the ground.

Those were the right words. Storm could tell the man no and he'd have to move off, but the woman and the animals looked like they couldn't take another step. He was sure Undar wasn't used to having to bow and scrape to get his way, but he was doing a good job of it.

"If you stay, you abide by my rules. If you break any of them, you lose the woman to me." Storm stepped up to him, using his height to continue to intimidate. He wanted this man to know he was serious.

"And what are those rules?" He frowned, clearly not liking Storm's proposal.

"I will not tolerate any sort of abuse." Storm smiled when the man's eyes widened. "I also expect the respect I and my property deserve."

"Property?" He scratched his shoulder.

"Everything I own is valuable to me. Any harm or destruction you might cause will forfeit your property to me as compensation."

He nodded, not happy with the turn of events, but Storm

could tell he didn't want to leave. Busandio had told him Undar would walk away at the threat of losing his property, unless his greed got in the way. If that happened, it meant he had an ulterior motive. His agreement worried Storm.

The young woman stood and started unpacking the animals to assemble the tent. She was exhausted and could barely lift the tent material off the back of the animal.

Just as Storm was about to have Fridon help her he heard Heather in his head.

The only one you can send to help her is me, my heart.

I wish to keep you safe.

Nothing will happen as long as you stand there and watch.

He stepped inside for a moment before walking out with Heather behind him.

She went to the young woman's side, who looked grateful when she saw her. Heather helped her erect the tent in a short time. Using the hand signals the women used to communicate with each other when the men were around, Heather asked if she needed help setting up the interior. The young woman shook her head no so Heather went back into their tent where Storm felt she was safest.

He didn't like the way the man was watching her every move.

And I don't like the way your frown deepens as you stare at him.

Storm stepped in behind her.

"Perhaps I shouldn't have let him stay with us." Storm noticed their food all laid out around the small section she had set up as a sitting area. "And what is this?"

She laughed but didn't answer him. The way that man watched her, he was probably listening in as well, and until Storm gave the command for her to talk, she wasn't going to take the chance the man would overhear her. She wasn't going to give him anything to use against them.

Storm called Fridon in. He sat first, then Fridon joined him. Heather knelt beside Storm, as she had done at Busandio's house, which frustrated Storm.

"I despise this." He looked at her. "I wish you to join us."

Heather gave him an 'are you crazy' look.

"Perhaps if you gave her permission to speak, sir." Fridon said it softly so he wouldn't be overheard.

"I have already given her permission." He glared at Heather.

"Yes, but the merchant joining us has made her hesitant. He doesn't know you gave her permission." Fridon picked up a piece of fruit and bit into it. "Perhaps if you give it again where he could hear you."

Storm turned his glare to Fridon, who wouldn't look at him. Heather touched his arm. The laughter in her eyes relaxed him. If the man was listening in, he knew she was allowed to speak.

"I wish to take care of you the way I'm supposed to." She offered him a small piece of fruit.

"You remember the last time you fed me like this?" Storm sucked in the piece of fruit, grabbing her hand so he could draw her fingers into the recesses of his mouth as well, licking the juices that ran down her fingers.

Desire filled her eyes.

"I think I'll finish my meal outside." Fridon took his plate and headed out of the tent.

"You scared him away, Storm." Heather spoke softly so no one would hear her, laughter lacing her voice.

"He will be fine." He pointed to the small drape she created to block his bed from theirs as he shifted his weight so he could close the distance between them. "I see you worked hard to keep our intimacy private. He just did the same thing."

"But you need to eat."

"So do you." He picked up a piece of fruit and offered it to her. Storm closed his eyes as her tongue licked off any excess juice from his fingers. "Keep that up though, and I'm going to want dessert before dinner."

"You started it." She offered him another piece. He took it then crawled over to where she knelt.

"And I plan on finishing it." He moved close, invading her space, and forcing her backwards until she was lying beneath him. "This is where I like you most." He placed a wet kiss against her stomach. "You taste so much better than anything you have to feed me."

Heather still held the plate, and popped another piece of fruit into her mouth, holding it in her teeth as an offering to Storm. He claimed the fruit and her lips at the same time. He swallowed it whole so he could deepen the kiss, his tongue delving into her mouth. Melting beneath him, she sighed.

Her fingers worked on the tunic he wore, maneuvering it up his chest so it would be easy to remove. She felt his fingers separating the closure of her top, then the heat of his hands on her breasts. His lips left her mouth and worked their way to her mark before he pushed up to look at her.

"I miss the computer where we could remove our clothes with a thought." He pulled his shirt off.

"You're just spoiled." She slipped the straps off her arms and pulled the top from under her. Storm sat up and slipped her skirt off. "And overdressed."

"That I can fix." He stood and dropped his pants before joining her back on the carpets.

"We could move to the bed."

"I'm quite happy right here." He leaned over her again and pressed his mouth to her mark. "And I know how to make you forget about that bed."

"Work your magic, my heart."

———

Fridon couldn't get out of the tent fast enough. The passion that flared between Heather and Storm was powerful and beautiful, but he didn't need to see it firsthand. Heather would never complain, but anyone who knew her knew she considered the intimacy she shared with Storm private. He didn't want to upset her by not leaving when he knew he should.

Time to check their perimeter, make sure the security he set up wouldn't be noticed, and still do its job. The planet had some strange rules. They didn't allow advanced technology unless it could be hidden from others. They worked along the lines of if they don't know about it then you're not doing anything wrong.

He turned the corner and spotted the young woman who traveled with the merchant. She was busy following the man's orders and it gave Fridon a moment to study her. A petite thing by Vespian standards, she was tall for this race. Her golden skin sparkled in the late day sunlight. Her dark hair hung down her back in one big plat. He wondered how it would look if it was free of its binds. She was also quite pretty now that the bruises had faded.

The way the man treated her angered him. No one had the right to cause such harm. Fridon smiled. Let the man try to discipline her while he was with them. He would learn fast that pissing off Vespian males was the wrong thing to do.

His smile got wider. He had picked up a lot of Earth words from Heather. Storm frowned at him when he used them, but he liked the way they sounded and their meanings. Pissed off worked in this situation.

The man in question stepped out of his tent, spotted him, hesitated then wandered behind it. Fridon wondered what he was doing back there and thought about following, but knew he'd be able to view it later. If the man was up to something, his presence might stop him, but the camera would pick up everything. The small devices they planted around the area before Undar arrived were undisturbed so would still keep the site safe and let them know anything he might be up to.

He watched as the large sun started to set. Twilight here was so different than on Vespia. The big disk dipped below the horizon, leaving a black sky. Stars started winking in, filling the sky with light.

Vespia's two suns kept the sky lit a lot longer than this planet, but they weren't as close to such a large cluster of stars that lit up the night sky here. He had seen his share of other planets' skies, but he always missed home.

Once the sky had darkened, he turned toward the tent and stopped in his tracks. There, silhouetted against the side of the tent, was Storm and Heather in an intimate embrace.

He was mesmerized by the image of them. The passion between them was amazing. They moved together with such joy. At first Storm was on top, but he pulled Heather into his embrace as he moved to a seated position. He could see how being intimate with Storm affected Heather by the way she moved. She arched against him, her head falling back. It reminded Fridon of the picture they had given the media. Beautiful, mesmerizing. Knowing how shy Heather was about intimacy, he turned away, only to find the merchant staring at their images on the tent as well.

This was going to cause problems.

———

Storm held her close. He always made her feel cherished when they were intimate. The way he touched her made her feel precious. His lips found her mark, which sent frissons of heat through her blood.

They had moved into a seated position, which she loved. One of his arms ran up her spine to help hold her in place while the other was at her core, stroking her the way she liked and pushing her toward her orgasm.

She moved against him, feeling her muscles tighten around his shaft. Her back arched when he hit just the right spot.

"Storm." She felt her climax start to unfurl. Little frissons of heat pooled in her core before they zinged through her blood. Her muscles clenched as the orgasm caught her up and took over everything.

"My heart." His voice came out softly against her ear. He shook as her muscles clamped down on him, his release starting. Heather's breath hitched when she felt his climax as well. Sharing their orgasms like this was something they kept to themselves. The specialness of feeling each other's euphoria wash over them as muscles relaxed and hearts calmed down was something they could never describe.

"Each time it is glorious." He captured her lips with his. "And I always want more."

———

Once they finally ate, Storm stepped out and approached Fridon.

"You seem deep in thought."

"I think we might have a problem." Fridon was a little hesitant. "I was checking the perimeter and found we should have lit the tent a little differently."

"Why?"

"I'm not sure how to explain this. Perhaps you stay out

here, and I'll show you." He stepped into the tent after asking Storm to stand in a particular place.

Storm looked at the tent, wondering what he was trying to prove. Fridon walked toward the canvas wall and his shadow went from being slightly fuzzy to a sharp image. Heather walked up to her friend and started to gesture. It didn't take much for him to go stomping into the tent.

"You watched?"

"It caught me unawares, but I did look away. I can't say the same thing about our company."

"Is there something wrong?" asked Heather.

"It seems we put on quite a show earlier."

"Show?" Her brow furrowed. She looked at the canvas wall and back at Storm. Her eyes widened. "Oh! You mean he saw everything?"

"I'm afraid so." Storm watched her as she digested the information. A slight blush filled her cheeks.

"Well, I hope he enjoyed the show." She kept her gaze down.

"Are you okay?" Storm placed fingers under her chin and lifted her face.

"I am fine."

"You don't sound it."

She touched his face. He could feel her frustration with the situation. Knowing Fridon saw didn't bother her as much as knowing the merchant did. The man gave her the creeps. He returned the gesture, knowing anything he said didn't really matter. What was done was done. They couldn't change the past, but they could use it to their advantage.

———

They couldn't travel far with Undar with them since Heather had to walk the whole way. Storm found his presence annoying. He missed being able to touch his mate whenever he wanted. Heather never would have said anything if he tried while traveling with this man, but he knew he would have the man's undivided attention the whole time, and Storm didn't want that.

All day he watched as Undar mistreated the young woman he had. Not enough for Storm to confront him, but he would pull on her chain for no apparent reason or push his horse into a quick trot so she had to run to keep up.

Fridon didn't like it any more than he did. Storm watched as his friend's hand tightened on his lead rope every time the young woman tried not to cry out. He ended up riding off to scout ahead, but Storm knew he couldn't watch anymore. When he came back, he spoke to Storm quietly about a small oasis ahead. It would give everyone a chance to refresh their water supply and bathe.

Storm found himself standing next to the man while the women put their tents up.

"I have a friend who lives nearby. I'm sure he would welcome us."

"We don't need to disturb your friend, but you don't have to stay here with us if you wish to visit him. We could part our ways now." Storm hoped he would leave them. Traveling with this little weasel angered him.

He didn't answer right away. "She has already put up the tent so I can't ask her to take it back down again. I will stay."

Storm wanted to know why he brought up the subject in the first place then. He knew if he had said yes then Undar would have demanded she take the damn thing down in his hurry to get them to his friend's.

Heather lifted the flap to let him know she was done, but

following his desires, she didn't come out. He gazed at her and felt his want grow. Storm had spent the whole day near her without being able to do anything about it and he needed a little physical contact. He strode in and swept her up in his arms.

"Miss me?" She grinned up at him.

"Very much." He paused long enough to drink from her lips for a moment. "I'm used to being able to touch you whenever I want."

"I was close by."

"Walking." He pressed a soft kiss against her mark. "I would have been much happier with you in my lap."

"Ah, but you could have brought me up anytime. We just would have had an audience."

"Which you don't like, and I have found I don't either. Our sex life is just between the two of us, and I don't care for others watching."

"Now wait a minute. Vespian culture allows couples to have sex wherever and whenever they want." She touched his face.

"Yes, but even though it is part of our culture we honor the intimacy." He returned the gesture. "Do you stop and stare when we pass by two people expressing their need for each other?"

"Well no. I normally turn away from it. It's for them to enjoy, not me."

"Exactly, because you understand our way and show respect to the act." He nuzzled her throat. "That man doesn't. He covets what I have and that bothers me. I have seen what he did to that poor girl and there were several times when I wanted to take a whip to him over the way he keeps harassing her."

"A lot of the men are like him."

"You feel that way because of what you went through

before, but I have seen different. The men at Busandio's home didn't treat their women harshly."

"They didn't treat their women the way you treat me."

"You are special." He carried her to their bed. "And I want to show you just how special you are to me."

"I hope you know your meal will be late because of this."

He laughed as he lowered her to the mattress. "It doesn't matter to me since I'm having my dessert right now."

Storm released the clasp on her top. He dipped his head to capture one peak in his mouth. The gentle sucking motion made Heather sigh. His hands worked on the skirt she wore, easing it off her hips. He placed a kiss against her stomach as he freed her from the garment.

"How about you?" She touched his shirt.

"It will be disappearing in just a second." He stood long enough to shed his clothes before joining her back on the bed. "There."

She laughed.

"What?" He had climbed up her body just as fast and brushed a few strands of her hair out of her face.

"You fill me with such happiness when you act like this. We have been together long enough for you to get a little bored with me, yet you still act like you did when we first met. Like you can't get enough."

"You have brought this up before. What is bothering you?" He touched her chin so she would look at him.

"I don't know. Maybe it is this place. These men don't seem to care about what happens to the women. So many rules harm the women more than help them."

"But you are looking at their world through your eyes, not theirs." He brushed his fingers against her mark. "This is the way they have lived for thousands of years. If you were to try to change it the women would fight you harder than the men, I think. They know what is expected of them. The men need them to do for them."

"But it's not right."

"Okay, you were a security officer on Earth. You were comfortable in that position, weren't you?" When she nodded, he continued. "Then you went to Vespia, totally out of your element and you struggled to fit in."

"But I did fit in." She slid one leg around his waist while the other wrapped around a thigh.

"But until then you feared our pleasurers, the fact that our people don't see sex the same way you had been taught. Now it doesn't bother you." He surged inside her. "I remember when you saw your picture for the very first time on one of the huge screens through the public newsfeed. You were embarrassed when I found it arousing."

"You still do."

"I know." He grinned as he lowered his mouth to her mark for a quick lathe. "But you need to see their way of life from their perspective. You need to forget what you have been through and look at this world with new eyes. And I know how to make you forget."

"You do, don't you?"

He pulled out and drove back in. Her muscles tightened against him. "What do you think?"

"I don't want to. I want you to work your magic, so I don't have to."

"That's my girl." His lips caressed her mark, drawing the soft tissue into his mouth. She moved beneath him as it went straight to her groin. He set a pace that allowed him to go deep as he made her body sing. Each stroke filled her completely.

Heather tilted her hips, her breath catching as he hit the right spot over and over. Her legs locked around his hips as she grew closer to her orgasm. Her body shook, muscles clamped down and she soared. Her world splintered around her. The power of it brought Storm right along with her.

His mouth found hers, their tongues danced together.

"My heart, you are amazing."

"You make me that way."

———

Storm stepped out of the tent to see Fridon waiting for him. His second had never looked so angry. "Problem?"

"To me? Yes." He waited until Storm cleared the opening of the tent. "He struck her."

"We didn't hear a thing." Storm looked toward Undar's structure.

Fridon pulled a small device out of his pocket. The item made Storm grin, a sound blocker.

"I knew you and Heather would want your privacy and if he heard anything he would be staring at that tent, hoping for a glimpse of something he shouldn't." He shrugged. "I had it on when you entered the tent. My goal was to shield you from him, but I ended up shielding him from you."

"What happened?"

"I don't know. She was working over there and must have done something that upset him because he back-handed her." He put the small device back in his pocket. "The bruise is already starting to show."

"I told him he would lose her if he mishandled her." The man was treading on thin ice.

"I reminded him of that. He balked at first, saying I had no right to speak to him because I was your man, but I reminded him that I am not your servant, but being trained by you. I also showed him that arguing with me wasn't a smart thing to do."

"And how did you do that?"

"I used one of Heather's joint locks." He grinned. "It is very persuasive."

"Make Heather aware of the young woman joining us sometime this evening." Storm crossed his arms over his chest. "I warned him he would lose her if he did anything that I would consider harmful. He didn't believe me. I will make him see the error of his ways, but I must do this properly and follow their rules. Once she is with us, I don't want him to find a way to get her back."

"Can I be of assistance?"

"I need to see the girl. See the proof of the damage and then I need to show him how to treat a woman properly."

"I hope Heather goes along with your plan."

"She'll have no choice."

———

Storm requested that they eat their meal outside this time. He wanted to see the young woman. He needed to see the evidence before he could act. Undar came out alone, watching Storm. He smiled as he scratched. His blemishes were fading, but he was still itching.

"Where is your property?" he asked as Heather knelt beside him, holding his plate as she offered him a bite of his food. Storm took the offered morsel and ate as he kept his gaze on Undar. "I wish to see her."

"She isn't feeling well."

"Is that because you hit her so hard you don't want me to see the damage?" Storm crossed his arms over his chest. "You think I don't know what happened while I was occupied?"

"She was slow."

"Sometimes slow is good." He gestured toward Undar's tent. "Bring her out. Now!"

He glared at Storm but did as he asked.

Undar dragged her out but kept her behind him. "See? She is fine."

Storm stood and walked over to where the young woman cowered. His size frightened her and as much as he wished to calm her fears, he had an image to portray. The bruise on her right cheek looked ugly. He wanted to throttle the man. How could he be so cruel? He gestured for Fridon to step forward to escort her to their tent. "Once you're done, clear his tent of any of her personal effects. Bed, clothing, you know what to look for."

Fridon nodded. He took her hand and urged her to follow him.

Heather stood. She wanted to help the young woman settle in, but Storm had other plans. She walked until she realized she could go no further. Her chain stopped her. Turning, she saw that Storm held the other end. She looked at him quizzically.

"It is sad to see that you don't know how to treat a woman." He tugged on the chain, drawing her to him. Storm hoped she would forgive him, but he wanted to prove a point.

"I know how to treat my property." Undar watched Heather with an unhealthy intensity. "You, on the other hand, are too lenient. You let your base desires rule you."

"Really? What makes you say that?" He looked up at his mate, silently letting her know what he wanted to do. He knew she didn't like it because of the way she glared at him.

"You have to discipline women from time to time to make them behave."

"Have you seen me ever raise my hand to mine? Yet she does what I ask of her. Kindness can work more than cruelty." He brought her to stand directly in front of him. Patting his lap, he waited for her to straddle him.

"A woman is like a fine wine. It takes a lot of work to get them to be the sweet nectar you want to enjoy. They need to know they are important in your life. Beating them doesn't make them want to do anything for you. It just makes them fear you." He touched Heather's face. Her silent anger told him she didn't like the way he was using her. There would be some explaining later, but he would enjoy making this up to her. "But the joy of the way they change your life is worth everything you own."

"They are only property."

"That is where you are wrong. Without them there are no children. Without children the race dies. To mistreat them goes against the reason they are here. Your line will die because you harm the vessel that brings your progeny forward." Storm undid the clasp that held Heather's top on. "Why would you want to do that?"

"I can always buy another one." He watched as Storm dropped her bra to the ground. The man tried to see what he exposed but he made sure Heather was at an angle that hid her from him.

"And mistreat her just as badly?" Storm shook his head. He slid a hand up her back, so soft it felt like velvet. "How can you harm something so precious?"

"What do you mean?" Undar shifted in his seat.

Storm watched as the man stared at his mate's back. Conscious of Heather's nudity, he pulled her close to help shield her body from Undar's prying eyes. "Have you ever noticed how soft women are? Their skin is like satin." His fingers glided down her back. "So soft. It begs for my touch."

"You spoil her."

"I do." Storm smiled. "But in return she trusts me. Even now, although she doesn't like the fact I am using her to prove a point, she knows I would never do anything to hurt her so she is sitting on my lap half naked. If you were to try this, your property wouldn't have the same trust and you would have probably beaten her to a pulp by now, trying to force her to do something I can do with just a nod."

"They need discipline."

"You said that before, yet I have never had to raise a hand to Heather. I show her compassion, devotion and kindness. In return I get trust, faith, and passion. I know just where to touch her to spark that passion." He slid his hand up her spine. "It is beautiful to see."

Heather sat straight in his embrace. Angry at what he was doing. He was sure he'd get an earful if she could speak freely, but he was proud she allowed him to put her through this. His fingers continued to glide up and down her spine. It was to calm her as well as show how she enjoyed his touch.

"Right now, she is frightened. I can see it in her posture. How she holds herself away from me. Can you see it?"

"Yet she seems to be tolerating your touch."

"Tolerating, that is a good word. She more than tolerates my touch though. Even now, with you watching, I know if I caress her just the right way she will melt in my arms because she trusts me and knows I would never harm her." Storm looked at the man. "You on the other hand only care about yourself. You don't care what people think of you."

"I am a merchant. It isn't my job to befriend every person I deal with."

"True, but how will you continue to make money when those people refuse to purchase from you a second time?" Storm pulled Heather's pelvis against his. He needed to be sure Undar couldn't see anything and having her body flush against his was one way to be sure. It also would help arouse her. The weasel needed to understand.

"What does this have to do with the way I treat my property?"

"Everything. When patrons see how you treat your property, they know you don't care. Why would they trust you and what you have to sell?" Storm wondered if his words were sinking in. "Every time you raise your hand against that young woman you show no respect. She does what you say out of fear, not because she trusts or respects you. Your cruelty has her cringing every time you come near her. Then you question why she fights you. You expect her to just do as you say because you think she is supposed to just take the abuse. You will never get the type of response I do with that attitude."

Storm brushed Heather's hair off her collarbone and started to press soft kisses against the skin he exposed. Little bumps raised on her arms. His lips found her mark and focused on that one spot for a few moments. He slipped his hands under her derriere and tilted her hips a bit more so her core was pressed intimately up against his erection. The thin cloth of his pants didn't give them much of a buffer so she could feel him as he pulsed against her heat. A shudder raced through her.

"Have you ever had a woman react to your touch like this?" Heather's demeanor had changed when he pulled her against him. She relaxed against him, desire taking control. Now he wanted to take that up a notch.

He slipped the hand not protecting her nudity between them and slid his fingers into her folds. The slight tension he felt in her body relaxed as he caressed her. Her anger hadn't dissipated. He could feel it through their connection, but she kept her thoughts to herself so he wouldn't get distracted. Each stroke lowered her anger and raised her desire. It didn't take too many caresses before she was lost in the sensations. Her head dropped back, and her breath came out in short pants. "She is so beautiful right now, so arousing, and all mine."

He stood with her in his arms, not wanting to exploit her anymore. He carried her into the tent. One look to Fridon and the area was cleared.

"My heart." He waited for the anger he knew she felt.

"I can't believe you did that to me." Her eyes held so much hurt. "And in front of him."

"Are you questioning me? My ability to protect you?" He hadn't set her down and tightened his grip a little in anger.

"I...no." She broke eye contact with him.

"He didn't see any more than what I wanted him to see." He used his free hand to lift her chin so she would look at him again. A single tear slid down her cheek. He gently wiped it away. "The man doesn't know how his cruelty affects the way women react to him."

"And he doesn't care." Her voice was flat like it was when she first learned of this mission. "All he knows now is that I am passionate with you and that will translate to money for him."

"So you think I made matters worse."

She didn't respond.

"Good. My goal was to goad him. If he wants you, then what he saw will push him to act faster." He touched her face. "But I have upset you and that wasn't my goal. Now what can I do to make you feel better?"

"How about loosening your grip?"

"And let you escape? Don't think so." He looked around. "I miss the ability to pin you to a wall. Canvas just isn't the same. If I could pin you like I want to, I would be able to free up my hands and use them to make you forget everything but you and me."

"So what are you going to do?"

"Hmmm. I'm thinking a bone melting kiss." His lips claimed hers. Soft at first, then demanding, his tongue delved into her mouth, searching for hers so they could dance the way they always did. She melted against him, falling into the sensations he brought forth. When he finally broke the kiss, they were both breathing a little hard. "Still mad at me?"

"You going to kiss me like that again?" She touched his face with a tender hand.

"Of course."

"Then yes, very and I think it's going to take a lot more of those kisses to make it go away."

"That's my girl." He carried her to the bed and laid her down. "But I know an even better way to change your mood."

After removing their remaining clothes, he joined her, his lips finding her mark. She arched up against him as he pulled the sensitive skin into his mouth. He knew what that did to her. His hand caressed their way down her arms until he reached her fingers. After lacing his with hers, he pinned her arms to the bed.

"Storm."

"My heart, you can be very demanding when in the throes of passion, and I want to prepare my playground properly." He nibbled his way down her collar to her breast. The heat of his mouth, focusing on her nipple, made her groan. His tongue swirled around the tip a few times before he latched on, sucking on her until it pebbled under his ministrations. Once he had the desired effect, he worked on the other one, paying homage to it until it reacted like the first. He lifted his head and smiled at her. "And I know just how to do that."

"I'm not sure I can wait any longer."

"I know, and the longer I prepare my favorite playground the better chance I have of drawing a scream from you. They are a rare gift." He moved down to dip his tongue into her belly button before moving to her mound. She came off the bed when she felt the heat of his mouth at her core. Oh, she was ready.

He focused on her core, drawing a moan this time. Good sign. She kept trying to move her hands. Which he allowed, but he didn't let go of her fingers so all she could do was move them around.

"Now. Please."

"I love it when you beg, my heart." He climbed back up her body, centered himself, and drove in deep. He was gifted with another moan. "Now that bodes well for my scream."

"My heart."

He latched on to her mark as he set a pace to drive her wild. Her breath came out in short pants as he pounded into her. Her muscles tightened against him, making him suck in his breath at the exquisite vise she created. Her hips tilted, and her legs slid up higher on his waist.

Storm changed the tempo, making it slower. His goal was to strike that spot that could make her scream, as many times as possible. That scream was music to his ears.

———

Fridon stood outside the tent with the young woman they liberated. He didn't know what to do with her. The young woman cowered in front of him, keeping her gaze to the ground. He didn't even know her name. Fridon couldn't handle the silence any longer. "You may speak."

She nodded but kept her gaze away from him and remained silent.

"I gave you permission to speak and I stand by it. We

don't strike our women." He wasn't sure if that would help, but he didn't know what he could say to get her to talk to him. He thought about reaching down and getting her to stand up and face him, but he feared she'd faint on him.

A moan filled the air. He looked at the tent. Not the perfect time for Heather to do that. The poor girl shook when she heard it.

"Will I have to satisfy him the way she does?" she asked, her voice barely a whisper.

"No. Heather is his only sex partner." He smiled. At least she was now speaking. She had noticed how often they were intimate, and they probably intimidated her.

"What about you?" She glanced up at him for a moment before lowering her gaze.

He wasn't sure how to answer that. For a second, he saw hope in her eyes. Was it because she did find him attractive or hope she wouldn't have to spread her legs for another heartless man? "What do you wish?"

"I listen to my owner." She kept her gaze down.

"You won't be forced into anything you don't wish to do." He stood up, needing to do something constructive. The moment he moved she cringed. "Why do you fear me?"

She looked at him again. Exotic eyes with every shade of brown. They started off dark but lightened toward the center. He found them beautiful.

"*He* would say such things, then hit me." Her voice was soft, as if she was afraid of the sound.

"You have no reason to be afraid anymore. Women are to be cherished, not beaten. I might yell, but I will never harm you. To do so goes against my nature." He laughed as he thought of the two stubborn people he traveled with. "Wait until the first time when Heather and Storm don't agree on something, and you'll see. Storm will get very angry with Heather, but he would never raise a hand to her."

"He is just so big." She looked back at the tent, then back at him. "But so are you."

"Yes, well, that is because people are much taller where we come from. Our size might be a little intimidating, but you'll find us to be very kind."

She nodded again, but didn't say anything else, just kept watching the tent and listening.

———

Every stroke sent little quakes through Heather. Storm had her body singing. Her legs moved against his as she felt her orgasm coming. He penetrated as deep as she could take him, yet she wished he could go deeper. Warmth filled her, starting at the pit of her stomach and spreading out to her arms and legs. Another moan escaped.

Storm's hot mouth tugged on her mark as he switched between lathing it and sucking it between his teeth. It made her shake. Her breath caught as she felt everything tighten. Then her orgasm roared through her. It wrapped around her spine, pulling her away from the world for a few moments. When she did return, she heard Storm's breath coming out in pants like hers.

"Sorry, there was no scream," she said once she found she could talk again.

"Oh, my heart, don't worry about it. I still made you boneless and make it possible for you to have your out of body experiences each time. As long as you enjoy each and every time with me, that's what matters." His lips claimed her mark once more.

"With the way you make my body want you all the time? I will always enjoy it." Her eyes closed as she felt desire unfurl again. "Um, we need to set the perimeters."

"Fridon can take care of it," he murmured against her throat.

"We also have a new guest who needs to learn the way we do things." Heather was torn between wanting to spend more time with Storm and helping their new guest fit in. "I'm sure she wonders what is expected of her."

He lifted his head up and looked at her.

"We're not the quietest couple." She touched his face. "I'm sure she wonders if she'll have to satisfy you as well."

"And you want to mark your territory?"

"Yes." She smiled at him. "You know I don't like to share."

He lowered his mouth to her throat once again. "In a few moments."

Heather felt very relaxed when she peeked out to find the young woman close to the tent. She kept looking over her shoulder as she sat there, waiting. Storm exited the tent, which had her scurrying to her feet. Once he went by, she spotted Heather at the flap. She straightened and waited.

"Come, let us talk." Heather held the flap open for the girl, then gestured to a small pile of pillows that she had put together for them to sit on. She had never been the lead woman before. This was new for her. "I know your last owner was cruel to you. I want to assure you that neither Storm nor Fridon will ever strike you. In fact, you're going to find them quite kind."

"He gave you permission to use his name?" Fear laced her voice.

"Yes." Heather smiled. A lot of women didn't have the same privileges she did. "But I bore him children, so he felt I deserved it."

"You did?" She looked around, not seeing any evidence of children. "Did he eat them?"

"No." Heather couldn't help but laugh. Storm's size had the young woman so nervous she didn't know what to think of him. "They are still small and are with family. He didn't think we should bring them on this trip."

She looked at the flap, still deciding if what had happened to her was a good thing.

"When it is just the four of us you will find the rules very relaxed." Heather watched her. What Heather was about to explain to her would go against everything she had been trained to do. "You will find it hard to under-stand in the beginning, but women are equal to men in Storm and Fridon's eyes. Where we come from men and women share the workload. Even though they can't help us physically here, these two men understand the value of our impute."

The young girl didn't look like she understood what Heather was saying so she tried again. "They know we're capable of knowing things they don't. In other words, they want your opinion if you know a better way to do things."

She just blinked at her.

Okay, so maybe she would need to be convinced of that before she believed it. Time to switch subjects.

"We didn't anticipate anyone joining us so I can't give you total privacy." Heather stood and took the girl back to the area where she would sleep. "I took a panel from Fridon's area and one from Storm's to give you what I could. We will pick up more panels when we reach the next town."

She touched her bed and the few items Fridon took as hers. Her hands lingered over a small bag. It had a few medicinal items and made Heather wonder if she was a healer.

Looking around, she didn't see a bed for Heather. "Where is yours?"

"There." She pointed to the area where she and Storm slept.

"You sleep with him all the time?" Shock laced her voice.

"Yes." Heather kept a straight face when all she wanted to do was laugh at her reaction. There was no other place she wanted to be.

"His desire for you is very strong."

"Yes." Heather smiled again. The young woman had no idea, but she'd see it firsthand very soon. Storm's eyes were already glowing when he left the tent earlier and they had just been intimate.

"I spoke to our owner's man, and he said you are his only sex partner. That I wouldn't have to satisfy him that way." She looked at Heather with a touch of fear in her eyes. "Is that true?"

"It is true." Heather touched her hand to make her look up at her. "I satisfy his needs."

"Are you trained well, or is it a natural talent?"

Heather felt her cheeks heat up as Storm sensed her embarrassment. *My heart, you know why I want only you. Tell her.*

"Um."

"I have embarrassed you." The young woman ducked her head. "I meant no disrespect."

"You haven't done anything wrong." Heather pushed her embarrassment away so she could calm the girl down. "I have always been shy about talking about sex. There is something about his touch that makes my body sing. There is an honesty between us that fills us with such joy. We can't get enough of each other."

"You like his touch?" she asked, her voice barely above a whisper.

"Very much."

"And what about his man?"

"He's all yours if you wish. You will find him to be a very good lover. He respects women." Heather stood. Time to let her think about what she was told. "It is time to make the meal."

"I wish to make it." She didn't look at Heather when she spoke.

"Really?" The request surprised Heather. Most women would stay in the background. Remain invisible as long as possible.

"I wish to show my thanks. I am a very good cook."

Heather smiled. Good, she was already trying to find her place. "What do you need?"

———

"Sir?"

Storm had sent Fridon off to check out where Undar was while he gave Heather time to speak to their newest addition. He looked up at Fridon as he rode back into camp.

"He is still following us, but at a safe distance. His camp is several rises behind us." He slid off his frulas.

"As long as he keeps that distance, he can follow us all he wants. I worry about him doing something stupid, like trying to get that young woman back." Storm looked at the tent where the two women were.

"What shall you do with her?"

"I don't know. Heather says I'll have to sell her before we leave here, but I don't think I can do that. It goes against everything we believe in."

"You going to bring her back to Vespia?"

"I can't do that either. Unless she is someone's mate."

Storm rubbed his chin. "Perhaps I can speak to Bear, and he can help me find her a safe home."

"And if he can't do anything?"

"You have been around my mate too long. You sound just like her right now." Storm saw Fridon's smile. "You think that is a compliment, don't you?"

"Yes, sir."

"I think she has corrupted you."

"No more than she has corrupted you, sir."

———

Heather helped the young woman when she needed to, but the girl did know what she was doing. She was amazed at their supplies. Undar must have had very little by the way she kept going on about what she was able to use.

"You know, you haven't told us your name."

"No one has ever asked me for it." She stopped what she was doing for a moment. "My parents called me Micali."

"Pretty name." Heather paused for a moment. She knew not all women gave their name to their owners. Of course, most of the time, the men didn't care to know anyway. "May I tell the others your name?"

"You ask my permission?"

"Yes." Heather smiled. "I tried to explain that the rules will be very relaxed. If you wish the men to use your name, I will tell them. If you wish to keep that power to yourself, I will keep it to myself."

"You may tell them."

"Good."

Once the meal was served, Heather gave all the credit to Micali. "She wished to thank you for taking her away from that madman."

"The meal is delicious." Storm smiled at her. "Thank you."

"Don't frighten her, my heart. I just got her talking," Heather teased.

"You can be as intimidating as I can."

"I have my moments." She winked at him. Heather was next to her mate and offered him a few bites from her plate. He took it as foreplay, sucking on her fingers a little bit longer than most men would. She felt it to her toes.

"Yes, you do." The glow in his eyes started a spark of desire deep inside her.

"I want to introduce you to Micali." Heather offered Storm another bite.

"A beautiful name." He took her offering, pulling her into his lap at the same time.

"Thank you," Micali said, her voice hesitant.

"There is no reason to fear us, Micali. You will find we don't believe in uncalled for violence." Storm pressed his lips to Heather's mark. "Can I assume you showed her where she'll sleep?"

"Yes. But we didn't discuss chores." She tilted her head to give him better access. "I wasn't sure how you wanted to break everything up."

"If it were up to me, Fridon and I would do most of it. Having to wait around while you do all the work grates on my nerves." He touched her face. "But I know you fear the repercussions if we were caught. I will leave how you separate the chores to you."

She nodded. "Then we'll work together to see which things one of us does better than the other."

"I need you two to stay inside tonight. Undar is following us."

"Figured as much. Do you know how far away he is?" Heather leaned her head against his chest.

"Of course, my heart. If I were to throw a rock east from this seat, you would hear his cry of pain from the contact."

Micali looked up in surprise.

"Have no fear, little one. We will protect you from the likes of him." Storm grinned.

Heather knew that smile. He was looking forward to the challenge.

———

Undar waited until after dark before leaving his camp. He knew they were aware of his presence and didn't want to alert them to his plans. If Storm's property was who he thought, she was worth a lot. That kind of money would line his pockets for years. He could even give up being a merchant if he wanted.

He approached the small shack with care. If he didn't announce his presence properly, he could end up with a hole in his chest. This man shot first, then asked questions when it came to strangers.

"Who is there?"

"Undar. I have news." He stood so the man could see him.

"You always say that." He lowered the crossbow he held in his hands. "I tend to disagree."

"But I have seen *her*." He pointed behind him. "She isn't far from here."

"And how do you know?"

"The woman I have seen is very tall, and violet eyes. That is how you described her." She wasn't fair skinned nor had the white hair he had described, but how many women had the violet eyes? It had to be her.

"She is close?"

"I can show you." He gestured for the man to follow

him. "But there are three things, Lewmard. She has no scars from your whip, has altered her looks, and she is guarded by her owner. Be warned, he is very protective of her."

"She was but a servant when I saw her last."

"Not now, and she has been trained to please her master."

"I don't care what she has been trained in. If you are right, I will finally get my revenge."

———

Storm's head snapped up. Someone was coming, his heightened sense of smell told him so. "You two need to go inside. Now."

Heather didn't question. She stood, took Micali's hand and headed into the tent.

Storm and Fridon stood and took guard.

"Two, Fridon, to our right." Storm kept his voice low. "The worm and someone new."

"Shall I circle behind them?"

"I want you to stay put. It shouldn't take much to scare them away. I can smell Undar's fear. The other man is angry and a bit confused." Storm turned to Fridon and smiled. "We have our sensors set up so they can't get too close without making us aware. Perhaps we should have a little fun this evening and let them know we know they are there."

———

"You sure she is here?" Lewmard studied the area, but all he saw was two huge men standing in front of the tent. They stared out at the night. Did they know they were there?

"Yes. I saw her."

"I don't see any women." He turned to glare at Undar.

"He has probably made them go inside." Undar pointed at Storm. "I told you he protected her."

"No one has seen her for years and now all of the sudden she is within a few minutes of where I live? I find that hard to believe." He moved to leave.

"The woman's name is Heather."

That stopped him. The woman who ruined his life was named Heather. The name was too rare for him to ignore. "I need proof."

"Stay with me tonight. You'll see her tomorrow when they break camp."

FIVE

Storm realized the other man was the one to watch when their little prank last night didn't deter them. Storm had shifted and ran off the frulas with all their food. The animals didn't go that far, but it should have kept those two occupied long enough for them to start traveling.

He didn't like knowing Undar and that other man was still watching them. He wanted to remain where they were and keep the women inside, but Heather reminded him they had to keep going. That young woman they were sent to rescue couldn't wait for Storm to get rid of this new nuisance. Even now, she could be out of reach for them.

"Why haven't they approached us?" Storm looked out the flap of the tent but hadn't given the women permission to leave it yet. "They stay close enough to see us, but no closer. Does the new one need to see you?"

"I don't know, my heart. I can cover up if you wish." She still had the cloak designed for that in her satchel.

"If you do, he will probably continue to follow until he can see your face." He stepped up to her and touched her cheek with care. "The more time I spend here, the more I understand your dislike for this planet."

"You have a good handle on the language now. I could go back to the safety of the embassy."

"True, but Micali needs to feel secure around us. I can't see her feeling that way without you and I can't send her with you. You know our protocols won't allow her on the ship and it would take too long to backtrack. We will keep you safe. I just wish we could go home now."

"We can leave the moment we find her." She placed her hand on his heart.

"Be prepared to ride today. Make sure Micali understands. I want to put as much distance between them and us as I can."

Heather nodded. After she explained everything to Micali the two women took down and stored the tent quickly, ready to leave when the men were. She stood waiting while Storm mounted his ride. A wave of hatred and recognition crashed into her, knocking her to her knees. She stood quickly, but not before Storm had dismounted and stood before her, concern etched on his face.

"Are you okay?"

She could only nod. The hatred surrounded her, choking any response she could give. Storm gripped her arms, making her look up at him. He searched her features for whatever caused her to fall.

What is wrong, my heart?

Whoever is out there knows me. I can feel their disgust at my presence. They want to harm me. We must be very careful. Undar knows I am important to you, but he believes it is because of sex. Don't give them any other reason to suspect your desire to protect me. Don't give them any ammunition they could use against you.

He stepped back then, wrapping her chain around the pummel of his saddle, he remounted. Giving the signal, they headed out. Wanting to protect her, he wished he could deal with the new threat and be done with it, but the rules of this planet forbade so many things. He had to tread carefully.

———

"It is *her*." Lewmard grinned. "I knew she would show up sooner or later. Now I will have my revenge."

"And my payment?" asked Undar. He wanted to rub his hands together. This could make him very wealthy. Lewmard had put a high bounty on the woman's head.

"You will be paid when she becomes my property. Until then, we travel together. First though, we need to even the odds." He pulled a small container from his pocket and opened it up. An insect hopped up onto his hand. "Go, my little friend, share your bite with one of the males. Once he is dead, we can take down the other one."

The bug flitted away, flying toward the two men on the animals.

"What are we going to do in the meantime?"

"Go get our pack frulas. They won't get far before that bug does its job."

———

Micali walked behind Fridon's animal, not sure what to think of these people. The men set an easy pace for her and Heather to keep up with. So far, they had been kind and considerate, just like Heather said, making sure she was happy with the choices they made. Undar had an evil streak and would make his animal trot just to see her run to keep up, but he had been nice in the beginning too. Could they be trusted?

Fridon slapped at his back a few times like he had been

bitten by one of the bugs that fed on the animals, but they normally didn't bite people. She found it odd that one did. Perhaps it was just sweat rolling down his back that he swatted at.

It didn't take long before he started to sway in his seat. She looked up at him and noticed his pallor was off. Micali touched his leg by slipping her hand up under his pants and found his skin cold and clammy. Something was wrong. How was she supposed to make Storm and Heather aware? When Fridon slipped out of his seat and tumbled to the ground, she cried out and got their attention.

Storm turned his animal around, dropped Heather's chain and charged over to their side. Heather ran toward them, racing to where Fridon lay.

"What happened?" Heather asked as she touched his cheek. "Good Lord, he's burning up."

"Micali? What caused this?" asked Storm.

She dropped to her knees, tears spilling down her cheeks.

"My heart, give her a moment." Heather knelt beside Micali and took her hands. "You aren't in trouble. Storm is hoping you saw something that could have caused this."

"He was swatting at his back earlier like he was being bit. I thought he might be swatting at sweat in the beginning, but now I fear it was a bug that bit him." She wiped at her eyes. Undar would have beaten her if this had happened to someone traveling with him. Micali spoke softly and looked only at Heather, but knew Storm listened as well. "The only insect I know that can do this kind of damage so fast is a frenisu. They are rare and quite deadly."

Heather looked up at Storm. Micali's voice was strained, and she started to shake as she spoke. Was she afraid of what would happen if they lost their friend? The poor thing still didn't understand. She looked back at Micali. "Do you know what the bite looks like?"

"It's hard to miss." Micali kept her gaze down and her voice soft. "My father was bitten once, and we came close to losing him. I was the one who treated him and brought him back."

"We need to put the tent up." Heather patted her on the shoulder. She stood and turned to Storm. "Then we need to get him out of his clothes."

"Why?" Storm slid off his animal.

"We have to find the bite. It needs to be treated first." She turned back to Micali. "Do you have what we need to heal him?"

"Yes. The one thing Undar liked was that I could heal. He always made sure I had medicinal items." The hope that filled Micali's eyes showed she believed Heather trusted her and she would do whatever it took to keep that trust.

"Good. Let's get the tent up as fast as we can." The two women put the tent up in record time. Not worrying about the cloth partitions right away, they put Fridon's bed together and waited for Storm to carry him in.

"Now what?" Storm asked as he laid him on his bed.

"You and I remove his clothes while Micali gets the remedy ready," Heather said.

"And what are we looking for?" He held Fridon in a sitting position while Heather worked on pulling his tunic up over his head. Storm lifted him up so Heather could loosen his trousers and got a good look at his back. "Is it a big ugly thing that is taking up half his back?"

"Oh dear." Micali came to look where Storm was talking about. She touched it with fear. "It has festered. He wasn't bit that long ago so it shouldn't have done that so fast."

"Is the medicine ready?" Heather asked.

"Not quite." She looked at her, sending silent signals to

thank Heather for helping her keep her focus. The water had come to a boil, and she dropped items into it from her bag. She sniffed and added a few more things. "It needs to boil for a few minutes once I have everything in it. He might start shaking in a minute or two. If he does, you'll need to hold him down. He could harm himself."

"Let's get the rest of his clothes off. Make sure there are no other bites." Heather released his trousers so they could pool at his feet as Storm maneuvered him onto his bed. Dealing with Fridon's dead weight took a little work, but he was able to get the man on his stomach.

Micali came with the medicine. Now she had to give orders. How would Storm take that? She took a deep breath and looked at Heather. "Hold him as I apply this on the bite. He will react violently."

Storm sat on their friend, locking his legs down with his own as he pulled his arms in and pinned them with his knees.

She poured part of the hot liquid on the wound and Fridon started to buck. It took a couple of grunts and a short wrestle before Storm got him back under control. The wound started to shrink almost immediately.

"It's working." Heather sounded relieved.

"Now I need to pour the rest down his throat. It is bile and he will fight harder." She looked at Storm's chest, not quite ready to look him in the face. That fact that he did as she asked without getting upset because she had to give him instructions had her hoping he was as nice as Heather had said.

"How long before I can flip him over?"

"We might do better if he stayed in that position." She looked at Heather, who hadn't left her side. Between the two of them, they put the antidote into a sling and forced it down his throat. Fridon fought it, but Storm was able to keep his hold on him long enough for the women to get the awful cure in him. "Now we need to rub his neck, so he won't try to force it back out."

Storm held him tight as Heather and Micali worked on keeping the bile stuff inside. Once she was sure he wouldn't throw it back up, she relaxed. "Now we wait."

"Will he be okay?" asked Storm as he climbed off his friend's body.

"I think I got it in time, but I can't be sure until his fever breaks." She glanced up at Storm for a second before dropping her gaze.

"Keep me posted." He placed a hand on her shoulder and waited until she looked up at him. "Thank you. Fridon wouldn't have had a chance if you hadn't been here."

She ducked her head at his compliment.

Storm gestured for Heather to step away from Fridon's side. Speaking to her in Vespian, he asked, "Why did you let her heal him instead of using the emergency medpack?"

"The local remedy is actually better than anything we could use out of the kit. He will recuperate a lot faster under her care. If she hadn't been here, we would have had to give him a shot, then send him back to the ship until he was better. This way he will heal within the day and be able to continue with us and she gets to see she has value."

"You have a good heart to allow her this." He took her hands in his and led her to the section they normally slept in. "I'm not sure Fridon will be happy with you, though. That stuff smelled awful."

"I know, but if we hadn't allowed her to cure him and sent him back to the ship, he wouldn't have been able to help us. He would have been in the medlab for a week or more. I'm sure he would agree it was the best way."

"Do you think his illness is a coincidence?" Storm looked back at his second in training.

"I don't know." Heather picked up several of the pillows and started working on putting their bed together. "I have heard of the bug, and the planet lore says they can be trained to kill, but no one believes the old tales. No one has been able to prove it."

"You know these stories?"

"I have heard a few. I'm sure Micali knows more." Heather looked at him. "Why?"

"It is the timing. He gets sick right after you feel the hatred of someone directed at you. Right after Undar picks up a new friend." He walked to the flap and lifted it. "I don't like it. If these bugs can be trained, who says whoever did this won't try again?"

"You want to investigate to see if he has more. You know he probably won't be parading them where you'll see them."

"I still need to see what he is up to, but I don't want to leave you two alone." He pressed his hand to her heart.

"You have trained me well, and out here no one would know if I had to defend us. It would be your word against his." She returned the intimate gesture. "It is when we're around other people I have to act like the rest of the women to protect myself and you."

"Me?" He touched his chest. "I'm here to protect you."

"Oh, my heart." She laughed. "You would jump to my defense if I was accused of something that could bring harm to me. If you did that, you could be punished as well."

"You worry too much." He pulled her into his embrace.

"I learned to be overprotective by my mate." She rested her head against his chest. "And he is very good at it."

He hooked a finger under her chin so he could lift her face to his. His lips claimed hers. His tongue searched her mouth, looking for its partner so they could dance together. He loved the way she opened for him, never holding back. When he broke the kiss, she sighed her satisfaction.

"Stay inside while I'm gone."

She nodded, watched as he walked out of the tent.

Storm moved to where he couldn't be seen and shifted into his favorite form. He ran from the area so he could circle around and see what their followers were up to. Knowing they were still there bothered him.

He ran a wide circle and got behind them. Staying downwind, Storm inched his way toward them, hoping to get close enough to hear what they were saying. If he was lucky enough, he would catch them plotting something.

"Should we put our tent up?" asked Undar. They had binoculars in their hands and were watching Storm's tent, not paying attention to his wolf form sneaking up on them.

"Where did the big one go?" Lewmard looked around. He searched for signs of him, but Storm made sure to stay out of sight.

Storm could see the newer man was the dangerous one when he showed concern because he couldn't see Storm anymore. If that man tried to approach the tent while he was in his wolf shape. He'd have to rip his throat out. If Heather didn't beat him to it. At least he knew what the man looked like now.

"I don't know. He went behind the tent earlier and I haven't seen him come back." Undar didn't seem concerned in the least.

"We need to move. He's probably scouting around for us." They pulled back from the small buff they were hiding behind and headed to their animals. "We'll make camp three rises back. That should be back far enough, so they won't know we're here and still let us keep an eye on them."

"Do you think the bug did its job?"

"We won't know until we see them bury the other man."

"And if it didn't?"

"I don't have another one, so we'll have to try something else."

Storm came back into the tent after watching the two men set up and bed down for the night. He didn't like those two being so close. He checked the perimeter to make sure everything was working right. If they tried to sneak into the tent while everyone was resting, they wouldn't get too far.

Heather had left a plate for him out near the fire. She must have done that when she came out to dampen it and put everything else away. He had asked her to stay inside but learned a while ago that she wasn't very good at following his requests when she felt something else was more important. A runaway fire could cause some damage, but she could have waited until he got back. Thank goodness he had been watching the two people he knew would attack if they had realized he was gone.

After eating, he entered the tent and found the lights had been dimmed as well. Fridon still lay on his back with Micali sitting on the floor next to his cot, resting her head on the mattress. She must still be worried about him, or she would be in her own bed, which Heather must have put together after he left. He hoped his friend would make it through this.

He found Heather curled up on their bed, naked, with a light cover draped over her. Her hair was spread out across the pillows, still the darker golden brown the chip had brought it to. Her skin sparkled in the low light. She had feared what Kuarto had done for them might disappear as time went on, since she had never been able to dye her hair or tan, but her brother was excellent at what he did. There had been no fading or odd glitches his mate kept looking for. He was getting used to her new color but missed her alabaster skin.

Storm removed his clothes and slipped in beside her, then pulled her into his arms. He heard her sigh as she settled against him. "I know you're not asleep."

"Very close. You were gone a long time."

"So long you felt you couldn't stay inside like I asked?" He brushed her hair away from her face and throat.

"There was no one else, and it needed to be done." She turned in his arms so she could gaze into his eyes. "My heart, I can take care of myself. I have proven that over and over."

"It doesn't stop me from worrying." He touched her face with gentle fingers. "Those two are dangerous and that one truly hates you."

"I promise to keep myself safe. I also have two of the best security men from Vespia to protect me." She placed her hand against his heart. "Now, do you want to talk about how I always seem to get into trouble all night long?"

"You know me too well." He chuckled. "I always have better things to do with you than talk about how I wish you would listen to me better."

"Thought so." She slid one of her legs around his. "I've been lying here thinking about all the delicious ways you have punished me in the past. What are you planning this time?"

"I knew you enjoyed your punishments too much." His lips caressed her mark, making her move beneath him. "But right now, all I can think of is being inside you."

"Shifting does make your desire spike."

He drove into her, making her suck in her breath. Her body shook at the sweet invasion.

"Wow. You must have just shifted."

"I did." He sighed with pleasure. "I love the way your body tightens against me. Holds me like it doesn't want to let go."

Heather wrapped her legs around his waist, feeling every slight movement as if it was the beginnings of an orgasm. He filled her so completely she didn't think her body could take too much before it skyrocketed. "You might get that supernova tonight."

"Really?" He slid out and drove back in.

"Oh my, yes." She arched up against him. "It feels too good."

"My heart, you haven't felt anything yet." He wrapped his arms around her and pulled her into a sitting position, still buried inside her. "Think I'll get that scream tonight?"

Heather cast a quick glance where Fridon lay. "You just might."

"You worried about what they might hear?" He pressed his lips against her mark.

She didn't answer as she sighed, but she didn't have to. He knew how she felt. The white noise machine was over near Fridon, and he wasn't about to move. Neither was she.

"Have you tried to turn on the machine with your mind?" He slid his arm up her back and pressed another kiss against her mark.

"No." Her muscles tightened against him as a slight crease furrowed her brow. "Do you think I can?"

"You have a very powerful mind and you've been able to move things with it before." He touched her face.

"But those items were touching me, it was easy to manipulate them because I could feel them against my skin. This is different. I've only tried this once before and wasn't very good at it."

"But you were able to move the picture." He knew she

meant the time she took over her daughter's body when she was in danger. It had only been a few months ago. She was able to move a picture enough to send it crashing to the ground and startle her daughter's abductors. "Try, my heart."

A thrill raced through her, causing her muscles to tighten against him again as she cleared her mind. Closing her eyes, she had to reopen one when she heard his quick intake of breath. "You liked that, didn't you?"

"Very much."

"Well, there might be more. I've never tried to do this on purpose before." She closed her eyes again and shifted her weight so she was comfortable.

"My heart, you can practice this every time we're intimate." His voice was soft and very close.

She didn't answer him. Heather pulled the image of the machine into her mind. Once she could see it clearly, she focused on the volume and turning it up. At first, she couldn't get it to move, but slowly she was able to raise it so no one would hear them. "Just like the picture."

"Next time you might find yourself distracted." He spoke softly. "You kept flexing against me, my heart. I can't take anymore."

"Then we need to put you out of your misery." She lifted up and slid back down his length. She was gifted with a shudder from him. His fingers slid into her folds, caressing her with just the right amount of pressure. Her head dropped back at the exquisite sensations. Each stroke brought her closer to the edge. Storm played her like a fine instrument as she rode him, bringing her to her orgasm quickly. It started in her core, unfurling through her bloodstream, racing through her body. It overtook her, making her whimper at first before it grabbed her with its full force, tearing a scream from her.

"That's my girl," Storm whispered near her ear as he reached his climax too.

———

Fridon opened his eyes to see a fuzzy brown haze in front of him. It took a few seconds for his vision to focus better and to realize it was Micali's hair. The faint scent of her soap filled his senses. He wanted to reach out and stroke her hair, but the woman was so frightened of everything he dared not. She was such a pretty thing too. He wished they had met before the damage to her was done. He bet she would have been a wonderful bed partner.

He lifted his head as the volume on the white noise machine went up and knew Heather and Storm were being intimate. Fridon was grateful they trusted him with their secrets. If they hadn't, he'd probably be yelling for them to come to his side, trying to explain what he just saw. All he'd end up doing would be to embarrass Heather and that was something he never wanted to do.

Micali's head lifted when they couldn't hear Heather and Storm anymore.

"It's okay. We have a machine that blocks sound, so we don't have to listen in on them." His voice came out a little raspy. Maybe he wouldn't have been able to yell after all.

"He won't hurt her, will he?"

He found it sweet that she worried about Heather and annoying that she thought every man would hurt a woman the way Undar had hurt her. The fact that she spoke to him at all spoke volumes about the trust she was putting in what they told her about no one harming her ever again.

"Storm cares for Heather very much. All he wants to do is give her pleasure."

"Pleasure?" She turned her face so she could look at him.

"She enjoys the act as much as he does." He saw the shock on her face. It was obvious she had been used by Undar. He didn't care about her, only his needs.

"How?"

"What did Undar do to you? You never had any joy from sex? Not once? No slight thrill? Or excitement?"

She didn't answer him.

"Did he ever kiss you?"

"No." She shook her head. The look on her face showed she was happy about it too.

"It's such a beautiful thing. I can't believe he never showed you the sweetness of a simple kiss."

She watched him, wondering if he spoke the truth, yet fearing the idea. He felt for her. He needed to show her how wonderful it could be when passion flared between two people, but would she be willing to allow him that chance? Had she been hurt too deeply to enjoy any level of intimacy?

"May I show you?" He knew he needed to be very gentle with her. She looked like a frightened animal, ready to bolt at any moment. Micali surprised him when she nodded her agreement. Fridon moved his face close enough to hers so he could brush his lips against hers. He did it several times until he felt her relax enough to accept him touching her, even if it was only with his mouth. He pressed his against hers, with a gentle pressure, hoping she would allow his entrance without having to ask for it. A sigh escaped her, and his tongue entered her mouth. She froze for just a moment before her curiosity got the best of her.

He wanted to draw her close, hold her against him as he explored her mouth, but knew she'd probably fight him. He had to let her feel safe, so he kept his hands to himself. Their tongues danced together, sparking need inside him. He had to stop before it got out of hand. When he broke the kiss, he was blessed with a sigh. She enjoyed that.

"Why did you stop?"

Now how was he going to answer that?

He was saved by the presence of Storm.

"I'm glad to see you awake. How are you feeling?" Storm flashed a smile that made most women swoon. Micali shrank away from him, his overpowering presence too much for her.

"I'm awake so that is a good thing. What happened?"

"You were bitten by a nasty little bug. If it hadn't been for Micali, we could have lost you."

He looked at her. "You took care of me?"

She nodded.

"Thank you."

Heather joined them, a bright smile on her face, happy to see her friend awake and alert. "If you feel up to it, I have saved you some of our meal."

"I am hungry." He swung his legs to the floor and felt lightheaded. "If my body will behave."

"Should we prepare him something else?" asked Heather. She looked at Micali and waited for an answer.

"He can eat normal food, although he might not eat as much as he thinks he wants," she said, her voice soft.

"Can he walk out to where I have it stored, or should we bring it back in here?"

Heather was worried about him, and he wished she wasn't. He would do this to prove to her he was fine. "I'm fine, Heather."

"He should be able to walk, with a little help." Micali looked up at him, faith in her eyes. If she said he could do it, he would.

Storm moved to help Fridon up.

"I can do this, sir."

"You couldn't even lift your head two hours ago. My mate would be very upset with me if I didn't offer my help.

You know how she favors you." Storm pulled him to his feet.

"And because of that, I must walk on my own." He steadied himself before he could take a step. "I am here to protect her. How would it look if I had to rely on you to get outside?"

Fridon took his time but was able to make it out to the fire on his own.

Heather stood as he stepped out of the tent. The look on her face to see him up and about made the effort it took to get there worth it. He took his seat, then gave her his best smile, even though he felt like he had walked a marathon.

Heather picked up the plate she had left for him earlier and sat it next to the fire for a few minutes to let it heat up. Once she felt everything was warm, she picked it back up and handed it to him.

Heather touched Micali's shoulder, but she shook her head.

"Are you two not eating?"

"We ate earlier, my heart," Heather explained. "But that frees me up to feed you if you wish."

A spark entered his eyes. "I have enjoyed that a lot, haven't I?"

"Very much." She smiled at Storm.

Fridon knew the white noise machine was going to get a workout this evening.

"Perhaps I should feed you, too?" Micali said softly.

Was that one of the reasons Heather offered? To put the idea out there? He looked at the plate and knew that trying to eat on his own would take more energy than he had at the moment. "That would be nice."

Micali nodded. She knelt in front of him and picked up the plate. Her hands shook as she offered him his first bite. He closed his mouth around her two fingers. Eyes widening, she looked up when he held onto her fingers a little longer than she expected.

Fridon saw desire fill her eyes for a moment before she became nervous and lowered her gaze. Perhaps there was a chance for them if he seduced her properly. So now he had to figure out how to go about it. Her training would force her to his bed, and he knew he could use that, but he wanted a willing partner, not one who would just lay there.

Heather and Storm had forgotten the meal once again and were heading into the tent. He shook his head.

Micali had offered him another bite of food when she saw him shake his head. "No?"

"Sorry." He smiled at her. "Heather and Storm are heading inside. We might want to stay out here for a while."

"But they were together barely an hour ago." Shock filled her face. "I only had to tolerate Undar once a night."

"That was because he didn't care about your needs." He touched her shoulder and allowed his fingers to trail down her arm, using feather-soft caresses. Little bumps rose up on her arm. "With the right partner, you'd understand why Heather and Storm are intimate so much."

"Would you like some more food?" She changed the subject.

He wondered if the idea frightened her or if she just didn't want to believe him. He knew this would take more than a few kisses and caresses to make her see so instead of trying to force the issue he just smiled. He always enjoyed a challenge anyway.

"I'm fine right now. Guess my appetite is off due to my illness."

"That isn't unusual." She lowered the plate. "I can keep this so you can nibble again later."

"Thanks."

"I don't understand how she can enjoy it." Micali

slapped her hand over her mouth the moment the words left her lips.

"It's okay." He smiled. She couldn't stop thinking about Heather and Storm's sexual appetite. It was a good sign.

———

They entered the tent when Fridon felt it was safe. Storm wouldn't care, but he waited because of Heather. This was the first time he had traveled with them where they didn't have their normal privacy. Heather tried to show she wasn't uncomfortable with the situation, but he could tell she was. She was modest, something new to him, but he found it endearing so respected her desire to keep their intimacy private.

A quick glance revealed Heather and Storm curled around each other.

As much as he wanted to move so it wouldn't seem like he was staring at them, he found walking fast beyond his ability. Micali helped him to his bed. Once he was settled, she knelt beside it.

"You don't have to watch over me." He spoke softly, even though he knew the noise machine would shield their voices from Heather and Storm.

"I did before you woke and need to be near in case you relapse." She looked at him, trying so hard not to show any fear. "Unless you wish me to leave."

"I only wish you to be comfortable and I know that floor can't be." He watched her face as he continued. There was confusion before curiosity filled her face. "You could lie here with me. I'd feel better knowing you were not sleeping on that hard ground."

She looked away.

"I promise not to touch you." He wasn't sure if he could

keep that promise, but he'd make sure she wanted him if he couldn't.

She seemed to sit there forever before she gave a slight nod. He knew she was nervous. She had been hurt before. Fridon moved back so there would be room for her beside him. Once she lay down, he drew a cloth over them.

"Is this normal for your people?"

"What?" He propped himself up on one elbow so he could see her face.

"Sleeping together." She looked up at him.

"Yes." He couldn't help but grin. "We like touching."

"Why?" Her look of curiosity touched him.

"Because it feels good. Would you like me to touch you? I can show you what I am talking about." He waited for what seemed like an eternity before she gave him a quick nod. "I'm going to start with your face, brushing the tips of my fingers there then I'm going to trail them down to your collarbone, across your chest and over your stomach."

His feather-like touch had her sucking in her breath as he moved them around her body. She was sensitive around her bellybutton. He heard a sharp intake of breath as he skimmed along the edge of her skirt. Her skin was so soft he found it hard to stop.

She looked up at him with a touch of fear, but he also saw desire. The two emotions warred against each other.

Fridon lowered his head to hers to capture her lips with his, making sure he stayed on his side so she wouldn't feel trapped. He had planned on giving her a chaste kiss, but when she opened her mouth for him, he deepened it instead, his tongue dipping in to draw hers to dance with his. Her actions surprised him. She was hesitant at first but responded to him. He hadn't expected that. How far would she let him go before she stopped him? His desire begged him to find out.

The top she wore became a barrier he needed to remove. How would she react when he took it off her?

His fingers found the clasp and released the closure. Before she could react, he used those feather soft touches that had her sucking in her breath earlier against the skin he had exposed. He brushed his fingers against the underside of her breasts, caressed the tips of her nipples. When he first released the catch on her top, Micali froze, her fear palpable, but when he started to touch her softly, she relaxed again. He could sense her indecision and her fear was still in control, but he knew she liked what he was doing.

Fridon broke the kiss, working his way to her throat, then collarbone. Moving slowly, he pressed open-mouthed kisses against her skin as he worked his way down the tender flesh of her breast. When his mouth closed over the tip of her breast, she whimpered. So, was it because she wanted him to stop or because she was enjoying it? He didn't know. When he felt her fingers in his hair, holding him against her, he got his answer.

Moving to her other breast was a little tricky since she had such a strong hold on his head, but he used his tongue to swirl around her nipple before he licked his way to her other breast where he paid the same amount of attention. His fingers replaced his mouth as he made his way back to her lips, delighting in the aggression she showed.

Breaking the kiss once again, he pulled himself up so he could look at her. He smiled at her, knowing she'd either be happy or angry. "Time to sleep."

Her jaw worked as she tried to speak.

"Something wrong?"

"Why did you stop? I could feel your hardness against my leg."

"Because you were always forced. I won't be lumped into the same group as Undar. When you're ready, you'll ask me for it. I want a willing bed partner, not one who feels she must because it is a duty." With his body screaming at him for not following through, he lay down and closed his eyes.

———

Heather looked at Micali as they broke down the tent the next morning. She seemed distracted. Heather had to call her attention back to the task at hand a few times.

"Are you alright?" She had noticed Micali had shared Fridon's bed when she rose earlier. Vespians didn't force anyone to have sex with them. They didn't need to because there were so many willing partners to choose from. But Fridon had been without a partner since they came to this planet, did he try, but was denied? Was the young woman upset, but afraid to say anything?

"Yes." She was quiet for a moment. "I wish to ask a question."

"Feel free to ask me anything."

"Why do you like sex?"

Her question was so heartfelt Heather couldn't help but laugh. "Because Storm is a wonderful partner. He wants me to enjoy our intimacy as much as he does so strives to let me have as many orgasms as I can handle."

"Oh." She was quiet as she thought about Heather's answer.

"May I ask a question?"

Micali nodded.

"Did you have sex with Fridon and not enjoy it?"

"No." She saw Heather's frown and hurried with her explanation. "No sex. He said he would wait until I want it." She sighed. "He kissed me and used his hands and mouth in a way Undar never did. I–I found it nice? I don't know."

"You had a horrible teacher before. Undar strikes me as a

man who only thought about his own needs. I can only assume he beat you when you tried anything other than just lying there."

She nodded again. "It was awful. I prayed he would finish quickly."

"Which he probably did." Heather paused for a moment. "Where we come from being intimate is a time for sharing. Each partner wants to be sure the other enjoys the coupling, culminating in a beautiful release. Something I don't think you have ever experienced."

"I liked his kisses."

"Fridon's?"

"Yes." She looked to make sure the men weren't close enough to hear. "At first, I feared it would be the same as before with Undar, but he made my body tingle as he touched me with his mouth and hands. I didn't want him to stop, but he did. That's when he said I had to ask for sex."

"You had your first taste of how I experience sex and believe me it gets better." They had finished packing everything inside and it was time to take the tent down. "We can speak of this later if you wish."

Micali nodded.

They stacked the last of the interior bags near the flap. Heather picked up several straps. "Ready to take this out?"

"Yes." They lifted the satchels they had filled and took them out to the frulas. Once they had the bags hooked to the animals, they took the tent down and loaded it as well. Once everything was done, they were ready to go.

Storm took Heather's chain and wrapped it around the pummel of his saddle. He now rode the stallion. The horse didn't like being used as a pack animal and it let her know when she and Micali unpacked when they stopped for the night. When they saddled the animals earlier, Heather made sure Storm got the stallion and Fridon got the mare. The animals seemed much happier.

Fridon wrapped Micali's chain around his hand. They headed out, taking their time because of the women walking. After a while, Storm pulled Heather close.

"My heart?" She looked up at him.

"I hate you walking while I ride."

"I know, but I must. Especially since we are being followed." She looked over her shoulder to see the small dust cloud their trackers were making. "It's a little too windy for them to be discreet today."

"From what I read in the files it is the time of year for the sandstorms." Storm scanned the horizon. "How fast can you get the tent up?"

"Pretty quickly, but if we get hit, you and Fridon can help. It is one of the few times the men can aid women." She grinned up at him. "A loophole."

"Have you ever been here when one hit?"

"Not traveling like this, but I have seen how fast they strike and how deadly they can be. We'll be safe in the tent but digging out afterward will be hard." She looked ahead of them. "Do you sense something?"

"I'm not sure. My heightened senses are still a little confusing to understand at times. Something is coming, but I'm not sure what I'm sensing yet." He looked down at her. "I noticed that Micali didn't sleep in her bed last night."

"It was hard to miss, wasn't it?" Heather looked behind them to see how close Fridon was. "Fridon is trying to woo her."

"Woo?"

"Seduce."

"Ah. Wondered how long it would take him. She is a beautiful woman, and he has been without for a while. I have heard his libido rivals mine." Storm looked back as well.

"Is that possible?" She was close enough to rest a hand on his thigh. The muscles there jumped at her touch.

"Keep that up and you'll be riding up here with me."

"I know." She smiled. "But my goal is to tease you until you can't handle it anymore. Just like you do to me all the time."

"I could pull you up here now." He leaned down like he was going to pull her up into his lap.

"You would take this wonderful opportunity away from me?" She shook her head. "That's not fair."

"I don't fight fair when it comes to you, you know that." He tightened his hold on her chain. "Just watching you move in that outfit makes me want to touch all that deliciously exposed skin. Then I would follow that with my mouth."

His words sparked her desire.

"I like the way these pants are loose on you." She slipped a hand inside one leg, caressing a sensitive spot on his upper thigh. "It allows me to touch you wherever I want."

A growl escaped him.

"And watch as that glow in your eyes gets brighter and brighter."

SIX

"Let's drop back a bit." Fridon slowed his animal so Heather and Storm could have some privacy.

"I can keep up. You set an easy pace."

"It's not that. Um, Heather and Storm."

"Again?" She looked ahead and saw Heather walking very close to Storm's mount. "They don't seem to be…" Her voice trailed off when Storm scooped Heather up in his arms, capturing her lips with his as he sat her in front of him.

"I know the signs." He watched the horizon before looking behind him. "We'll take our time for now. We'll keep them in sight but stay back far enough to give them some privacy."

"Is privacy important?" She looked up at him.

"To Heather it is."

"She is important to you."

"She's my best friend." He looked down at her. "She saved my life."

"How?"

"She was there when I got hurt, if she hadn't been I

would have died." He wasn't sure what he should tell her. They weren't keeping the fact they were from another planet a secret, yet they weren't broadcasting it either.

"You don't have to tell me." She dropped her gaze.

"It's not that." He wished he knew what he could say.

"I know you're not from here." She spoke softly, as if unsure how he would take her words. "Heather is more than property to Storm. He's protective of her."

"What has Heather told you about us?"

"That I don't have to stay on this planet when you leave. I can go anywhere. No one would be wiser, and she'd make sure my family knows I am happy."

"Ever heard of Vespia?" He decided to tell her the truth. If he was wrong, he'd take the reprimand.

She shook her head.

"That is my home. Our home. Men and women are equal there, and Heather and I are trained as security officers for two different governments. We were doing a security exercise designed to test Heather's ability to work with Vespian security. Someone tried to kidnap her. I happened to be at the wrong place at the wrong time and was shot in the face. She activated a medical device in my uniform that kept me from dying. We've been close ever since."

"And Storm isn't jealous?" She looked at the small silhouette of the couple. "He is very possessive of her."

"Noticed that? Huh?" He grinned. "Heather is his mate and where we come from it is a bond that can't be broken. He knows how we became close and understands it. Believe me, if I were to stand a little too close to her, I'd get a look, but he knows her heart belongs to him."

"They are in love then."

"You could call it that." He watched them for a moment.

"But you don't."

"The word love doesn't translate in my language." He

then looked behind them to make sure their shadows were staying out of sight and not trying to take advantage of the fact that they were apart at the moment.

"How do you speak our language so well?"

"Heather taught me."

"How did she know our language?"

"She's been here before."

"Really?" She was quiet for a moment as everything clicked into place. "She is the woman Undar's friend rants on and on about! She humiliated him and he wants revenge."

"We know. That is who Undar is traveling with now."

"He is dangerous." She grabbed his pant leg. "I heard them talk. The horrible things they plan to do to her. They will cause her great harm."

"Don't worry." He covered her hand with his as he tried to comfort her. He looked at Storm's silhouette. "They have no idea who they are dealing with."

———

"She is no longer walking! He is breaking the rules." Lewmard stood in the saddle, filled with excitement.

"No, he isn't." Undar shook his head. "She is pleasuring him."

"How do you know?"

"Because he demands it from her all the time." Undar looked at his friend. "I watched one time when they were in their tent. She was very sensual with him. Made me hard just watching them. She must have been trained in the art of sex before he bought her, which is why he won't sell her."

"So you have tried to buy her?"

"Several people tried at my brother's party, but he wouldn't part with her. In fact, he got angry when people kept asking him." Undar shrugged. "I can't blame him. Who wouldn't want a woman who knew how to act like sex was the best thing she ever had?"

"This I must see." Lewmard spurred his mount to race along a parallel path to catch up with the couple in question.

Undar whipped his frulas to get it to run hard so he could catch up with Heather and Storm as well. He didn't want to let Lewmard out of his sight before he got paid, but there was another baser reason he raced to catch-up. The thought of viewing what he saw without the block of the tent had his desire spiraling.

Lewmard made sure they stayed out of sight from Heather and Storm, which made it hard for them to watch as they were intimate. But Undar saw enough. Storm held Heather as she arched against him, ecstasy etched on her face. It was beautiful, arousing, and it made him want her more. He looked at Lewmard. The man hated her so much Undar wasn't sure if he would get a taste of her before the man exacted his revenge.

He had to find a way to be with her before Lewmard did any damage to her.

———

Heather clung to Storm as her orgasm started to dissipate. She looked up at him with a smile. "Wow."

"You never cease to amaze me, my heart." He caught her lips for a quick but heated kiss.

"You can't say our sex life is tame now." She leaned back and touched his face.

"That bothered you, didn't it?"

"No." But she wouldn't look at him. It did bother her. He was so used to the way Vespians handled sex yet had accepted her shyness and went out of his way to be sure their intimacy was for their enjoyment only. She didn't feel she had the right to complain.

"You are a terrible liar." He pressed a kiss against her mark. "I didn't mean I was bored with you or our sex life, only that our children had changed it a little. I shouldn't have said a thing, although I have enjoyed how you keep trying to prove to me that you don't want to be thought of as tame."

"I don't want you to get bored." She looked at him.

"With you?" He laughed. "How can I get bored when you keep me so sated?"

She looked over his shoulder and noticed Fridon coming up on them fast. "I need my top. We're about to have company."

"I think I know why." He watched the horizon as he helped her back into it. "Looks like a storm."

"Crap." Heather turned in the seat once it was secure. "And it looks like a big one."

Storm stopped the stallion and allowed Heather to slip off the animal. She went to the pack animals the moment Fridon was close enough for her to reach it. With Micali's help, they had the tent spread out just as the wind started to kick up. Storm and Fridon secured it to the ground while Heather and Micali worked on putting the framework up inside. Their quickness had the tent up and ready before Storm or Fridon could do much to pitch in, but it freed them up to make sure everything else was secure before the storm hit.

Storm and Fridon came in, leading the animals inside.

"It is going to be a bad one," said Fridon, as he tied one of the pack animals to a section of the infrastructure. He then worked with Storm to reinforce it so it would withstand the strong winds and sand. They set the corners to climb up the sand as it built against the tent so the tent wouldn't get buried too deeply. Depending on how bad the storm would be, the tent should be close to the surface so they wouldn't have to climb out the top. One of the few pieces of technology they were allowed to use.

The storm lasted for hours. The wind howled around them. Storm found he had to calm his new mare a few times to keep her from rearing. The stallion had taken a liking to Heather, which helped him settle in with the pack animals. She crooned to it and petted it when he had to deal with the mare while they waited for the wind to die down. Once it had passed, they were ready to exit. Even with the climbers built into the tent to keep it from being buried by standard winds and drifts, the sand was too deep for them to use the main flap.

"Micali and I will climb up the frame and clear the door so you two can exit."

"With those two out there?" Storm shook his head and crossed his arms over his chest. "Don't think so."

"And they are the reason we must follow the rules." Heather had seen that particular stance too many times to let it get to her. "At least let us go up first, then you and Fridon follow. Then you can watch as we dig out the tent."

"How about I go first and if it is clear, you can follow me."

"Storm." She mimicked his pose.

He couldn't help but grin.

"How about I go first with you right on my heels? That way, you can check to see if we're safe and we're still following the rules."

"I don't like some of these rules. It's hard to keep you safe."

"I'll be fine." She walked up to the main frame, tucked her skirt the way Usatha taught her and started climbing, Storm right behind her.

"What is this?" He tugged at the skirt she had tucked. It didn't take much to free it.

"I was told I could do this to keep my skirt out of the way." She looked down at him. "At least until you knocked it loose again."

"Have to say I do like this view much better than seeing your skirt hiding everything."

She looked down and found him looking up. The skirt swirled out as she climbed, allowing him to see up inside. She laughed as she continued to climb. Her mate had a one-track mind. As she got to the top, she found someone grabbed her arms and hauled her up.

"Crap." She felt Storm grabbing her ankles. She felt like a piece of taffy. Fighting the hold on her arms, she screamed. "Let go!"

The hands that had her didn't stop though, and Storm continued to hang on. Whoever had a hold of her ended up pulling Storm up with her.

"You are heavy for a slip of a woman."

She wanted to say if you only knew but knew better and remained silent. Once she cleared the opening, and Storm had reached the top so he could climb out, he let go. The sudden lack of weight had her assailants losing their balance. They let go too, allowing Heather to land on her feet.

She positioned herself away from the tent so the two men getting to their feet wouldn't spot Storm climbing out. Undar stood back behind Lewmard, holding a crossbow on her. The first man she recognized instantly. "Lewmard."

"I didn't give you permission to speak." He lifted his hand to strike her, but found it caught in a powerful grip. He turned to find Storm holding his arm with one hand and Undar by the neck with the other.

"You do not have my permission to touch her." He

towered over him, using his height to intimidate. Heather was used to his size, but most men found the breadth of his shoulders coupled with his seven-foot-four-inch height to be more than they wanted to tangle with.

Heather picked up the crossbow that Undar had dropped. She made sure the weapon was loaded and aimed it at Lewmard.

"She isn't allowed to touch a weapon!"

"Really?" Storm gave Undar's neck a squeeze that knocked him unconscious. The moment his hand was free, she gave him the crossbow. "I don't see her holding anything."

Lewmard glared at him but didn't comment. "What happened to her back?"

"Nothing. It is flawless."

"I'm talking about the scars she should have," Lewmard snapped. "How did you get those removed?"

"It doesn't matter since they are gone." Storm released his arm then he pointed to Undar. "Now I want you to take this piece of trash and go. If I catch you following us again, I will make sure you won't be able to do it anymore. She is my property and I protect that which is mine."

"She needs to pay for her crimes."

"What crimes? She saved a man's life. Doesn't that clear her of any crimes? You were the one who could have caused the death of the one she saved because of your brutality." He stepped over to where Heather stood and blocked her from Lewmard's view. "She has my protection, and you are going to have to come through me to get to her. Remember that."

———

"That might not have been the smartest thing to say to a crazy man," Heather commented softly as she watched

Lewmard load the unconscious Undar onto an animal and lead him away. "The man has an unhealthy hatred of me to still want to punish me for something that happened years ago."

"He won't be able to get close enough to you to harm a hair on your head." Storm pulled her into his embrace as he watched them leave as well. "But I will have words with Bear when this is done. Putting you in a situation like this is wrong."

"I'm still a member of Earth security. It's part of my job." She turned to look at him.

He kept the hold on her, so she remained in his protective embrace. "You are my mate. Nothing can happen to you."

She hugged him, thankful he was hers. "And I'm sure you will make sure nothing does. Now we need to get Fridon and Micali out of there."

Storm looked at the top of the tent poking up out of the sand, nodding his agreement. He wanted to put a few miles between them and the other two before nightfall.

Storm kept an eye on their surroundings as they continued to travel and was happy to know that Lewmard and Undar heeded his warning. He hadn't seen anything that would make him think they were following them anymore.

They made it to the next large city two days later. After flashing the proper amount of power and a few coins, Storm found out when and where the coming-of-age party was. He sent Fridon to the home of the man having the festivities with the missive Busandio wrote for him so he would be accepted into the man's home. Once Fridon dropped it off, he was to return to the tent.

Heather had recommended they stay in their tent just on the outskirts of town since Storm didn't want her or Micali to be sent to the central sleeping quarters for women if he and Fridon were to stay in one of the public hotels.

Storm stepped outside the tent to see if Fridon was in view and found three riders coming toward them. As they drew closer, he spotted Fridon amongst them.

"Sir, Nasturo has invited you to his home." He slid off his animal. "I explained your wants, and he has agreed to allow Heather and Micali to remain with us at night."

"Thank you." He was glad the man went along with his demands. "Any sign of Undar or Lewmard?"

"No, sir."

"Good." Storm turned and entered the tent. With the audience they had, he needed to be sure they didn't break some small infraction that could cause trouble. "We are to go to Nasturo's now. There are about six guards from his home right outside."

"We are to cover up until we reach his home then." Heather walked to their bed and started to pull it apart.

"We could make use of that one more time before you pack it up." He had come to enjoy the massive thing.

"You want to keep your host waiting to dally with your property?" She gave him a sultry smile.

"Especially when that property is you." He pulled her into his arms and nibbled on her mark.

"My heart, you do have a one-track mind, but it wouldn't be polite to keep him waiting." She danced out of his hold and went back to work on the bed. "We'll be out as soon as we're ready."

It didn't take the women long to pack everything onto the animals. They followed the group as they headed to the house of Nasturo, who greeted Storm at the gates of his home. He had two of his guards show Storm and Fridon where they would sleep.

"These quarters will do nicely." Storm then dismissed the men properly with mental prompting from Heather, wanting to focus on his mate. He looked around the room. The design of it was a little different than the last place. He noticed a small alcove up near the ceiling. He looked at Heather. "What is that for?"

"My sleeping area." She looked around the room as well. As she picked up her things and headed to the ladder. "They are a little more lenient when it comes to women if they have a place built in for women to sleep in."

"You know you're not going to sleep up there." He came up behind her and wrapped his arms around her, stopping her.

"I have to make it look good." She turned in his arms. "Our host should be here in about three minutes, and I'm supposed to be busy settling you in."

"And you don't think it would be good for him to catch us being intimate instead?" He nibbled on her mark. "He would know you're taking care of my needs."

"He might want to join in."

Storm pulled back, the glow in his eyes fading just a bit. "Really?"

She shrugged.

"Since I don't like to share, I will let you get to your work, but the moment he is gone I plan on taking advantage of at least one of these walls." He pressed a kiss to her mark.

"He will probably have everything brought in for a bath." The glow in his eyes brightened again. He did enjoy the last bath she gave him.

A knock on the door interrupted them.

"Enter." He hadn't let go of Heather when Nasturo entered the room.

"I wish to welcome you to my home." He slowed when he noticed their intimate embrace.

Heather dropped her gaze and backed away.

"I am honored." His handle on the language was one hundred percent now. He wanted to sigh when Heather stepped away from him to go about settling him in. She kept busy while he continued to talk to Nasturo.

"I assume you'd like to freshen up before dinner." He clapped his hands, and a small group of women came in carrying oils and soaps. Once they set the trays down, they removed the cover on the sunken tub. "If you have any need for any of these women just ask."

"Thank you, but she provides for my every need." Storm looked at his mate.

"Very good, then." He turned to leave.

"And my man?" The last time they treated him as a servant, and he wanted to make sure that didn't happen again.

Storm's words stopped him, and he turned back. "He is in the room next to yours. I plan on speaking to him next. Shall I pass on a message?"

Storm looked at Heather for a moment. He had better things to do than follow the man around, but he wanted to be sure Fridon was treated properly. "I shall join you."

Nasturo gestured for him to come with him, and they entered the room next door. Just as spacious, Storm was happy to know he wasn't in some cramped little room like the last time. The women did the same thing in Fridon's room with Micali working in one corner, unpacking for him.

"I will also offer you the use of any of my women."

"Thank you." Fridon turned to look at Micali for a moment before he faced his host. "I shall decline for now. This one is new to us, and I don't want to frighten her by having other women do what she is being trained to do. She might think we're not happy with her."

"Very good." He clapped his hands once again and the women filed out. "Dinner is in two hours. I hope that will give you both ample time to freshen up."

Storm nodded to the man, and he followed the women out. "I know those two aren't going to stop so be diligent."

"Of course, sir." He looked at Micali again. "You don't think they'll be so brazen as to enter a man's house without permission, do you?"

"Maybe not the house, but possibly the property. If they think they can catch Heather alone, I think they'll try anything."

Once Storm headed back to his room, Fridon turned to Micali. She looked frightened. Perhaps he should have taken his host up on the offer of the women. So she wouldn't have to worry about what he might want from her.

Steam rose from the sunken tub, beckoning him. He stripped and climbed in. The heat from the water seeped into his skin. It felt good. He closed his eyes and rested his head back on the edge of the floor. He wasn't used to women not wanting to share with him. This wasn't easy on his libido.

Micali watched as Fridon removed his clothing and stepped into the tub. When he closed his eyes and leaned his head back on the edge of the tub, she found herself admiring his looks. He had beautiful hair, jet black, that brushed the collar of his tunic. He kept his shorter than most men she had known, but she felt it suited him. Long dark lashes rested on his high cheekbones, hiding his eyes from her view, but that didn't matter. The golden tone of those wonderful eyes had her dreaming about them in her sleep. And now she had his wonderfully sculpted body to add to her fantasies.

Was she attracted to him because he had been so kind to her? Undar had been so cruel, ridiculing her at every turn. Striking her when she didn't move fast enough. Forcing her to have sex, then getting angry when she didn't respond the way he thought she should. He would pinch her and slap her just to get her muscles to contract the way he wanted them to. It was awful.

Yet here was a man who was willing to put her needs first. Could she take a chance that he would be true to his word? Her mother told her when a man knew what he was doing it was enjoyable. Not knowing what her future held had her wondering if she should take a chance with him. What if she trusted him and found that all of this was nothing but a ruse and he turned out to be as cruel as Undar? If he was honest and showed her how wonderful sex could be, how would she handle being sold to someone else when they left this planet and her new owner turned out to be as bad as Undar?

She hated not knowing what to do. This could be her only chance to see what it should be like. And if the way he treated her the last time was any indication she'd be crazy to not take advantage of it. Memories to help her cope with her fate once he left.

Taking a deep breath, she removed her clothing and climbed into the tub with him. He opened his golden eyes and lifted his head when she caused the water to move. His look held the unspoken question in his mind.

She got up on her knees and picked up the cleansing oil. "I wish to help you bathe."

He didn't say anything, but when his fingers brushed her hair out of her face, she knew he wasn't going to send her away. Time to be brave.

She couldn't look him in the face. Her nerves wouldn't let her. Pouring the oil into her hands, she started to spread it across his chest. Undar was soft all over. Micali was surprised to find the muscles Fridon had were hard under the soft texture of his skin. Her finger dipped into valleys as they slid over his torso.

Then she felt his hands on her. He started in a safe place, her shoulders. Micali looked up at him.

"I'm sure you would like to clean up as well. This will save time." He gave her a sexy smile that made her knees weak. Fridon pulled her against his body and started to rub oil into her back.

"I…"

"Thought this would make it easier to clean each other's back. Do you disagree?" He pulled back enough to look down at her.

She didn't know what to say. Delight and desire filled her over the physical contact. Wrapping her arms around him, she rubbed the oil wherever she could reach, but his broad shoulders made it hard for her to reach the areas above his shoulder blades. Her hands slid down the tight muscles on his back and kneaded his buttocks. His staff jumped against her stomach.

Excitement and a touch of fear filled her.

"Stand for me." His voice came out husky.

So used to obeying commands, she did as he asked.

Fridon wrapped his left arm around her slender waist and pulled her close. His head was now level with her breasts, and he took advantage of that by taking one of the tips into his mouth. She felt his right hand sliding up the inside of her right thigh. Her knees buckled again when his fingers slid into her soft folds at her core.

Sensations she never felt before raced through her blood. Excitement, need, and a pressure that built as he continued to caress her. She leaned into the caress as her body started to tingle all over. It felt like she was reaching for something but didn't know what. It continued to build, causing her breath to shorten. Her body tightened, coiling like a spring. Whatever was racing toward her was almost there. Her breath caught as her body clenched. Suddenly she soared, a release she had never experienced grabbed her and sent her flying.

Fridon still held her, waiting for her to speak, but words failed her. The beauty of what she just experienced brought tears to her eyes.

"Why are you crying?" He brushed a tear off her cheek. He seemed confused by her reaction.

"I never experienced anything like that." She couldn't stop the smile that spread across her face. "Is it like that each time?"

He smiled back, that wonderful bone-melting one that made her knees quake. "It gets better."

"Really?"

"I promise."

———

Storm knocked on the massive doors, then he caught the whiff of something. "Perhaps we should come back in a few minutes."

"Why?" Heather kept her voice at a whisper.

"I believe they are engaged." He touched his nose.

"You can smell that?"

"Yes." He pulled her into his embrace. "I can pick up so many nuances in scents I can smell things that most don't even know have fragrances. Like passion. Your skin has a distinct aroma as you reach your climax. I can smell your need, your frustration, your joy."

The door opened. Fridon's hair, slicked back, showed he was fresh from a bath. Fully dressed, he smiled as he opened the door wider so Micali could step out and follow them.

Fridon is frustrated but Micali seems to have found release.

You think the Virgin Slayer has struck again?

Storm grinned. That was a nickname Heather gave him when she learned that he was sought out by parents to introduce their daughters to sex. He was very gentle with the young girls and the mothers were normally very grateful. *It sure looks like it.*

They were led to the dining area by one of the household guards. Storm had never been one to enjoy the formal meals at home and these were even worse. He was bored the moment he took his seat. Heather took her place as his property beside him, wearing her formal gauze attachment. She looked as bored as he felt. *Do you think the young woman we are looking for is here?*

It's hard to tell. If he has already gotten his gifts, you'll have to let me mingle with the other women again so I can see if she is being prepared for him.

I don't like letting you out of my sight with those two out there somewhere.

Your decision.

He hated it when she did that. Deferring to him when she was right. The only way to be sure was for her and Micali to go into the women's quarters. *Let's see what happens tonight.*

As friends and relatives offered their gifts to the boy coming of age, Storm realized that the woman wasn't among them. Could she have been given to him earlier and being kept hidden? He didn't think so but couldn't be sure. Against his wants, Heather would have to infiltrate the women's area.

Nasturo made his job easy by asking if he could use Heather and Micali while the women prepared for the continued festivities tomorrow. Storm agreed. If the young woman was being hidden somewhere, Heather would find her.

The meal was long and tedious, but it did finally end, and they headed back to their rooms.

"My heart, I have one request to ask of you." Storm had a hand on each of Heather's arms.

"Oh, boy, when you speak to me so formally you normally want something big."

"I wish to switch bodies tomorrow. Let me look for her."

"You?" Heather started to laugh. He wasn't sure why she found it so funny. "You have problems manipulating my body, and the things they have us do calls for dexterity. You think you can arrange flowers, fold linens? I can see you pounding carpets, but that keeps you away from the main room so you'd never be able to look for the girl."

"I have gotten better. I can handle it." He knew she was right, but this was one way he knew he could keep her safe. He would do his best to do the tasks expected from his mate.

"You worry too much." She touched his face tenderly. "How about I let your mind come with me? You'll have to find a way to stay in the room all day, unless you think you can split your focus."

"You know I will do anything to protect you. I'll find a way to be with you tomorrow."

———

Fridon was happy to be back in the room. He found the whole night boring. The only bright thing was Micali and the way she kept looking at him. He wanted her to trust him not to hurt her, and he thought he might have made headway earlier. He'd know for sure when she finally gave herself to him. His constant erection had him hoping it would happen soon.

Micali stood in the middle of the room, looking confused.

"Everything okay?" He walked over to the large bed and sat on the array of pillows she had set up for him.

"Um, yes." She moved, but it was in small circles.

Then it dawned on him. She wasn't sure where she should sleep and was waiting for him to tell her. He couldn't make that decision for her. Fridon stood, stripped off his clothes and climbed into the bed, pulling the soft sheet over the lower half of his body. Lying down, he crossed his arms behind his head and closed his eyes. He waited a few more minutes before talking. "Where you sleep is up to you. You're more than welcome to share my bed but know that I won't be able to keep my hands to myself. I've already proven that twice."

Then he waited. Now it was up to her.

SEVEN

A little thrill ran through her at his words. She found him so different from Undar. That man would have demanded and forced her to do what he wanted, but Fridon didn't. She knew he wanted her. His need was evident. Yet he was letting her make all the decisions. Right now, it would be so much easier if he just told her what to do.

She swallowed. Once she made this choice there was no going back. If he was pretending all along, she could be in real trouble, but she saw how Storm was with Heather and that man scared her. Removing her clothes, she climbed into bed with Fridon, her heart hammering in her chest.

Now what?

Fridon rolled to his side and propped his head up on his elbow. "I see you have decided."

She nodded, afraid to say anything. He sighed, probably upset with her reaction. He didn't seem happy with her fear.

"Micali, each time I have touched you, have I caused you pain or pleasure?" He placed his hand on her stomach.

"Pleasure." She looked at him, her words barely above a whisper.

"So why do you fear me?" He started to draw little circles on her skin, filling her with excitement.

"I don't know." She swallowed again. "I think I am just scared. I have no idea what to do now."

"Ah, but that's okay, because I do." He widened the area where he drew the circles. "But understand tonight we will be intimate. I can't hold myself back anymore. Your body is too delectable for me to ignore."

She could see his desire for her in his eyes. Like a fire, it blazed brightly. No one had ever looked at her with such need.

He lowered his head to hers and claimed her lips. She felt a fluttering in her stomach when she opened her mouth for him, and his tongue swept in. His hands still drew the soft circles on her skin. Micali wanted more. The need to touch him drove her to place a hand against his chest. The smoothness of his skin over the hard muscles delighted her. Soft fingers traced one of the muscles.

His mouth left hers and blazed a trail down to her breast. The heat of his mouth sent warmth through her. He shifted his body so she couldn't touch him anymore but when she felt his fingers at her folds once again, she found herself lost in the sensations he elicited from her. Desire swirled around her. Now that she knew what it felt like, she wanted it to go on forever. Then she felt him slide a finger up inside her. Micali froze for a moment. But then he pulled one finger out and slid two in. He did it slowly, caressing her inside and out, and she felt her need spike. The fluttering in her stomach intensified and she felt her world explode. She floated along, wrapped in a blanket of ecstasy.

Fridon's mouth moved from her breast to her stomach, placing soft kisses all along the way. He seemed to be waiting for something. His fingers were still inside her as the aftershocks continued.

She sighed when her body finally relaxed.

Fridon wasn't done though. He moved lower until she felt his tongue against her, lathing her as his fingers started to slide in and out again. She felt everything clinch again. Another one? So fast?

His hands moved, grasping her hips, as he climbed back up her body. "Are you ready?"

She nodded as she tried to move.

"Where are you going?"

"Oh, assuming the position?"

"Vespians like to watch their partners' faces as they are intimate. I want to see your release. Have you see mine."

She felt his hardened staff slowly enter her. Micali wasn't sure if she would be able to handle his length and size, but his gentleness gave her body time to adjust to him. He started to move then, pulling out only to slide back in. The pace he set was slow, but each time he filled her she felt her muscles squeeze him. The rhythm started a delicious friction between them.

Her shock must have been on her face because he chuckled. "Not what you expected?"

"I never felt anything like this." She arched up against him as her body reached for something. "Is it like this every time?"

"As long as your partner knows what he is doing. Yes." He stopped talking when she gripped him tight for a moment. "I find it gets better and better."

"Oh, my."

"You want to see what I am talking about?" At her nod, he continued. "Wrap your legs around my waist."

They had been lying against the bed before this. How could moving her legs make a difference? But she trusted him. The moment she lifted her legs she felt a whole new set of sensations. The changed angle intensified everything she felt.

He started moving faster, increasing the friction. "Don't be afraid to tell me what you like or what you don't like."

"What?" Undar never wanted her input. He took what he wanted and left. "Oh!"

"This is mutual, my little flower. It's not all about me or you."

His endearing name reminded her of home. A tear escaped. She tried to hide it by turning her face, but Fridon spotted it before she moved.

"You're crying. Why?" he wiped away the tear sliding down her cheek.

"My father called me his tiny blossom."

"I struck a chord, didn't I?"

"Yes." She took a tentative hand and touched his face. "It is the first time I have thought about them in a positive light since they sold me to Undar. Thank you. I know they didn't know what type of man he was, but I kept hoping my father or brother would learn the truth and come to help me. I felt so alone for so long, but now I don't. You did that for me."

"You deserve so much more than he ever gave you." He pulsed inside of her.

"Oh!"

"Like enjoying sex and having your first set of multiple orgasms."

"Multiple?"

"Let me show you." He had stopped moving when he caught her tear, but he picked up the pace again. Watching her for something. He shifted his weight and continued to move.

The change in his position intensified the friction. She found it hard to breathe.

"Oh, my!"

"I'll take that as you like the change?"

She could only nod.

"Tell me what you like. It will only make it better." He continued to move in and out, caressing a particular spot that had her close to keening.

She was close, everything tightened inside her. She felt her blood zinging through her veins, and she wasn't sure if she could take much more. A strange pressure built in her core. Her legs slid against him as she felt everything coil before it released. Color filled her vision as she arched against him. Her world splintered around her. "Oh, oh, oh oh!"

She floated along on an invisible cloud. A euphoria filled her, and it lasted until she realized she was laying on the bed once again.

Fridon propped himself up and smiled down at her. "Enjoyed that?"

"Immensely." She gave him a hesitant smile back.

"Good." He rolled them over, keeping their bodies locked together so he stayed inside her. "What I find fascinating is that women can have multiple orgasms whereas men can only have one. Women have the advantage. But I'm lucky enough to have the stamina to withstand those orgasms so I can be sure my woman has several before I have mine." His hands touched her gently, caressing her hip, skimming over her belly button. "You ready for round two?"

She felt him pulse inside her and she nodded.

"Good, this time you get to be on top."

———

The next morning Heather and Micali headed for the woman's section. Heather noticed the smile on her new friend's face. "You look happy."

"I am." She didn't elaborate so Heather had to keep her questions to herself.

They entered the massive area where most of the work was to be done and found the women scrambling. Whoever was in charge seemed to have lost control.

Heather looked around to see if she could find someone to speak to, but the rest of the women ignored her. A clump of women stood nearby speaking quietly. As she approached them, she heard the fear in their voices.

"I don't know what to do. I have never seen anything like this."

"He will kill us all if they die."

Heather pushed her way into the center of the group to find one of the women in labor, her body racked with pain. Her skin was blue, not a good sign, and there was a lot of blood, but no baby. Where was Kuarto when she needed him?

Storm felt her stress at what she found because his mind brushed up against hers. Once she assured him she wasn't in any danger she tried to figure out what to do.

Their anatomy wasn't that different, perhaps the baby was turned the wrong way. Heather knelt beside her and pressed on the stomach to see if she could feel the baby's position. The idea of putting her hands up inside the woman without getting her permission didn't sit right, and the woman wasn't talking to anyone right now.

"What is her name?" She looked up when no one answered her. What happened to the head woman? Why wasn't she here calling for help? "Do you want to be responsible for this?"

Several shook their heads.

"Then tell me her name."

"She is Formeen."

"Formeen, can you hear me?" Heather was greeted with a groan. Now wasn't the time to ask a lot of questions. "I want to help you."

"Baby..." she screamed then, her body stiffening.

Micali knelt beside them. "I have seen this before. We have little time."

"What do you need?" Heather was grateful Micali had the healing touch. They needed it right now.

"Pillows, and we need to get her flat and elevate her hips."

Heather looked at the women standing there. Standing, she put her hands on her hips. "What is wrong with you? Start moving!"

Several took off at that point. Heather knelt back down. "What first?"

"We need to get her flat."

Heather pushed the woman down.

"No! Baby..."

"You want to have this child? Then lie down." She held her shoulders to the ground until the woman stopped fighting her. Stark fear shone in Formeen's eyes. Heather spoke to her to soothe her. Her fear wasn't helping her baby. "It's okay. We're here to help."

She nodded.

"Where is your healer?"

The woman touched her chest.

Great. The healer they needed was the one who needed healing. Heather bet she was also the head woman. She looked at Micali. "You can do this?"

Micali nodded as she set the healer's legs for delivery. The pillows arrived and she placed them under her hips. She checked Formeen's eyes and temperature before she reached in to see what was keeping the baby from traveling down the birth canal. She sat back on her heels. "Oh dear. I see the problem."

"What?"

"There are two, and they are fighting to come out at the same time."

"Twins?" Heather touched the woman's arm. "Did you know you carried two?"

"No." Another contraction grabbed her, causing her to cry out at the pain. "Had hoped, but never felt the other child."

Heather looked at Micali. This could be a real problem. If the woman didn't feel a second heartbeat did that mean the second child would be stillborn?

"They are both moving." Micali grinned. "A lot. I'd say they are anxious to come out and meet their mother."

Heather let out a pent-up breath. She was happy to hear that.

"I need to move them." Micali pointed to the healer's arms. "It will hurt. You must hold her still or it will make matters worse."

Heather nodded. She looked at several of the women standing nearby. They joined her to help hold her down. At least she didn't need to yell at them again.

Micali reached inside to push one child back so they both could come out, but the pain had the healer arching up off the floor. She heard Heather yell, and the three women came close to sitting on her to keep her still. The moment she untangled the twins the first one slid down the canal. It was a boy and as blue as his mother.

Heather picked him up by an ankle and gave him a few light, but deliberate strikes. It took a second or two, but then he started with a nice healthy cry. One of the other women handed her a cloth to wrap him in. His color returned by the time she had him wrapped up, but there were still hints of the trauma he went through. Once she was sure the second child had been born without any complications, she took the boy to the head guard. The father needed to know.

She took the proper stance and announced. "It is a boy."

———

Storm felt so many emotions from his mate. All of them had him on edge. He had wanted to switch with her, but she had asked him to let her go into the female quarters first to see what they would have her do. After that, she ignored his requests to take over. Something was going on and she wouldn't tell him what. One of the guards came in with a small bundle. He held it up for Nasturo. "A boy, sir."

Not five minutes later came another guard. "Another boy, sir."

"Two? I have two boys!" He cradled them close, a bright smile on his face, proud of his sons. "I wish to see her."

Now Storm understood why she kept ignoring him. She must have had a hand in the births.

The man studied the two boys, marveling at the twins. He touched their tiny hands and feet. Storm watched as his face went from the beaming smile to a frown.

"These two show signs of a stressful birth. Why wasn't I told?" He stood and handed the infants back to the guards. "Take me to her."

"Sir?"

"I am master of this house. I can break the rules. Take me to her now." He strode out of the room, leaving everyone behind.

What is going on, my heart?

Busy.

Nasturo just stormed out of here heading in your direction.

The woman who just gave birth isn't stable. I need to focus.

Storm growled his frustration. His mate could be in trouble, and he couldn't help her. He started pacing, wanting to know what was going on. It didn't take too long before one of the guards came back for him.

"He wishes you to join him."

Storm nodded, deciding the guards must have told him Heather was involved. Fridon stood as well, but Storm shook his head. He had to go alone. No man would barge into another man's female quarters without permission. He hoped Heather hadn't done anything to jeopardize their mission. Hopefully, the man only asked him to accompany him because he wanted someone to speak for her and probably Micali.

Storm followed. His thoughts on how they could escape if things went wrong.

They arrive at the woman's quarters, guards standing nearby, looking like they had been threatened with their lives.

Nasturo was already in the room shouting.

We need you.

How did you know I was here?

I can read your thoughts, remember?

He stepped in and found most of the women cowering in a corner. Heather was shielding the new mother from a screaming Nasturo. Storm glared at her as he addressed the man. "Is there a problem?"

"I wish to see my favorite and yours is keeping me from her side."

"She did just give birth." Storm could smell his frustration. Heather needed him to keep the man away from her so he wouldn't see the harm giving birth had done to her. He wasn't sure how he was supposed to accomplish that.

"I am the master here. I will not be denied."

"Did she ever have two at the same time before?" He needed to defuse the man's anger, maybe getting him to see it from a different perspective might be the answer.

"No."

"Then give the rest of the women time to clean her up for you." When the man just stood there glaring, he turned to his mate. "Heather, why can't he see his property?"

She took the proper stance and kept her voice low as she answered him. "She wishes to be presentable. Bringing two into the world was a little more complicated than expected."

"Then there was a problem." Nasturo glared at Heather. He looked like he wanted to strike her, but Storm would never allow that. "She wouldn't tell me there was something wrong, but I could see my son's colors were off. I wish to be sure she is healthy."

"She worked hard to bring your sons into this world." Heather kept her head down. "Your two sons were fighting over who would come out first."

He laughed. "I want to see her, now. It doesn't matter how presentable she is."

Heather nodded and stepped aside. The young woman was pale, far too pale for this race. Pain racked her body from time to time.

"You said she is healthy. This birth harmed her."

Storm could smell his fear that he would lose her because of this.

Nasturo knelt beside his favorite. "Thank you for my sons."

The moment his knees hit the ground Heather got Micali to help her send the women running. This was a private moment. *Help me, Storm. This could be their last. She has lost a lot of blood.*

He worked on the guards so they would be left alone.

"You can't die. I need you. Our sons need you." He touched her face with tenderness.

"I don't plan on leaving you, or our sons." She grasped his hand in hers. "But I need healing. These two helped save your sons. I'm not sure if they can save me."

"They must." Fear laced his voice. "There is no healer close that can help you."

Contact Bear. See what he can do. She shouldn't have to die because of their rules.

Is there nothing you can do?

Micali is doing everything she can, but I fear it isn't enough.

He excused himself and stepped out. Using his communication implant, he told Fridon what needed to be done. They were going to break a lot of laws, but it was worth saving a life. His first was convincing the new father to let him stay and make sure she was readied for him. Storm was able to talk Nasturo into going back to his guests, promising to make sure nothing would go wrong, while the women readied the healer to be brought to him.

Once he stepped back in, he worked on clearing the area. The guards were easy. They went back to their posts. The women were different. They worried about her and kept trying to get close to the healer to show their support. It took a few growls and glares to get them to stay in the other section of the building.

He heard back from Fridon. Heather was going to have to push herself to keep them safe. *How strong is your mind?*

Why? What do they want to do?

Transport her to the embassy.

I'll see what I can do.

———

Heather pulled Micali with her, away from the other women peeking into the area. Storm had tried, but they were worried about their healer so snuck in when they didn't see him looking. "We need to make all the women go into the other areas. No one can be here but you, me and Formeen."

Micali nodded. Heather could see she wanted to ask why, but she trusted Heather so accepted what she said without question. Heather touched her arm. "If we get caught, we will be punished, but it's the only way to save her life."

There has been a change of plans. Someone is coming to us. They will teleport when I give the all clear. I am going to be outside to keep the guards away so no one will see them from here.

Heather gave Micali a look so she could get the women to return to their jobs or give them chores that would help the new mother. The moment the doorway was clear Heather sat on the floor and stared intently at the place where Formeen lay. Opening her mind, she created the image that was in front of her in her head then projected it out so it overlapped over the real one.

Now. She watched as one of the embassy doctors transported into the area. Heather blocked her from sight as she fought to keep the image up. The drain was horrendous on her. She couldn't keep it up for long.

My heart?

Not now. This is taking all my concentration.

Why not just put the image in the head of the people looking?

Need clear line of sight. Someone could look in and if I'm not aware of it could set off an alarm.

Can you borrow strength from me?

Don't know how. Her body slumped against the floor. She was losing the image; she could feel it slip from her fingers. Closing her eyes, she forced the last of her strength to solidify and keep the image until the doctor left. Conscious-ness slipped away.

She awoke to find several women around her. Micali knelt to her right and the healer, now completely well, to her left. Storm was frantically trying to contact her mentally. *I'm fine, my heart.*

Don't do that again.

You are my heart.

And you are mine.

She smiled, knowing how lucky she was to have such a mate.

"Are you alright?" asked Micali.

"Yes." She sat up. She was still very weak, but she couldn't show it. Heather doubted anyone here had an ability like hers.

Formeen offered her a cup. "This will help you regain your strength." She leaned close to help Heather drink and whispered, "And thank you."

Whatever was in the drink did help. She was able to stand, allowing Micali to help her keep her feet. Heather swayed a little as she felt a little lightheaded, but her strength was returning a lot quicker than she expected. "We promised your owner we would bring you to him when you were presentable."

"I'm not leaving you until you can join me." She gripped Heather's arm. "You saved my life, and my owner needs to honor that."

"By breaking the rules." She wasn't sure how that would go over once the woman told her owner about how she survived.

"I didn't see any rules broken." She smiled at Heather, letting her know she wouldn't tell what really happened.

Heather breathed a sigh of relief. One less thing to worry about. The moment they stepped out of the women's area

Storm was there. He had a frown on his face. She knew it was because he was worried about her, not because he was angry at her.

"I wish to speak to my property for a moment?" His voice came out as a growl.

Formeen and Micali stepped to the side, fear etched on their faces. Both kept their gaze to the floor, but Heather spotted Micali glancing up when she thought it was safe.

"They are afraid of me?" He spoke to her in Vespian so no one would understand them. Frustration filled his words.

"You were frowning, and they are worried about me." She smiled at him. His concern for her so strong.

"I would never harm you. You know that."

"I know my heart."

He wrapped his arms around her and lifted her off her feet. His actions spoke volumes. Holding her close, he brushed his fingers through her hair while he studied her face. "You are too pale."

"I shall be fine." Her smile softened as she touched his face.

"You need to rest." He touched her face the same way, showing the women he cherished her. "I don't like it when you push yourself this way. It makes me feel helpless."

"I know, but I want to use my ability to help others. It would be selfish for me to keep it to myself. If I just stood by when I knew I could have done something, I would feel inadequate, and you know I can't do that." His concern for her welfare had her defending what she did at times.

He growled but didn't argue. "One of the reasons you seem to get into trouble all the time."

"And one of the reasons I'm your heart."

"True." He lowered her feet back to the ground.

"We will have time to rest after the meal." She rested her

head against his chest, loving the strong beat of his heart. "I promised Nasturo she would join him."

"You are not responsible and as your mate I feel your need to rest is more important than making sure she sees her master."

"Storm." She would still do what she thought was right. "I have an obligation."

"The stupid rules again?"

She nodded.

"Fine, then I am your owner. If anyone is responsible, it will be me." She knew he would take the blame too.

"Owners are never charged with the faulty behavior of their property," Heather reminded him. No matter what he said or did, she would be punished if someone knew what happened.

"No harm will come to her. No one will know because no one saw." Formeen had taken a couple of hesitant steps forward and touched Heather's arm before she spoke softly. Her words were aimed at Storm. "Do you wish to get out of the heat? I'm sure the meal is ready to be served and my master will wait until you return."

They had spoken in Vespian the whole time, but the women had picked up on what Storm was worried about.

He switched his hold on Heather to an arm around her waist and nodded. Storm entered the eating area first, followed by Heather and Micali. They took their places before Formeen entered.

Nasturo stood and crossed to her. "I am very happy with you. Two sons."

She smiled and nodded. "A great gift for my owner."

"And you?" He touched her shoulder.

"Ready to serve you." She touched his hand. His fingers clasped hers for a moment before he crossed to his seat and waited for her to join him.

Heather noticed how their touch lingered. There was something between them. Was she wrong about the way the men here felt about their women? She had seen how these men treated their favorites and they rivaled Storm's care at times.

———

Once the meal was served, Nasturo released them for a few hours. Heather wondered if it was because he wanted to speak to his favorite in private.

Storm half dragged Heather with him when he left. The moment the doors closed he backed her up against them. "You frightened me to death. I am so used to this connection now, having it stop while you were unconscious had me fearing the worst."

"My heart, we don't share dreams."

"I know, but there is still a connection." He touched the side of her head. "Your mind is always active. When you went down there was a void there."

"I'm sorry, but I did the only thing I could think of." She pressed the palm of her hand against one of his cheeks. "I felt the drain too quickly so I need to learn how to build up my strength or learn to borrow from others so I can sustain something like that better, but it worked."

"You're not thinking of trying that again, are you?" He ran the tips of his fingers along her jaw.

"Only in the safety of our rooms on Vespia."

"And never alone." His lips claimed hers. His tongue begged for entrance, wanting to touch her deeply, prove she was still there for him.

She opened for him gladly, knowing he needed this. The heat of his hands on her thighs had her reaching for her skirt. She sucked in her breath when she felt him enter her, driving in deep. Heather wrapped her arms around his neck and her legs around his waist. His need for her always amazed her. He never tired of wanting her. When he worried about her safety, it drove him close to a frenzy that only taking her like this would help make it disappear.

Then he would wipe away any of the wildness by taking her again and again with a tenderness that brought tears to her eyes.

"My heart." Her words came out breathless as he pounded into her. The friction was exquisite and had her muscles tightening against him. A growl escaped him as his mouth found her mark, intensifying everything. A moan, deep inside, worked its way up as an orgasm raced through her.

He continued to pound into her until he reached his climax. He rested his head atop hers as he waited for his heart to slow down. "You liked that."

"Oh, yes." She clung to him, still feeling a little boneless. "I know you like to be in control the whole time, but I like it when you lose control a little."

"I love it when you moan." Holding her in his arms, he walked to the bed. "Let's see if I can get another one."

EIGHT

"I thought your goal was to get a scream from me."

"Those are very precious, but the moans are just as good from a woman who barely made a sound when we were first intimate." He laid her down, then joined her. "Knowing I can get them when I least expect it makes me want to try even harder."

"We have about two hours before it is time to ready your bath." She smiled up at him.

"Good. I might be able to get a moan or two."

"Or if you are really lucky you just might get a scream."

———

Micali stopped in front of Heather and Storm's door, but Fridon wrapped an arm around her waist and brought her to their room instead.

"I just wanted to make sure Heather is okay."

"Not right now." He pulled her into the room and closed the door.

"Again?"

"Always." He glanced at the wall that separated their room. "Storm has a very strong libido. If their door is closed, we're not to disturb them. If Storm needs me, he'll come to me. Same with Heather."

"She just crumpled. It frightened me." Micali pressed her hand to her heart. "I feared she was dead. That was what my father did when he died. Just fell to the ground."

"I'm sorry, Micali." He placed a hand on each of her arms. He wanted to tell her about Heather's mental abilities but knew it wasn't his place. "She's made of sterner stuff. When you get a chance ask her about what happened. She'll probably tell you the same thing."

Micali nodded.

"So how much time do we have before we're interrupted?" He lifted her chin so she would look at him.

"About two hours before it will be time to ready your bath."

"Sure did enjoy that last bath." He gave her a sultry smile. "I believe you did too."

"I did." A blush filled her cheeks. "I never experienced anything like that before."

"We have time for you to experience it again before the bath, if you'd like."

"Really?" She looked up at him through her lashes. "And after?"

He laughed as he picked her up and carried her to the bed. "As many times as you wish."

———

Micali felt a thrill run through her at his words. She had trusted him and with that trust she learned it could be quite beautiful between a couple. Undar had come close to ruining this for her. If she hadn't met Fridon, she would have always feared sex. Now she knew better and wanted to get as much as she could before he left her.

He laid her on the bed and shed his clothes before joining her.

"But I am still dressed."

"I know, but that will be remedied quickly." He pressed a kiss against her stomach. "I wish to undress you."

She wasn't quite sure what to think of that. Undar sometimes didn't even let her remove her clothes before he was on her.

Fridon nibbled his way up to her top. She felt the clasp release just before she felt the heat of his mouth on one of her breasts. He was gentle as his hands skimmed across her skin to the edge of her skirt. His fingers dipped under the band, sending little fissions of desire racing through her blood. He sucked on one, then the other breast as he took his time inching her skirt off her hips. The brush of his fingers had her wanting more.

She felt a fire start deep inside, spreading through her body. He then kissed his way down her stomach as he eased her skirt down her legs to let it flutter to the floor. The flames she felt climbed as he slowly worked his way down to her core, his mouth blazing a trail of erotic kisses to her mound. Never had anyone touched her like this, paid homage to her, or made her feel things she didn't know were possible. Tears filled her eyes at the tenderness he showed her.

The gentle caresses she felt against her skin as his touch became intimate tightened her muscles. He lathed her core, making her shake with need, and tears spilled again. She wiped at them when he started to climb back up her body.

"Please tell me those are tears of joy." He touched her face as he entered her.

He filled her completely, the sensations he caused as he

stretched her had her quaking in his arms. Before she could answer him, she arched against him. Her release exploded all around her. Filling her with a euphoria she had just started to recognize. More tears flowed.

"After that, I'm going to assume it is happiness that is making you cry."

"Very much." She dashed at the tears once more, hoping to remove them before they upset Fridon.

"Ready for more?"

"Really?"

He pulled out and drove back in.

"Oh, yes." She couldn't stop the smile that spread across her face.

———

Desire raced through Heather's blood. Storm's warm breath fanned the area of her mark, making her want more. She tilted her hips. A gasp escaped her when his strokes touched a very sensitive spot. Her body shook at the intense wave of need that swept over her.

She was so close. Her hands slid up his back before sliding back down again and gripping his buttocks. The simple movement had him shaking as he pounded into her.

He was close too. She knew his release was imminent when he changed the pace to long deep strokes that took her breath away. Muscles tightened as her orgasm unfurled inside her, racing through her blood, making her body vibrate with the joy it filled her with. She floated along with the intense emotions washing against her.

Storm held Heather close as he pressed gentle kisses along her jawline. His release had followed hers, and he loved their combined climax. "My heart, as much as I enjoy all this leisure time with you, we need to finish our mission and get home."

"You mean to the safety of Vespia." They still didn't know if the girl they were searching for had been given as a gift. Heather didn't get a chance to look for her before. She needed to go back to the women's quarters to search for her. Storm didn't like it one bit.

A quick knock startled them.

"It's not Fridon. He knows better." Storm gave her a quick kiss before he got up from the bed and walked to the door.

"My heart, you're naked."

"So are you, and this will teach them not to interrupt me." He whipped open the door to find Nasturo and Formeen standing there.

"Oh, sorry to intrude." His eyes widened at Storm's state of undress. "We can come back."

Storm looked back at his mate to find she had sat up, clutching the sheet against her. He sighed as he stepped out of the way. "No, come in."

"I only wish to thank you. I have been told that your properties saved my favorite's life today." They walked into the room, and Storm closed the door. He grabbed his pants from the floor and slipped them on before joining Heather on the bed.

"I did what needed to be done." Heather held herself proudly, ready for any retribution she might have to take.

"I will not allow her to be punished." Storm stood in front of Nasturo, blocking Heather from view.

"No. You misunderstand. I don't know what I would have done if I had lost Formeen today." He took his favorite's hand and brought it to his lips. "She is my world." He then turned his attention to Storm. "Busandio's note said you were looking for something?"

"Yes," said Storm. "A young woman. She was stolen from her parents, not purchased, and we want to bring her home. Has your son received any women as a gift?"

"My son received three women as gifts. I'll have them brought here." He stepped outside for a few moments. When he came back in, he took Formeen's hand again. "I hate to bring this up but there are two men here claiming you stole from them."

"Let me guess, one is the merchant, Undar." Storm growled. If those two were going to continue to annoy him he would have to do something about it.

"Yes. I have to give him an audience." He didn't look happy with the idea. "Is it true? Did you take what he considers his?"

"He was abusive. I took her to protect her. Your laws are quite explicit about how to deal with owners such as him. I followed those laws."

"Can you prove it?"

"She has healed, thanks to the salve Busandio's favorite gave us, but he saw the damage Undar caused. He will collaborate my story. We had to take the salve with us because she was so badly bruised."

"The rest of her scars aren't ones you can see." Heather spoke softly, as she was supposed to, but everyone heard her.

"I wish to speak to the young woman," said Formeen.

Storm nodded and banged on the wall separating their rooms. Fridon hurried into the room, pulling his tunic on as he entered. Storm gave him a knowing smile. "Sorry. Those two idiots are here. The healer wishes to speak to Micali."

"I'll go get her."

He was back in moments with Micali in tow. She stayed behind Fridon, her gaze to the floor.

"Undar and Lewmard are questioning our possession of

her." Storm directed the comment at Fridon but his words had a strong effect on Micali. Tears started sliding down her cheek.

"The healer wishes to speak to you, Micali," said Heather. Lack of clothing kept her on the bed, but Storm knew she wanted to go and hug the poor girl. "Just tell her the truth."

She nodded and allowed Formeen to escort her to a quiet corner. They only spoke for a moment or two before the healer came back. Micali took a few more moments to compose herself before she retook her place behind Fridon once again.

"We have to give them an audience tonight at dinner." He looked at Formeen who gave him a slight nod. "Hear their side of the story."

"Understand they will not leave here with either woman. I will not stand for that." Storm stood. "If they try, I know one sure way to make sure they never bother us again."

"I'm going to pretend I didn't hear that. What they accuse you of is a grievous offense, but if what you say is true, then they will learn what happens to liars. As you said, our laws are quite explicit." He walked to the door. "We will see you at dinner."

The moment the door closed, Storm growled, "Pack. We're leaving now."

"We can't."

"Why not?" Storm turned to glare at his mate. Didn't she understand?

"Because if we run Nasturo will assume what they say is true and there will be a price on our heads. We have the truth on our side. I know you're not going to believe this but trust them to do what is right."

"All we have is a jar and a mouse of a girl who won't

stand up for herself." He waved his hand at Micali who ducked behind Fridon when he gestured toward her.

"If she acted any differently it would prove she wasn't abused." Heather looked at Fridon who gave her a slight nod before he turned his back to her. Without words, he knew what she wanted. She climbed out of the bed and placed her hand on Storm's chest. "I have seen a different side of these people and believe they will do what is right. Nasturo is the law here, and he can make sure those two leave us alone."

"I don't like it." He pulled her into his embrace.

"I know."

———

The meal had been cleared when Lewmard and Undar were allowed in. They weren't offered any food, only the chance to plead their case. They stood in front of Nasturo, looking a little too smug.

"You accuse my guest of stealing your property." Nasturo reclined on his pillows, playing the role of owner well. He looked bored and annoyed.

"That man decided his man needed a woman to occupy his time." Undar went first. He stepped forward and pointed at Storm then Fridon. Then he turned his attention to Heather. "He abuses his property all time by forcing her to have sex."

Storm coughed as his drink went down the wrong pipe. Forced her? There were times when she wouldn't take no for an answer. He looked at his mate who was fighting hard not to laugh. She was thinking the same thing.

"Interesting. She doesn't look abused. If anything, I would say she was spoiled properly, which is the way a woman should be treated." Nasturo took a sip of his drink. "Can you prove she was abused?"

"I saw her holding a weapon," Lewmard interrupted when Undar couldn't answer.

"Really?" He turned to Fridon. "Did you see Storm's favorite hold a weapon?"

"No." He shook his head. "Property isn't allowed."

"He wasn't there," Lewmard snapped.

"Then who was?" Nasturo looked at him.

"Her owner," he said, his voice flat.

"So it is your word against his. You know who normally wins in those arguments unless you have evidence." He paused as his favorite offered him a bit of his meal. Nasturo took his time chewing and swallowing. "So that is a closed matter. You say he stole your property. Which one is the woman in question?"

Undar pointed to Micali.

"I thought you said that Storm was the one who took her from you." He looked at Storm who held his hands up. "She is property of his man, not him. If property has already changed hands, there is nothing I can do and you know that."

"But he works for Storm and not allowed to have property."

"Is that true, Storm? Does Fridon work for you?"

"If you are asking if he is my property, then no. He is a free man. If you are asking if I am training him to be a leader, then yes." Storm smiled, understanding that Undar and his partner had nothing to fight for now.

"And does the woman belong to Fridon or you?"

"I gave her to him as a gift. He has worked hard to learn all I can teach and felt he deserved her."

"Was she damaged when you confiscated her?"

"Yes. Undar was quite cruel to her. Something I don't

tolerate. I even warned him ahead of time that if he mistreated her while traveling with me, I would take her from him and give her to Fridon."

"But he…" Undar sighed, realizing he wasn't going to win.

"So he traveled with you?"

"For several days. I tried to be hospitable, but he pushed too far." Storm shrugged. "To me women should be protected not beaten. They respond to kindness, not cruelty."

Nasturo took another bite offered to him. "I have to agree. I was gifted with two boys today and I believe it was because I have been kind to that which is mine." He wiped his mouth with a cloth as he thought about what he would say. "I'm sorry, Undar, but your case isn't a strong one. Storm's is. He shall keep his property and Fridon may keep the one you claim. This matter may not be disputed again."

Undar hung his head and headed out. Storm found Lewmard glaring at him as he left. They weren't done with these two, but at least they knew nothing more would come of him trying to take Micali and his mate away.

———

Micali shook her head. She had been saved by something so simple. "I am yours?"

"In a manner of speaking." Fridon closed the door once they were back in their room. "Storm did give you to me."

She laughed. Joy shot through her. She never had to worry about that man taking her away from Fridon again.

"I hope you do that a lot more."

"What?" She stopped and looked at him.

"Laugh. It is a beautiful sound, coming from you." He

crossed to where she stood. "You do realize they will try another tactic."

"Yes. I know all the ways they can try, but none will work." She didn't care what they tried. For the first time in her life, she felt safe. "They have already lost one confrontation and soon all families will know this. They can't try the same thing twice."

"But you know other ways they can try to take you and Heather?" He ran a hand up her arm.

"Of course, and I want to tell you everything they can try, but first I wish to celebrate." She smiled up at him.

"And how did you hope to celebrate?" His eyes held a spark of desire.

"Perhaps another bath? I can show my gratitude by bathing you." Micali crossed to the sunken tub. She dipped a few fingers into the water. "I can reheat some of the water on the fireplace. It won't take long. The water is still warm."

"If it is warm enough you don't need to reheat it." He stepped up to the tub and dipped his hand in. Turning to her, he smiled. "I think we can heat this up on our own."

"Are you sure?" Her heart fluttered in her chest. Knowing he wanted her filled her with a strength she never felt before. He did this for her.

He pulled his tunic off, then slipped his pants down his hips. Climbing into the tub, his smile brightened. "I am sure."

She removed her clothing and joined him. Picking up the oils, she started on his chest. The hard muscles under the soft skin amazed her. "How could Storm say you're soft? I touch you and feel nothing but hardness."

"At this particular time, I should hope so."

She blushed. "I meant your muscles."

He wrapped his arms around her, pulling her softness against him. "You are very beautiful when you blush."

It made her blush more. "I'm not done with your bath."

"Oh, but I am, unless you wish me to bathe you as well." She didn't answer, but he saw the spark in her eyes. "I'll take that as a yes."

"Not 'til I'm done." She picked up the oil. "There are a few places I haven't focused on."

"In that case." The smile he gave her held such promise she felt that weird fluttering in her stomach again.

Micali smiled back as she poured more oil into her hands. He wasn't going to deter her. "Where would you like me to start?"

"How about right here?" His hands slid down her stomach to her core.

Desire raced through her. She placed her hands on his chest and pushed him back gently. "I am to bathe you?"

"Later." He pulled her closed once again, then his head dipped toward hers, capturing her lips with his. "I want to feel when you have another fabulous orgasm around me."

"You can feel that?"

"Oh, yes. Your muscles tighten against me, your breath comes out in short little pants, and my favorite is the way you clutch at me when you are in the throes of your release. It is wonderful."

"You enjoy that?"

"You can't compare what we share with what you had with Undar. He is a very stupid man who didn't know how to treat you." He touched her face with the tips of his fingers. "I do and I find the way you react to my touch so beautiful. I want to erase every horrible memory you have from that man."

"That could take a while."

"I am up to it."

"I can tell."

He laughed as he lifted her up, braced them against the

edge of the tub and drove into her. She was still a little shy about facing him while they were intimate, but she showed how she trusted him by making herself look at him as he set a pace that would bring them both such joy. Wrapping her legs around his waist, she felt her breath catch in her throat as the new angle changed the friction she was feeling and intensified it. Muscles tightened inside. Fridon picked up the pace and she felt her body shake. It wouldn't take long.

He watched her face for subtle little things that let him know how close she was. She closed her eyes. He knew what to do to heighten what she was feeling. If she held her breath for a moment, he would make a change.

"You watch me too much." She dropped her head forward as she felt the heat starting in her stomach.

"I have to. You are too beautiful to ignore." He slipped a finger under her chin and lifted her face so he could see her eyes again. "Especially now, when you are so close."

And she was. Her body tingled as she felt the flames start deep inside. They licked at her insides, spreading deliciously along her veins, filling her with a warmth that had her reaching for the wonderful euphoria she knew she could feel. Then it started. It raced through her blood, igniting her release. It took her to the stars, filling her with a joy that brought tears to her eyes.

"You're crying again." He kissed her tears away.

"I can't help it. You have changed my whole life by your kindness. I never knew and if you hadn't come into my life, I would have lived it oblivious to what sex should be." She knew her words were a little sappy, but she couldn't help it. He had changed her world, and she was grateful.

———

Storm paced his room while he waited for Heather to return. He turned when the door finally opened.

"What took you so long?"

"Sorry, my heart. Formeen wanted to be sure I saw all the women there, including their guests. She isn't here." She placed her hand on his heart.

"Then we can leave."

"Yes. They are preparing a big sendoff for us. I have let Micali know so she can pack hers and Fridon's belongings."

"I will help you."

"You need to meet with Nasturo so he can make a big deal of our leaving." She looked around the room. "This won't take me long."

"And if those two idiots try to take you? I don't think so."

"There are two guards outside the door. They are to make sure nothing happens while Micali and I are alone. They will bring us to you when we're ready."

"Heather."

"We have to do this their way, Storm. It will be okay."

He didn't like it, but knew she was right. The sooner they left the happier he would be.

———

Storm breathed a sigh of relief once they were on their way again. "The next place is four days away. With those two out there, I must force you two to walk again."

Heather knew her mate. It wouldn't be too long before he pulled her up on the animal anyway. His view of her body from above heightened his libido. He kept watching the top of her outfit like he was willing it to fall off. Even now, his eyes were glowing. It never distracted him though. She also knew he was aware of what was going on around them. He knew where Undar and Lewmard were.

They kept moving, making good time. Their shadows followed but never came close.

They found a wonderful little oasis when they stopped on the second night. The lush shade and pool of fresh water offered them something they didn't think they'd be able to experience since their arrival. It would have been wonderful if they could spend an extra day but every minute they delayed could mean failure to find their target. Their tent went up with ease. Once the women finished setting up the insides, they began the meal.

Storm and Fridon worked on the perimeter security, making sure their followers couldn't get too close without their knowledge.

"I'm going to scout out our unwanted guests," Storm told Fridon.

"Do you wish me to stay here or join you?"

"Keep an eye on the women." Storm looked at his mate, who happened to be bending over at that moment in a very provocative manner. Maybe he should stay if she was going to continue to do that.

"Sir?" Fridon tried to regain his attention.

"Right." He grinned at getting caught staring at his mate. "I won't be long."

Fridon nodded and headed back to where Heather and Micali worked on their dinner.

Storm walked until he was sure he was out of sight before removing his clothes and shifting. He still hadn't learned how to shift back with clothes. Hiding them in the sandy ground, he cleared his mind and allowed his body to change. Now on all fours, he raced across the sand, using his senses to sniff out Undar and Lewmard's location.

It didn't take him long to find them. He needed to make

sure they understood he meant business. The animals weren't tethered very well and a deep growl from his throat spooked them off. The two men hadn't been smart enough to remove their saddle bags so their food as well as anything else they left in the bags took off with the animals.

That should set them back a few days.

———

Storm came back to find their dinner ready. Heather handed him a plate when he walked up.

"They won't be bothering us anytime soon." He took the plate from her and sat next to Fridon.

"How did you manage that?"

"Scared off their pack animals. They'll be too busy chasing them down." Storm grinned.

"You think we could take advantage of the pond?" asked Heather. Her gaze moved to the small body of water.

"Maybe in the morning. I'd want to make sure they are still occupied." He touched her face with tenderness. "But we can relax a little tonight. Nasturo gave us some of his wine."

"Shall I get the cups?" asked Heather. She stood, figuring he would say yes. With a quick nod from him, she went into the tent.

Storm went to the bag that held the skins. Tossing one to Fridon, he took his seat and opened it.

Heather came out with four cups.

Alcohol doesn't affect you or Fridon, so why would you want to drink wine?

Because if those two aren't chasing their frulas then they will be watching and think they can take advantage of us. If they leave us be, I will feel we are safe.

*Which is why you want us to wait until tomorrow to bathe.
What if they catch their animals faster than you hope?*
Then we'll use your bathing time as a trap for them.

———

The next morning, after they broke their fast, the women
readied for their bath.

"Why aren't they joining us?" asked Micali as she put
her cape on to hide her nakedness. She lifted the basket that
held their cleaning supplies.

"They bathed earlier. This way, they can talk while they
wait for us." They were bait. But Heather didn't want to
worry the young woman. "Are you ready?"

Micali nodded, steadying the basket on her arm. "What
would they wish to talk about?"

"They are planning our trip to the next city."

They walked out to the pool. Heather discreetly looked
around to make sure she didn't see evidence of their followers. Once they reached the edge, the women dropped the
capes onto the ground and climbed into the pool. The cape
would double as a towel later. The water was warm on the
top but cool below their knees. Heather dove, hitting icy
water pretty quickly.

"Wow!" She shook her head as she slicked her hair back.

"Warm?" asked Storm as he came up to the edge of the
water.

"Ice cold several meters down." She treaded water near
the center of the pond. "Warm at the top."

"Anything in there besides you two?"

"Not that I'm aware of." She grinned at him. "We should
be safe."

"Then I'm going to look around. Make sure." He winked
at her and headed behind the tent.

Fridon headed off in the opposite direction from Storm, leaving the two of them alone.

"How fast can you move if you need to?" Heather asked Micali.

"Why?" She looked at Heather with a frightened gaze.

"Curious." She continued treading water. "Did you put the cleansers over there, near the trees? It's getting a little too cold for me."

"I'll get them." She swam to the side and picked up the bottles they needed to wash their hair and bodies. She handed Heather the hair cleanser while she swam to a shallower spot to use the oils to clean her body. She propped them up against a few plants while she used them.

Heather lathered her hair and dipped her head below the water. When she came up, she saw two extra shadows on the shore. It didn't surprise her. Storm probably left just to see what they would do. She looked at Micali who must have spotted them while she was underwater and had moved into the deeper section, fear in her eyes.

"You do realize when Storm catches you here, he will kill you. You have ignored his demands time and again." Heather swam to where the oils were and picked up a bottle. Finding a spot to stand she stood, exposing herself to their gaze, using the oils to clean any grime away.

"We didn't give you permission to speak!" Lewmard screamed at her.

Heather gave him a bored look. His anger was so strong he didn't pay attention to her body. On the other hand, Undar did, which made her feel uneasy when his gaze filled with lust. Storm wanted to see which one wanted her so asked her to expose herself to see who reacted. She didn't like the idea but went along with his request. "And who is going to know I spoke? You think anyone is going to listen to you now? Storm has already proved he owns us outright. Nothing you can do or say will change that."

"He will be too late."

"I doubt that." She spotted Storm in his wolf form, sitting just a few yards behind them. She dipped back down into the water. "I hope you have put your lives in order because they won't last much longer."

A low, guttural growl filled the air.

Undar reacted to the sound by turning around. He turned white and fainted.

"Worthless cure!" Lewmard shouted at the unconscious Undar. He wasn't frightened as easily. Pulling a blade out of one of his pant legs, he dropped into a crouched position.

Storm hadn't moved. Fridon, on the other hand, stepped up behind the man and whacked him in the back of his head with a large piece of firewood. He dropped to the ground in a heap.

Heather swam to the shore and climbed out. She pulled the cloak back around her, signaling for Micali to stay in the water. Fridon was tying up Lewmard first, since he was the most dangerous of the two, while Heather took care of Undar. He then dragged the men back to their fire.

The moment the two men were away from the pond Heather signaled Micali to get out. "Go get dressed. I'll be there shortly."

"What was that?" She wrapped her cloak around her, apprehensive about the strange animal she had just seen.

Heather looked to where Storm had sat only seconds ago. "He won't harm any of us. Think of him as a protector. Now go get dressed."

Micali nodded and ran to the tent.

Heather moved to the back where she knew Storm waited.

"Undar wants you." Storm stood there proud and naked.

"Stupid man wants what he can't have." She wrapped her arms around Storm's waist. "He doesn't frighten me. Lewmard, though, is quite dangerous."

"I can handle him." He ran his fingers along her jawline and lifted her face so he could capture her lips with his. His tongue dove into her mouth, drinking from it, sharing the joy he felt for her. When he broke the kiss, they were both breathing a little hard. "I need to take care of those two before I can take care of our needs. Go get dressed, just understand you won't be in your clothes for long."

"I hope not." She pressed a quick kiss to his mark before turning and doing as he asked.

Storm went to where he had stashed his clothes, dressed then went to confront the two men.

They were just coming around when he got there. Storm crossed his arms over his chest and stared at them. "You just don't get the point I've been trying to make, do you?"

"That you're driven by your body when it comes to that woman? I don't care," spat Lewmard. "She ruined me and has to pay."

"No, she doesn't. I have heard the story and she did what needed to be done."

"You only heard her side and I bet that was while she had you between her legs."

Storm grabbed Lewmard by his throat and lifted him so they were eye to eye. He didn't care if the ropes they tied around him choked him a little as he dangled in Storm's grasp. He was lucky Storm didn't just squeeze the life out of him. "You will not speak about her that way or I'll show you that I am far more dangerous than you are. I heard the story from the child she saved when she stopped you from beating a woman who had only gone to get medicines to save that child. He was the heir to his father's fortune."

Storm dropped him at his feet. "But if you feel you can give me a clearer version of the story, go right ahead."

Lewmard looked at the ground.

"I see. Then I do have the right story." He stepped back so Lewmard couldn't touch him. "I want you to know who you are dealing with. I am skilled in the art of combat. There is nothing you can try that I can't counter. It is within my rights to kill you and leave you out here for the birds to pick apart, but because of my favorite's tender heart I will allow you to live. For now. Understand that Heather is mine and I protect what is mine. Now you shall remain my guest until we reach our next destination, then I'll turn you over to the authorities. Maybe that will keep you out of my hair."

Fridon stepped forward to secure them to a line he had erected earlier. They would have very little movement, and he and Storm could watch them easily.

Heather was waiting for her mate when he stepped into the tent. She didn't question his decision, but he noticed how many times she kept looking outside.

"You're not happy about this."

"I have felt his wrath personally. Having him this close makes me nervous. That's all." She clasped her hands behind her back when she wanted to wrap them around herself.

He pulled her into his embrace. "My heart, he will not be able to lay a hand on you. I will make sure of that."

"I know. But the memory of what he did is still here." She tapped her head. "Every time I see him, I relive those horrible moments. A part of me wants to run. A part of me wants to drive a knife into his heart."

"Then let me fill your head with much better memories as we make a few new ones." He picked her up so they could look eye to eye as he claimed her lips. His tongue begged for entrance which she gladly gave. With each sweep of his tongue, he tried to wipe away the memories that plagued her.

He carried her to their bed as their tongues continued to dance. His deft fingers released her top and it dropped to the floor. "Much better."

"You would be happiest if I were naked all the time." She wrapped her arms around his neck.

"Only because I'd have easy access to your body. But the clothing you choose, especially when you're trying to tease me is highly erotic." He pressed a kiss to her mark as his hands slid down her hips to remove her skirt. "If you were naked all the time, I wouldn't get the thrill of undressing you."

"That's true." She slipped her hands up under his tunic. "Now it's your turn."

He set her on the floor, then pulled his shirt off and let it flutter to the ground.

"So, that is how you're going to play it?" She slid her hands inside the waistband of his pants. "What about the thrill of me undressing you? Of you not knowing where my hands will touch next?"

"All I have to do is look at you and I get hard. I can't always handle your teasing. Besides, this is to help you forget. Next time I promise to take it like a man." He shucked in his breath when her exploring hands closed around his staff. "Of course, if you keep that up you might find yourself up against the wall again."

She released the closure of his pants and they dropped to the ground. "Now we're even. And the canvas walls won't withstand your amorous ways."

"I'm sure if I worked on this dilemma long enough, I'd find a solution." Storm urged her back toward their bed, easing her onto the soft pillows. "You, my heart, are something I can never get enough of."

Heather lay down, opening her body for him. A sigh escaped her as he drove his way home. His lips caressed her mark as he set a pace that had her breathing hard rather quickly. Each time he slid out, then drove back in again, had her body tightening. Wrapping her legs high on his waist, she met him stroke for stroke. She could never get enough of him, either.

Each stroke brought her closer to the edge. He caused the wonderful friction between them to build, blossoming into the beginning of her release. Little tell-tale quakes from Storm showed he was getting close, too. She felt the first tendril of her orgasm wrap around her when Storm shifted his weight.

"Not too soon, my heart." He brushed a few strands of hair from her face. "I want to prolong this as much as I can."

But she couldn't wait. When he shifted, he started hitting the one spot that made her scream. It built quickly, drawing a moan from her before she felt her world explode all around her.

"My heart," said Storm. "You were supposed to extend your orgasm, not reach it faster."

"Couldn't help it. You were hitting all the right spots."

"You know what this means don't you?" He pressed a kiss against her mark.

"We have to do this all over again?" she asked hopefully.

"That's my girl."

———

Heather looked over at the two men all trussed up. Storm and Fridon had made good use of the extra rope they had. Undar and Lewmard's upper torso was completely covered from the way Storm wrapped it around them as he bound them together, their arms secure against their sides, and then the remainder of the rope was wrapped around their feet so they couldn't run.

Heather had a plate in her hand. After feeding Storm, she was going to feed the prisoners. Just as she lifted a bit of meat to Undar's mouth, she heard Storm's voice.

"What are you doing?"

"Feeding our guests?" Her gaze dropped to the ground the same time she lowered her hand to her lap. Out of the corner of her eye, she saw Undar's mouth hang open for a moment or two before he realized he wasn't going to be fed.

"No." His voice came out sharp and she flinched, acting the way she was supposed to. "They shall eat like the animals they act like. Put a plate of food and a bowl of water down for them. That is all they get. No hand feeding."

She dropped the piece she had been holding onto the dirt and stood. Crossing to the path where their meal had been warming, Heather spooned out enough for two people and set it between the two men. Micali came up behind her with a larger bowl of water. They stepped back as Storm went to stand in front of the two men.

"Oh, and since you two don't have any hands to clean your face with, you might want to drink first so your water is clean." Storm dropped his little bombshell and turned on his heel.

They looked at each other before they conked heads racing for the water dish.

Heather kept her head down so they wouldn't see her laugh. It might not be the smartest thing to do, but it should make them think twice before they try to cross swords with Storm again and she knew that was what he was going for.

———

They traveled at a slow pace, more for the women than the men they now had in tow. As much as Storm would have loved to pull Heather up with him and make the other two run, he knew they would grab the first chance they got to tell on him. He had them tied to a second frulas that he had secured to his stallion. He didn't want them getting anywhere near his mate.

Not that Heather couldn't take care of herself. He didn't want to risk any confrontation between them with them heading to another populated area.

You know you could give my chain to Fridon if you really want to take them for a run.

I had thought of that but decided against it for now. Keeping them behind you should be just as humiliating as being dragged behind my animal and I plan on doing that when we get closer to town.

"You know the moment you turn them over they will be released," she said quietly.

"Maybe, but if the town sees me dragging them to their security, I'm hoping it will make them highly visible and that should keep them away from us." He looked down at Heather. "How far away do you think we are?"

"About four hours at the speed we're moving at." She was quiet for a moment. "I doubt that will stop them. Lewmard has been holding this grudge too long for him to give up."

"You are my mate. He will learn my desire for you is much stronger than his hate. Nothing will happen to you. I will kill him before he harms a hair on your head." He leaned down and touched her face. "When we're closer I'm going to hand you off to Fridon and drag these two behind my horse into town."

"We have been traveling for a while now." Heather

checked to make sure they were still on their feet. "We should stop and offer them food and drink."

"Would they have thought of that?" He looked back at the two men.

"No."

"They will be treated the same way you would be if they were the ones with the upper hand."

She didn't say anything more.

———

Storm smiled as he looked back to see how Lewmard and Undar were doing now that he had given Heather to Fridon to bring into town. He kept his horse moving at a good pace. Not so fast that they wouldn't be able to keep up, but they still had to run or end up being dragged. They were breathing heavily by the time he trotted into the center of a cluster of buildings with them in tow. The area was crowded, and it took him a few minutes to make it through the throngs to the law enforcement office. He slid off his stallion and pulled the men behind him.

The interior was quiet. Storm didn't see anyone at the large desk that dominated the room. Who was making sure these people were protected?

Papers were strewn everywhere, rotting food sat on the desk. It looked like no one cared. He wasn't happy because he realized Heather was right. The moment he turned these men over to the law they would probably weasel their way out. He needed to secure enough time for them to get to the next house, which was still several days away.

How was he going to do that?

"You having a problem here?" A guard came from a back room. He smelled of alcohol and some sort of burnt herb.

"Yes. These two men are thieves. They have stolen from me, then accused me of stealing from them."

"We haven't stolen from him. He stole from us."

"Really?" Storm stood there with his arms crossed over his chest. "And which one of us came in here trussed up like animals? They are untrustworthy. Lies flow from their lips like wine from a bottle."

"And how do I know you tell the truth?"

"This man," he grabbed Undar by the hair and pulled on it until his face could be seen. "Is Undar the merchant. He has never gotten any of his sellable items properly. Instead, he steals from one to sell to another. I'm sure you have heard of him."

"He does have a record." He pointed to Lewmard. "And that one?"

"Lewmard. He was bested by a woman."

"Heard of him, too." He used a fingernail to pick at his teeth. "What do you want me to do with them?"

"How much to get you to keep them for a day or two?" He knew he had to pay. His prisoners had nothing to barter with so if he offered enough, he might get the head start he needed.

———

Storm got back to Heather and the others as fast as he could. They had waited on the outskirts of town for him. "I bought us a few hours at best. They are in the middle of some sort of celebration so I'm not expecting the guards to pay a whole lot of attention to their new guests."

Fridon handed him Heather's chain. "I take it the women will ride then?"

"Yes. We need to check our supplies before we ride. Make sure everything is secure." Storm slid off his animal and started checking the ties on the pack animals. "We're still two days away from our goal if the women walk, but if we break a few rules and ride hard we should be able to cut a lot of time off our arrival."

"What if we run into other riders?" Fridon joined him, checking knots and shifting items around to help balance the weight better.

"We'll have to see how that goes." Storm pulled Heather up into his lap, making sure she was facing him, just in case. Fridon did the same thing. They rode as hard as they could for as long as they could, but after a while they had to slow down for the animals.

Heather and Micali fixed a quick lunch while they watered the frulas and the stallion.

"Why are we racing across the land?" asked Micali as she stirred the food.

"Storm gave Undar and Lewmard to the authorities and fears they will be released before we can get to our next destination." Heather stuck a finger in the meal, smiled, and nodded.

"And they will try. They talked while they were tied up but didn't pay attention to me as I worked." Micali brought out the plates they used. "They plan on kidnapping you when we've set up camp. Maybe when we're at the next city. They weren't sure when, but they will be looking for a chance."

"Storm won't let them get close to me."

"They know that." Micali held the plates while Heather filled them. "That is why they are going to go to the next city instead of following us. They want to get there ahead of us to make a plan."

Heather looked up to see Storm standing there.

The thunderous look on his face showed his displeasure. "Then we need to get there first."

———

Once they reached their destination, they erected their tent just outside the town walls. The moment the women started working on the tent, Storm and Fridon set up their security sensors. Completing their task, Fridon went into the town to see if he could spot Undar and Lewmard.

"Do you sense them?"

Heather shook her head. "Too many minds together for me to try to pick out two. Especially since I've never touched theirs. I don't want to know their thoughts."

"What about Fridon?"

"Nope." She pressed her hand against his chest. "Only you, my heart, and the children."

"You still don't like pushing this, do you?"

"Some of the thoughts I have caught from time to time bother me. Touching a stranger's mind makes me uneasy. What if they aren't as nice as they pretend to be? If there is evil lurking beneath, I don't know if I can keep my mind from being soiled."

"I see. My pure mind has spoiled you." He wrapped his arms around her.

"Ha! You don't have any pure thoughts when it comes to me. All you can think of is when you can get inside of me." She hugged him. "Thanks. I needed that."

"You're going to have to learn how to do this, though. Your mind keeps expanding, and sooner or later it will happen, whether you want it or not."

"I know." She sighed as she rested her head against his chest.

"Try to reach out for Fridon's mind. I'd like to think his would be safe. And he knows what you're capable of so it shouldn't surprise or frighten him."

She nodded. Leaning against him for support, she

opened her mind, reaching for Fridon's. It was weird to send her consciousness out like this. It touched several thoughts, but when she didn't recognize them, she moved on. Then she touched on a small and frightened mind. "Storm, there is a child lost."

"Heather, we don't have time for that. You need to find Fridon."

"But the child." She looked up at him.

"My heart, we can't rescue every child out there." He touched her cheek.

"And what if it was one of our children lost?" She knew he was right but couldn't help but feel for the youngster. "Would you expect people who realized they were lost to leave them because they know they can't rescue every child?"

"Heather, I don't want you leaving the safety of this tent."

"I hadn't planned on it." She smiled at him.

"So you want to send Fridon after the child?" He shook his head, knowing he wouldn't be able to talk her out of it. "Have you found him? Has he said he would rescue the child?"

She sighed. He was being stubborn. She tried, but there were just too many thoughts. And the lost child kept distracting her. "I'm sorry."

"What seems to be the problem?"

"So many people to work through." She rubbed her forehead.

"When you went through my mother's mind for the memories on Ialog, how did you do it?"

"That was different. I had help and knew what to look for."

"Perhaps you need to think the same way now. A Vespian mind has to look different from the people of this planet. Have you tried that? Look for the mind that is different by design or color or whatever allows you to tell us apart when you touch our minds. How can you tell my mind from the children?"

"I just know. It's like we have this cord between us."

"What about your brother or my mother?"

"Same idea, but they are different." She looked up at him. "It's not like I see anything to separate you from anyone else."

"Keep trying, my heart." He brought her to their bed and gestured for her to sit. He went down on one knee so he could look her in the eyes. "Think about what you see or feel when we connect."

"I always feel your desire for me." She smiled at the thought. "No matter what, it is always there."

"And the children?" He took her hands in his.

"I know you don't understand the word, but I feel their love. A pure thing that wraps me in a warm blanket." She sat there for a moment. "It's recognition. My mind knows who you are and lets you in. I need to do that with all these minds. Look for the one I recognize."

Heather closed her eyes as she held his hands. Her anchor. Sending her mind out again, she flitted along the minds she came into contact with. None of them she recognized. Then she felt him. The thoughts were a lot like Storm's.

Fridon?

What? Who is this?

Heather. Storm pushed me to reach for your mind.

Is he asking if I found them? The tone in his mind was slight exasperation. *The answer is no.*

I wanted to contact you because I have found a child who is lost.

Where?

I don't know. That's part of the problem. I touched the boy's mind, but I don't know where he is. All I can sense is he's being shadowed by something large, and he is very frightened.

How old is this boy?

His mind is still young. I'd say five or six.

You have a soft heart, Heather.

I know, my mate tells me that all the time.

I'll see what I can do but make no promises.

Heather opened her eyes and smiled at Storm.

"You found him."

"I did, and he will try to find the child."

"But you are still going to worry, aren't you?" He touched her chin to make her look at him.

She smiled, feeling a little guilty about how she worried about a child that didn't belong to her. "Blame my mothering instincts."

"How about I distract you?" He pulled her to her feet so he could wrap his arms around her and spread small kisses across her cheek before his lips moved down her throat to her mark.

"You are very good at that." She sighed as she felt his mouth suck on the sensitive tissue. "What about Micali? We can't leave her outside alone."

"She isn't outside. I saw her go toward her bed while you were reaching for Fridon's mind. And she knows how we are. She has already turned on the noise canceling machine." He released her top and let it drop to the floor. "So you have nothing to worry about and can take it like a woman."

His mouth closed on a nipple, and she came close to moaning. She felt him smile against her skin.

"What?"

"That was an almost moan." He kissed the skin between her breasts. "I might get a scream today."

"And you know how to make me scream." She stopped talking as he took her other breast into the heat of his mouth.

Storm worked his way down her body to her belly button, causing goose bumps to rise on her skin. "You are very aroused. As much as I'd like to think it is because of me, I'm curious why."

"I don't know." She sucked in her breath when his tongue dipped into her navel.

"It reminds me of the time when Kuarto worked with you to develop that block to keep him out of our intimate moments."

"You think I get aroused every time I push my mind a little." More goosebumps rose when he slid his fingers under the band of her skirt to ease it down her hips. He pressed a kiss against her mound, and her knees went weak.

"It is something we'll have to test, isn't it?" He kissed his way back up her body.

"But I didn't do it when my mind broke that device Ialog had placed on my forehead."

"True, but that was a little different. Your protective protocol caused that." He touched her face gently before he trailed a hand down one arm.

"What about when I kept taking over your body? I was pushing my mind then." She shuddered at his touch.

"And we were both aroused all the time because our intimacy was limited. I don't think we would have noticed the difference because of our need for each other." He urged her back down on their bed. "I don't want you crumpling at my feet while I pay homage to your body."

"You don't need to pay homage to my body. I need to feel you inside me." She wrapped her legs around him.

"Oh, no you don't." He dropped his knees to the floor so

she couldn't draw him toward her. "I want to take my time with you. Draw the moans I love to hear so much."

"Storm."

"Shh, you talk too much, and I know just how to quiet you." He rested his hands on her waist before he inched his way up the soft skin to her breasts. His mouth started working on where he left off, moving slowly down to her mound then to her core. One lick quieted her, two had her breathing hard. She was so close so quickly he knew better than to torture her anymore. Climbing up her body, planting a kiss here and there he touched her face as he entered her.

She arched against him, sucking in her breath as her muscles clamped down on him.

"My heart, you are ready to explode and all I have done is fill you."

"I know. Can't help myself." She tilted her hips. "Stay...right...Oh!"

It started as a ripple, flowing through her until all she knew was her impending orgasm. She felt like she was free-falling when everything tightened for a moment then released itself. Her body shook from the intensity. "Wow."

Storm brushed a few hairs out of her face as he smiled down at her. "Are you ready for more?"

"Oh, yes."

He started a slow pace. "Are you going to take off on me again?"

"I don't know." She slid her legs high on his hips. "Got to say that feels really good."

"It always is good, my heart. Are you saying it feels more intense?"

All she could do was moan as she tilted her hips again. "Faster."

"I'll take that as a yes." He changed the pace, slowing it down with a quick grind of his hips as he plunged in as deep as he could. Heather wasn't happy when he first started, but then she met him thrust for thrust. Her body quaked as she grew close again.

Storm.

Enjoy it, my heart.

Not without you. She tried to stop the overpowering wave of joy but couldn't. Once again, she was swept away by the power of her release.

"Each time you do that I get closer to mine. Keep it up and we'll both explode into that supernova you keep promising me."

"Promise?" she slid a leg down one of his.

"With all my heart."

NINE

Fridon wasn't sure if he should go back to the tent. He hadn't found the child Heather asked him to find. Would she be upset with him? He also hadn't found their two shadows and knew Storm wouldn't be happy.

When he came to the tent, he found Micali outside.

"Not a good time to interrupt?" He sat beside her.

"No." She stirred the fire she had started. "They have been at it for quite a while."

"And you have been trapped out here?"

"I was in the tent when they started. That is where I felt trapped, even with that machine of yours. Out here, at least I don't have to worry about them worrying about me being in the same place while they share with each other."

"I am sorry." He sat down beside her. "The relationship they share is exalted at home. Storm is our next leader, and the fact that Heather keeps him satisfied is very important to my people."

"Well, if they ever need a witness, I can vouch for them." She looked at Fridon. "They strive to keep each other satisfied."

He laughed. All he could do was wait now. Heather would probably sense his presence and want to find out what had happened.

———

"Fridon is back." Heather touched Storm's face just above hers. "He doesn't seem happy."

"So you think he didn't succeed?"

"As far as finding our troublemakers? I'm not sure. He could be upset because of the little boy, but I don't feel the fear from the child I felt earlier. Either he found his family or something else distracted me." She smiled up at him.

"I take my job very seriously." He pressed a kiss to her mark before rolling over and taking her into his arms.

She laughed. "You enjoy distracting me, even when I shouldn't be distracted."

"You mean when you don't want to be distracted." He gave her a wicked grin. "But you can never say no to me. You love the way I distract you."

"I do, but we have monopolized this tent for long enough." She stretched before she planted her feet on the ground and stood. Heather dressed quickly and walked out of the tent before Storm could stop her. If she didn't, they'd be occupied for another hour or so.

Fridon stood when she came out.

"You couldn't find the child, could you?"

"Sorry."

"It's okay. I didn't get a good feel for where he was anyway." She sat nearby. "Did you find the other two?"

"No." He growled like Storm would when he was frustrated. "But heard a few stories of men fitting their description. I believe they are here."

Storm stepped out of the tent at Fridon's last remark.

"We must be vigilant then. Lewmard will try to strike again."

"How?" Fridon turned to Storm. "He can't get in the tent. As long as the women stay inside, they are safe."

"True, but the laws here won't allow us to hide while there is work to do," Heather interjected. "He's going to find a way when we have to fulfill our duties."

"Why don't you give them what they want?" asked Micali.

"What?" Storm turned to look at her, a frown creasing his brow.

"Lewmard won't stop until he gets Heather, but she is protected by the chain she wears. No matter what he tries, that can't be removed. The only way he can properly own her is for you to sell her to him." Micali kept her gaze to the floor as she spoke. They had taught her to not be afraid to tell them her thoughts, but a lifetime of training was hard to fight. "Even if they try something underhanded, like selling her without your approval, they can't. They must have a bill of sale with your signature. If they try to take her, they have to make it legal for them to keep her."

"So you're saying they must have my signature? They could forge it."

"No." She shook her head. "It has to be the real signature."

"How can they prove anything they have is real?" Storm didn't like the way this conversation was going at all.

"Your signature is on file." She looked at Heather. "You might not see too much technology around here, but when it comes to personal property, the men use the highest. Nothing can be sold without the proper papers. It was designed to protect owners from unscrupulous merchants and property from being stolen."

"Are you saying these dealers are above reproach?" Storm didn't look convinced. "They can't be bribed?"

"That I don't know." Micali paused for a moment. "But taking a bribe is bad for business. If your buyers learn you take bribes, they will question the value of your merchandise. This place is known for its market. I know because I was sold here. They have a reputation to uphold."

"Then why would Undar and Lewmard want to use this place?"

"I know if they take Heather, they will try to put her in the market to buy her legally. If they can get her from this market, their purchase will be beyond approach."

"Beyond approach? I thought you said they couldn't be sold without proper papers."

"She can't." Micali looked up at him for a moment before she looked away. "But that won't stop them from trying. All you need to do is go to the owner and record your information. If they know who your property is they will make you aware if she is going to be put up on the block. You have the right to stop the sale before it happens."

"I won't let Heather be put through that."

"It is worth checking out," commented Fridon.

"Storm, I have been trained by the best." Heather placed her hand on his chest. "You'll be there to make sure nothing goes wrong, and it would make them a menace to society. It is illegal to sell another man's property if they are caught."

Storm was getting a bad feeling from this, but the three faces looking at him wanted him to go along with the idea. "We'll see."

———

Heather convinced him to go speak to the man in charge of the sales. He smiled at the memory of how she did it. Not wanting her to be in any jeopardy he had refused in the beginning. But she had her ways.

Now Storm wanted to know if these men could be bribed. How he would find out he wasn't sure, but he needed proof that his mate would be safe if they went through with this scheme.

He also expected if they took Heather, they would take Micali and he needed to secure her safety too. But he knew that would be easy. He had evidence of her mistreatment and two major families to back him up if anyone questioned Fridon's ownership of her.

"So all I have to do is sign paperwork? How do you know I am telling you the truth?" He handed back the pen. "I could say I own them but not be the right owner."

"This is how." He set the pen in a stand. Within seconds a green light flashed. A few moments later a printer filled a piece of paper with all his information. "You are Storm, proper owner of Heather. You are training Fridon, who is now proper owner of Micali. You are tied to the Earth embassy and backed by the Basuya embassy. You also have the backing of Busandio and Nasturo." He looked up at Storm. "You are a very powerful man here."

"Glad to hear it." He smiled, knowing he had found at least one honest man. "I need a favor."

———

Fridon kept getting an odd reading from the security grid. One he didn't understand. They had assembled everything right, so why did it keep showing that there was something wrong?

He had to check it out.

"I need to check the sensors."

Heather and Micali were preparing the meal for the evening. Heather looked up at him. "Okay."

"I wish you two to come with me."

"Fridon, we should be safe for the few moments you'll be out of sight." She smiled at him. "And I can take care of us if we're not."

"Storm will not be happy with me if I leave you alone, even if it is for a few moments."

"I'll take care of Storm." She made a shooing motion. "Go on. We'll be fine."

He sighed as he nodded. Fridon approached the spot, giving him the weird readings but found nothing wrong. Then he heard the scream. He raced back to the front of the tent to find the women gone. Oh, was he going to be in so much trouble.

———

Heather was laughing with Micali when she felt the odd sting against the back of her neck. Micali's face distorted as she screamed. Then Heather's world went black.

———

"Quiet." Lewmard held a knife against Micali's throat. "If you wish to live you won't scream again."

"Leave her. This is the one I want." Undar threw Heather over his shoulder. He staggered a little under her weight. Although thin, being tall and muscled made it hard for him to handle her.

"And have this one tell these men what we did?" Lewmard growled at him. He tightened his hold. "If she stays we need to kill her."

Undar looked at her. "Or we could sell her. She is my property. I think she'll bring in a few extra coins."

"Fine. Let your greed control you. Now get her secured before any of the men come back." Undar threw Heather's body over the back of his animal while Lewmard did the same with Micali. Breaking the law was nothing compared to what would happen if they were caught before they escaped.

———

Storm felt Heather's mind separate from his. No matter how hard he tried he couldn't reach her. Something was wrong. He pushed his stallion to race back to the tent, frightened at what he would find. As he pulled his animal to a stop, he found Fridon standing outside the tent, alone.

"What happened?" He slid from the horse before it stopped moving.

"I am sorry, Storm." Fridon hung his head. "Something was wrong with the security grid. It only took me a few minutes to check it out and that was all it took for them to take the women."

"What did they do to the grid?"

"Staked rocks on top of the sensor. I don't know how they knew about it."

"Undar might not be as stupid as he acts. He was with us long enough to know we set them up every night. We might not see the technology this planet uses every day, but I just saw proof they have it and use it when they need to. They might not train the women to understand it, but I wonder about the men."

"What do we do now?"

"Find them." He looked at the tent. "Heather has been drugged. I can't hear her thoughts."

"They couldn't know, could they?"

"I think they knocked her out because they knew she would fight them, and they knew they would lose. Unless they have the same ability as my mate there is no way they could know about her mental strength. She hasn't done anything to make herself stand out while Undar was with us."

"Micali was right. They're going to try to put her on the market so they can buy her."

"I'm not quite sure what they plan for her." Storm went inside the tent to find nothing out of order. "I'm going to assume they are going to try to sell the women. So we need to be there to see the sale. I have already bought us seats. This stupid plan is being played out even though I was against it."

"You want those two to know we're there?"

"Oh yes. The rules are very clear. They have taken my mate and your partner. We need to be very visible to be able to stop any sale they might be involved in."

———

Micali feared Heather was dead. She showed no sign of life, but then she noticed Heather's chest rise and fall in shallow breaths on the blanket the men had lowered her to. When they weren't looking, she tried to revive her, but she received no response.

What did they do to her? Heather had fallen to the ground just before they appeared. They must have shot her with something powerful to do this kind of damage.

Without Heather's help, she was forced to prepare a meal from the meager supplies they had. A lot of it was spoiled, but since she knew they wouldn't feed her she used it anyway. Maybe she could poison them, or at least make them sick enough where she could get away and find Fridon.

As the sun started to set, she feared what they would want from her. Undar had been watching her the way he always did when he wanted her to pleasure him. The thought of that man touching her after Fridon made her feel ill. But how could she stop him if that was what he wanted? A shudder ran through her. She'd do what she had to if it would keep her and Heather safe.

"We have her now," said Undar. "She will make us both very rich."

Micali kept her head down as she worked. Most of the time, they ignored her, believing they could say what they wanted. Property was something to ignore. They couldn't speak so there was no fear of someone else learning their plans. In the past that was true, but that was before she met the people who showed her kindness and compassion and taught her she had the right to speak for herself.

"Yes, we do, but I don't plan on selling her once we make Heather my property." Micali glanced up to see Lewmard look at Heather with a strange glint in his eyes. It frightened her.

"I thought we were going to split the profits?" Undar hesitated when Lewmard looked at him. "That we would sell her. You still owe me my payment for finding her and now you tell me you don't wish to sell her? How do you plan on paying me?"

There was a slight whine to his voice. He had been talking about how he would be rich since he first saw her. Heather meant nothing more than money to him.

"You'll be paid when she is mine."

"But that wasn't the arrangement. You promised to pay me when I delivered her. Then you promised more when we sold her. I have kept up my end of the bargain. Why do you keep changing things? Do you never plan on paying me?"

"So you want to move on then? Not see this through? I will pay you a bonus if you stay until the sale tomorrow." There was something in his voice that made Micali cringe.

"I will stay if I have to, but I wish to be paid now."

"You are afraid of the big one."

"Aren't you? His desire for this woman is all consuming. He will kill us if we are caught. I'd rather be gone before he finds us."

"Fine." Lewmard stood. "I'll get what is owed to you."

Undar looked giddy. He already had his animal packed and ready to go. Micali had watched him prepare his frulas earlier.

Lewmard came out of the tent with a small satchel in his right hand. His left was behind his back. Micali felt her blood run cold. She knew what was going to happen next. "You have earned every coin here."

Undar took the bag and opened it up. He poured the contents into his hands and found nothing but rocks.

"What—"

Micali saw shock on his face as he dropped to his knees. Lewmard had shoved a long blade into Undar's stomach and blood started to pour.

"You are worthless. Why would you think I would pay you when you've been more of a hindrance than a help?" He pulled out the blade so he could wipe it on a cloth.

"But you are my brother."

"Only by blood, not by thought." He turned away from the dying man and glared at Micali. "Bury him so there is no evidence."

Micali nodded. What else could she do?

———

Undar took a long time to die. Micali didn't like leaving Heather alone with Lewmard, but she had to play her role and do what he expected to keep them safe. She dug the hole she planned on rolling his body into while he lay there gasping for breath.

"Help me, Micali."

"Show you the compassion you never showed me?" She stopped what she was doing long enough to look him in the eyes, her fear of him gone. A dying man couldn't harm her. "Your greed put you in this situation. I am nothing but a woman and must do as I'm told." She repeated the words he had said to her over and over again. Going back to her chore, she continued to shovel out dirt. "I recommend you die soon, or I'll have to put you in here before you stop breathing."

———

Lewmard sat at the fire, watching Heather intently. He held a whip in his hand and ran his fingers up and down the length. Micali knelt in front of him when she finished burying Undar. He had been happy with how fast she got the job done.

She had prepared his meal and was in the process of feeding him. Each time his lips touched her fingers she had to fight the chill that raced through her. Right now, he was her lord and master and she had to show proper behavior. She cringed when he flexed the arm with the whip. He must have noticed her reaction because he spoke.

"You are not what I want. Undar might have used you this evening because he didn't care where he got his release, but my focus is on her. She bested me the last time, and that will not happen again. That woman will scream for me, in either pleasure or pain. I don't care which."

Micali relaxed back on her heels. She wasn't sure what she was supposed to do now.

"Get her ready for travel. We're heading into town now."

It was still early in the evening. Nothing could be sold until the next day. Didn't he understand the bond Storm and Heather had? The man wouldn't stop until he found her again. If Storm followed her idea, he would be registered and waiting.

She went to Heather's side and pulled her into a sitting position. The strain had her struggling before she could get her upright. Micali wrapped a hand around her neck as she worked on getting her to stay seated. In the back of Heather's neck, she found a small barb protruding out. Micali tried to pull it but found it impossible to remove.

"There is only one way to remove that." Lewmard's voice, close to her ear, slithered up her spine, causing shills to course through her. He pulled Heather up and dumped her onto the back of an animal. "Let's go."

She wished there was something she could do. Some way to warn Storm and Fridon. She touched the chain that had been given to her when Undar bought her. With his death, it had changed color and become brittle. Micali looked at the chain and smiled, realizing she had just the thing.

———

It didn't take the men long to break down their tent. Storm kept trying to reach Heather's mind. The link they shared was still there, but something was stopping them from connecting. He sighed his frustration as he secured the last of their items then climbed up on a frulas. He thought the animal would traverse the town better than the stallion. The last time the horse had some trouble working its way through some of the narrow streets. The animal started rearing when Storm tried to move the frulas. Now what?

He jumped down to calm the horse, but nothing worked. "You are upset about her disappearance as well, aren't you?"

The stallion neighed his displeasure.

"How about I ride you? Then we can look for her together." It understood him because it calmed down and allowed Storm to move the saddle, he had on his frulas to his back. He and Fridon worked to put the pack saddle on the frulas he had planned on riding. Storm climbed into the saddle and got the animals moving.

"I'm sorry." Fridon started his animal after Storm took the lead.

"This was the plan, wasn't it?" Storm knew he felt the same frustration over what had happened.

"Yes, sir. But we were supposed to be here when they took them so we could follow. That didn't happen."

"I have learned when it comes to Heather things don't always happen the way you plan." Storm weaved his animal through the small town to their law office. His first goal was to make them aware of the theft. Then he would go and speak to the man running the sale. One way or the other, he was going to make this as difficult as possible for Lewmard and Undar.

His sensitive nose caught something in the air. He stopped his mount, closing his eyes and allowing his nose to guide him.

"Sir?"

"I'm sensing something." He turned the horse to the right. "Come on." Storm urged the animal to move as fast as it could through the crowd, making several turns in the process. He started to slow when they reached the outskirts of town. Something was here, something out of place. The scent was familiar.

Studying the dirt around them he noticed a long silver chain and a freshly dug area.

"Fridon." He pointed to the chain as he dismounted and went to the area where the loosened dirt was.

"This is Micali's chain." Fridon picked it up and ran it through his fingers. "But only the one from Undar. Your chain isn't here."

"From what Heather said, the chain can't be removed unless the owner dies." He dug into the dirt and hit a hand. "And I'd say we have a dead man here."

"Undar?" He came to Storm's side and helped him unearth the body until they could see the face.

"Guess he wasn't of any value to Lewmard anymore." Storm sat back on his haunches. "The chain can't be cut off. How did she remove it?"

"Look." Fridon held up the chain so Storm could see its discoloration. "It seems to be part of that technology you mentioned earlier. It must be tied to the host somehow when he died so did this."

Storm took the chain and found it broke apart when he snagged it on a bit of Fridon's clothes. Yet when they first acquired Micali nothing would remove it, which is why he had to add his chain to this one. "It seems that Lewmard just made a major mistake. Without a trader, he will have a harder time doing whatever he plans."

"Unless he feels safe with whom he is dealing with."

"Which is why we're going to see the man running things." Storm stood and headed back to his animal. "I won't be happy until I have my mate back."

———

Lewmard tethered his animal outside the main building that led to the sale. He wasn't happy to find the place empty. He thought they would be here getting ready for the auction.

A young kid walked in to grab a big ring of keys. He spotted Lewmard and frowned. "You have to come back tomorrow."

"What? Why?" Lewmard needed to leave Micali there tonight before Heather's master came looking for him.

"The sale roster is full for this sale."

"That can't be." He frowned as he shifted Heather's weight from one shoulder to another. "I wish to speak to the owner."

"He's busy." The boy ran back into the main part of the market.

Lewmard followed him. The man who was in charge stood in the middle of a small crowd, barking out orders. Lewmard dragged Micali behind him and marched up to the man. He jerked on Micali's chain. "I wish to sell this one."

"We're full."

"You can't take one more?"

The man looked at Micali, then Heather, whom he still carried. "What about that one?"

"No. I wish to keep her." He let her slip down so he could lay her on the ground.

The man studied Heather for a moment before looking at Micali. "You have papers for them?" He moved to a group of three women and checked their collars to make sure they were marked properly.

"With my things." He pointed to his frulas.

"I want both or none." He nodded to the boy Lewmard had spoken to earlier who moved the women to a large building.

"Why?" Lewmard frowned.

"Her hair is different. It will cause a lot of buyers to come and see her. The other one I have too many of now." He pulled a small pad out of his pocket and made a few notes. "If you want me to add one more to my already full roster, then I want something that will draw buyers."

"But I don't want to sell both females." Lewmard's voice had a whine in it. Heather was not something he wanted to part with. He had gone through too much to get her. He also didn't have the papers the man asked for. He would lose both if he continued. "I think I will withdraw my offer."

"Why?"

"Because I don't want to sell both of them."

"Or is it because you don't have the papers to sell them?" He nodded to his guards who grabbed the women before Lewmard could react. "Now you will have to bid with all my other buyers for the one you want. If you can afford her, you will own her properly."

Micali followed the man who now had a hold of her chain. Another carried Heather out of the area where Lewmard stood. He stared at them, his face red with anger. He just lost both women. That made him even more danger-ous, and Micali hoped Storm realized that.

———

Heather rubbed her hand against her forehead. Damn, everything hurt. What happened? She tried to open her eyes. They didn't want to listen to her at first, but she finally pried them open. Her mouth felt dry, and she had a horrible headache. Once everything stopped swimming in front of her, she looked around and she wished she hadn't. She was inside a strange tent with thirty other women. She only saw one familiar face, Micali, who came to her side the moment she realized Heather was awake. Sitting up, Heather asked, "What happened?"

"Lewmard and Undar. They kidnapped us and knocked you out. Some sort of dart in your neck." She pulled Heather's hair aside and looked at the spot where the barb had been. "It is gone now."

"And this?" Heather lifted her hand to show the clamp around it.

"We are to be sold. Actually, I was to be sold, but you got caught up in this because of a technicality." Micali sat beside Heather. "Lewmard didn't want to part with you but didn't have the proper paperwork to keep you from being part of the auction." She paused before she spoke again. "He killed Undar."

Heather wasn't surprised. She figured the moment the merchant became unneeded, Lewmard would get rid of him. "Did either harm you?"

"No. He killed Undar before he could do anything, and Lewmard had no desire for me. Just kept watching you." She shuddered a little. "He terrified me."

"But you survived and made sure nothing happened to me. Thank you." She grasped her shoulder. "That shows how much you have grown."

"Thanks to you. I never would have been able to do that before."

"Any sign of Storm?" Heather changed the subject.

"No, but no one has been able to view us yet." Micali gestured to the guards at the opening.

"Is this all of us?" Heather glimpsed at the different groups of women in the area.

"Not sure. There is a rumor that there are a few more in another tent. Some daughter of a dignitary and a few more exotic looking women they hope to fetch a high price for.

You'd be there with them if they thought you were still a virgin."

"I'm surprised they didn't check to be sure."

"They brought in a healer who took one look at your hips and said you had given birth. That settled any question."

Heather grinned. With the way Storm had her working out, she had a lot of people commenting about her figure and how she didn't look like she had carried children, but these women only had to look at her to know the truth. She looked behind them and wondered who was back there. The women around them didn't look like the girl they were looking for, but she could be in the special tent. "Have they said we were banned from going in there?"

"Not that I'm aware of, but with the bracelets no one has moved from where they were placed."

Heather nodded. She stood. The moment she moved, their handler came to her side. "I will let the seller know you are awake."

She remained standing, waiting for the man to come and check her. It didn't take long for him to show up.

Heather knew she should keep her gaze down and show the respect all women were supposed to give men, but she didn't feel like it. With a toss of her hair, she looked right at him.

"I see you have backbone." He looked at his papers and made a few notes. "I need your name so you have permission to speak."

"My name is Heather."

"Duly noted." He made a few marks on his sheets. "I have several prebids for you so you will be moved into the other tent, but I will wait until after the viewing. The more people who see you the better your price will be."

It figured. She wanted to get inside the tent. How could she get in there before the viewing?

He lifted the chains she carried. "Do you know where your owner is right now?"

Unfortunately, she didn't. The chemical Lewmard and Undar had given her still affected her system and she hadn't reconnected with him yet. Knowing Storm, he was close. She shook her head. It wouldn't take him too long before he found her.

"Until he shows up you will remain a part of the auction." He dropped her chain. "All women will be allowed to bathe for fifteen minutes before the viewing. Do your best to look good. The whip will be used against anyone who refuses."

He looked at Heather as he said the last words. She knew better than to fight against them anyway. If all the women were bathing at the same time, it would give her time to see who was there and hopefully warn Storm if their target was there with her and Micali.

———

Storm felt the soft brushes of Heather's thoughts. *Thank goodness, where are you?* He didn't hear a response. *My heart? Can you hear me?*

"Sir?" Fridon must have noticed he had drifted off for a moment.

"I'm fine." He clasped him on the shoulder. "I believe my mate has come to. I can feel her mind, but she hasn't spoken to me yet. That worries me."

"Could it be because of the drugs she had been given? Some will keep the mind muddled when the body seems clear of it."

"You are probably right. I was just hoping I could

connect with her." He looked at his second-in-training and smiled, trying to show he wasn't too worried about Heather. "Has the auctioneer contacted you?"

"No." Fridon shook his head. "He did say it could take him a few hours before he'd let us know if your prebid is needed."

"Micali said this was the only place close where Lewmard could take her to make her legally his."

"I don't understand how he can buy her when he doesn't have the proper papers." Fridon walked around the interior of the tent. "Why isn't he arrested instead?"

"That would make our lives better, but they have loopholes that allow a man to acquire another man's property without the proper documents. She can be sold and bought without those papers if I'm not here to stop the sale." Storm hated not knowing where his mate was. He wished their link would hook back up so he could be sure she was safe.

The flap of their tent parted, making them turn. Storm was ready to kill Lewmard if he walked through that opening.

"My trainer sent me to tell you that both bids will be accepted. The viewing is in two hours. Prebids will be in a special tent, and you will be given a specific time to see the women you bid on, but you may look at all the women outside while you wait your turn." He bowed and exited.

"Well, we have our answer now. Heather and Micali are up for auction."

———

Heather kept trying to touch Storm's mind but found she couldn't do it. Her mind was still feeling foggy around the edges. Whatever Lewmard used on her had some strong mental residual effects.

All the women were brought together to bathe. Good, this would give her the chance she needed to see if the girl was here. She walked outside with the other women. A large, sunken pond glistened in front of her. They were allowed in the pond five at a time. Groups of women in the different stages of taking advantage of the bath covered the area. Some were already dressed and having their bodies powered. Others were having their hair worked on. Those who had just finished bathing were either drying themselves by the use of towels or allowing the sun to dry their skin.

Micali stayed close to her.

"Nothing is going to happen to us." Heather said it softly so no one would hear her.

Micali nodded.

They stepped into the pond together. They were part of the last group to bathe it looked like. Oils were handed to them so they could clean the grime off their bodies. Heather looked up when they were joined by another woman and her eyes widened when she recognized her. The puffiness of her eyes showed the girl had been crying. There were a few red marks on her arms from where she had been roughly handled. Her face looked thinner than her picture, but other than that she looked healthy.

Heather gestured for her to join them. Elated to know the girl was well, she had been afraid they'd never find her. So much time had passed. Wishing she could console the young woman, she knew better than to talk. The guards were right at the edge of the pond and here speaking could bring out the whip. She did use the silent signaling women used when around men, but the girl didn't understand. She never learned the hand language.

They moved out of the bath and dried off. There was constantly someone with them to make sure they did as they were told so speaking was off-limits. After they finished with their preparations, they were put in the big tent erected toward the back of the selling area.

"You will be chained to these poles," the guard said, pointing. "We expect you to show your training. Smile, do not make eye contact. Show proper respect to your potential owner. If you disobey, you will be punished."

Heather hated the threats. This was what she remembered of this place. That constant fear that if you made one wrong move you would feel the bite of the whip or the slap of a hand.

Their chains were wrapped around the poles, keeping them apart so Heather still couldn't talk to the young girl. She wished her mind would clear so she could contact Storm and at least let him know she found their target.

———

Heather heard the girl make a sobbing sound when the tent flap opened and the first of the men came in to see them. She skittered away when they tried to touch her, forcing the guard to hold her still as they inspected her skin, hair, teeth, or whatever else they wanted to look at. The garments they wore were see-through, but at least they didn't have to stand there naked like the women outside the tent.

Heather hated the pawing and poking she was receiving. Keeping her composure was hard when she was touched a little too intimately or grabbed a little too hard. Her mind reached out for comfort and found Storm.

My heart, are you alright?

Yes. She knew better than to complain about being handled by these potential owners, but Storm must have picked up something from her mind.

I'll get you out now.

Please don't.

What? She could hear the disbelief in his thoughts.

I found her, Storm. She's between Micali and me. You must go through with the bidding and add her to your purchase.

He didn't say anything else, but she could feel he wasn't pleased with her.

Heather watched as the next group of men came in. Lewmard was amongst them. He came straight at her.

Crap. Lewmard is here.

"I want this one." He looked at the salesman nearby. "I don't care how high the bids are."

"She is very expensive. The bid on her is the highest on record."

"How much?" He pulled out his purse.

Heather wondered if that was his life savings.

"Three hundred thousand solsas."

Lewmard blanched. He looked at her with such hatred, but Heather refused to show him the respect he thought he deserved. She looked him right in the eye and arched a brow. Her faint smile made him red in the face.

"You will show me more respect."

"You aren't worth my respect." Heather crossed her arms over her chest. Speaking to a man this way begged for punishment and she knew it but didn't care. Keeping her head held high, she waited for the bite of the whip on the guard's hip.

"You broke the law." The guard stepped up to her in a threatening manner with his hand on his hip where his whip rested.

She dropped her head, showing him proper respect. In a low tone, she spoke. "He has been trying to steal me from my owner for weeks. I know what I did was wrong, but he deserves no one's respect. My master would expect nothing less from me and I follow his desires."

"You stole her from her owner?" The guard turned his threatening stance toward Lewmard.

"It doesn't matter! She disrespected me." Lewmard gestured toward Heather. When the guard didn't move, he grabbed the whip from the guard and unfurled it. "You will kneel before me, woman. I am tired of your disrespect."

The snap of the whip filled the air before she felt its bite. It wrapped around her, the tip of the whip digging into her back. Excruciating pain filled her.

"I don't know what happened to the lashes I gave you before, but I will mar that beautiful body again to prove you are nothing but a piece of property." He pulled the whip back to strike her again. "Now kneel!"

TEN

S torm felt an intense pain sear into his back. It forced him to his knees. The pain stopped, but so did the link he and Heather shared. She was blocking him from feeling what was happening to her. Anger lanced him as he realized his mate was being whipped and there was only one person who would have the audacity to do it. He left explicit rules about how he wanted his 'property' returned to him. Rules or not, he was going to put a stop to it now. He barged into the tent and found Lewmard pulling back to strike his mate again.

Heather had taken each blow without reacting. She stood tall and proud. The lashes she'd already received had shredded her top to pieces, which lay at her feet. Ugly welts peeked out from the blood welling up on her back. It took him three steps to reach her. One hand grabbed the whip, wrapping it around his arm so Lewmard couldn't strike Heather again. The other went up to stop the guard trying to run interference. "This is my property he is damaging. My property he stole. I protect what is mine."

The guard backed off when he heard Storm.

"You truly have a death wish, don't you?" Storm growled. He jerked the whip out of Lewmard's hand. "Perhaps I should use this on you, so you know how it feels."

"You don't frighten me." He turned toward Storm. His words were brave, but color drained from his face when he saw the anger etched on Storm's.

"Really?" Storm grabbed him by the throat, his fingers cutting into the side of his neck, and lifted Lewmard off his feet. "You do realize I am trained to kill. It would only take one finger and all I have to do is press it against your throat here to end your life."

Lewmard started to gag as Storm pressed a finger against the spot on his throat. Not enough to cut all his air off, but enough to let the man know he meant business.

"But you don't deserve to die quickly. You took a whip and damaged something very dear to me." Storm dropped him at his feet. "So I'm going to mark you so you will never forget that crossing me is the wrong thing to do."

Storm unfurled the whip and gave it a light flick so it grazed Lewmard's face. Blood welled from the wound he created on his left cheek. He then snapped the whip hard, allowing it to wrap around the man's body a few times, cutting into skin as it wound around him, before the tip slapped against his back. Lewmard cried at the pain inflicted.

"You scream like a woman, yet Heather, who is a woman, didn't scream at all. She took it with a grace few have. You feel she is beneath you, whereas I feel you are beneath her. You see the problem, don't you?" Storm shook out the whip, readying it for another strike.

"She ruined my life!" He staggered to his feet.

"You ruined your life, not her. She stopped you from harming a woman who was only trying to save her child. If the boy had died, the father would have come after you for interfering with an order he gave. Your life would have been worse if not forfeited. Now if you wish to continue with this grudge, I can end your life right now." He grabbed Lewmard by the throat again, tightening his hold so the man struggled to breathe and pulled him up, so he was only inches from his face. "I protect what is mine."

The man made a few mewling sounds but didn't respond. Storm shook his head before handing him to Fridon. "I'm not done with him."

Heather smiled at her mate as he walked to her, happy it was over. This is what she had to endure before? Why would Bear allow this a second time? Earth should just use their strength to subdue this planet and be done with it.

Earth doesn't do that. Our history is covered with war because one group wanted to dominate another. We strive to use peace now.

Even on planets where they harm your people?

Yes. It's not perfect, but it is better than a war where millions die.

Seeing what he did to you I want to disagree.

It's not as bad as the last time.

He walked around her, frowning at the whip marks she had endured. *He tore your back up. How bad was it the last time?*

She didn't answer.

The man running the sale entered the tent, followed by the guard who had tried to stop Storm. He slowed when he noticed that Fridon had Lewmard sitting at his feet, wrapped in the whip. Every time Lewmard shifted Fridon clamped a hand on his shoulder, giving it a hard squeeze.

"She is damaged." Storm glared at the man. "Why weren't your prized sales protected properly? I had to stop him before she was beyond any worth."

"I am sorry." He looked at her back and blanched. He

could see she had been struck a half a dozen times before Storm interfered. "I will knock twenty percent off her price."

"Not enough."

"Thirty percent."

"She will be marred for life."

The man knew he was right. A sigh escaped him. "What do you wish, then?"

"Add that woman for the price I offered for the two." He pointed to the young woman they came to save. "No matter what bids have been offered over mine." Storm crossed his arms over his chest. "Or I will take all three anyway."

The man looked at Heather with sadness. He barely looked at Micali. Storm was probably the only one who bid on her so far. He then looked at the ambassador's daughter. She would have brought a high price, but Storm just killed that. "Agreed."

"Good." Storm touched Heather's cheek. "Free them now, and I will leave before the auction starts. No one will know how you allowed one man to mistreat your items."

He nodded to the guard nearby who stepped up and released their chains. Storm took his shirt off and dropped it over Heather's head.

Don't.

My heart, it hurts me to see what he did to you.

I won't let Lewmard get the best of me by hiding what he did. I want to wear them with pride. Prove to Lewmard that I am better than him. Besides, you tell me to be proud of my body yet expect me to hide this? I don't understand.

I am thinking more of how painful the sand will make it feel. I only wanted to protect you.

And the cloth of this shirt won't irritate the wounds?

Then I shall leave it to you. He knew she was right.

Heather picked up his top from the ground and held it close, just in case she needed it. She went to the young girl, able to talk to her for the first time. "We are going to take you back to your parents."

"No!" Tears streamed down her face. "He said the only way we could be together was for me to go through this sale."

"Who is he?" asked Storm. Frustration filled him when she spoke. Did they go through all of this for nothing?

She shrank back when he walked up to them with a thunderous look on his face. "His name is Retorin."

"Find him." Storm looked at the seller in charge. He should know who all his potential clients were.

The man came back with a boy in tow.

Storm looked at the kid quaking in front of him. "You are the reason my property was whipped?"

"What? I—I didn't touch her." Fear filled him when he found he was the center of attention.

"Really? You kidnapped this girl so you could make her your favorite, didn't you?" Storm pointed to the girl.

"I guess." The boy looked so confused. "We wanted to be together, and it was the only way."

"It is clear you didn't think this through. What you did caused Heather's government to get involved and send my favorite here to rescue your girlfriend. Her family wants her back and they asked us to rescue her. That man had a vendetta against my woman, and he ended up doing this." He turned Heather around so the boy could see her torn up back. "I can blame you for this. Why would you tell this girl the only way you could be together would be through a sale when you know that isn't true?"

"Her parents would never gift her to me. To be together, I had to buy her."

"Did you ask?"

He hung his head and shook it. "No."

"You are coming with us as well." He grabbed the boy

by the back of the neck and steered him out of the tent. Heather and Micali followed him, making sure the girl they were after followed as well.

Fridon came up behind them, half dragging Lewmard with him. "Sir? What about this one?"

"Like I said, Fridon. I'm not done with him yet. He committed a crime against my mate. Vespian law is very specific and when it is dealing with the mate of the next ruler the law can be quite cruel." Storm looked at Lewmard. "He will never see this planet again."

"You can't take me from my home."

"I can." Storm turned to face the man; the boy forgotten at the moment. He closed the distance between them, so they were barely inches apart. Grabbing his throat again, he lifted him as he growled, "You chose the wrong man to anger. No one harms my mate. She and the children she bore me are the most precious things in my life and anyone who threatens that will taste the full extent of my wrath. Too bad you killed Undar before he got a chance to do the same thing to you because you are going to wish you had died."

———

Fridon handed Lewmard off to Earth security when they arrived back at the embassy. Storm brought Heather directly to the medlab to have her back looked at.

The doctor on call took one look and disappeared.

"He leaves?" Storm growled.

"He'll be back." Heather still held his shirt against her chest.

Bear walked in as she touched Storm's face tenderly. One look at her back and he frowned. "Damn, Heather, not again."

"Yes, again." Storm squared off with Bear. "How could you put her in harm's way like that?"

"One, she is an officer of Earth, and this is part of her job. Two, you signed off on this mission when you joined her." Bear didn't back down. "She knew the danger and you saw the file from the last mission, so you knew it too. It was the reason I allowed you to go on this mission with her. I expected you to keep her safe."

The doctor walked back in with the piece of equipment he needed to repair her back. He listened to Storm and Bear arguing as he healed her. "They at it because of this?"

"Yes, my husband doesn't understand that shit happens."

"Commander, I know better. I have seen my share of wounds over the years and have learned a few things when it comes to spouses. He's blaming himself because you got hurt and shouldn't have." He ran the small wand over her back, blanketing it in a deep maroon beam.

"Is that true, Storm. You think this is your fault?" She said it loud enough to cut through their argument.

"That little snake of a man shouldn't have been able to cause this kind of damage." He gestured to her back, growing quiet as the ugly welts started to disappear.

"And you feel if you had been doing your job this never would have happened."

"You are my mate, and I am supposed to keep you safe."

"We all know I have a knack for getting into danger. How do you plan on keeping me from stubbing my toe, or getting a hang nail?"

"Heather."

"This is repairable. There won't be any scars. If he had threatened my life, I would have taken his." The doctor touched her shoulder, letting her know he was done. She stood and faced the two men arguing over her, still clutching Storm's shirt to her since she hadn't had time to change clothes yet. "I won't let you take the blame for this, Storm, because that is your nature. I did know the risks, but Admiral, someone didn't do their homework because we should have been aware that Lewmard was there and still held a grudge. We would have been better prepared."

"I'm already checking into why we weren't aware of his location."

"Thank you. Now if you two promise not to tear each other limb from limb, I'd like to change."

"We both should change." Storm pressed a hand to the small of her back to escort her out of medlab.

"Then are you two done throwing the blame?" She looked at her mate then Bear. The sooner she could put this in the past the happier she would be.

"Yes." Storm looked down at her. "But the next time we do anything like this for Earth you shall wear your protective forcefield. You talked me out of it, and I regret that decision now."

"Imagine how crazy Lewmard would have gotten if he found he couldn't mar me. I think leaving it behind was a smart thing to do."

"My heart, you are going to drive me crazy."

"Ha! You are using an earth idiom." She wrapped an arm around his waist as she continued to hold his shirt in place. "I knew I could corrupt you."

"You did that a long time ago."

———

Heather smoothed her gown as she went to the room where Micali and the young girl had been placed in. She needed to speak to the girl before they took her to her parents. This mess with the boy had to be addressed. Taking a deep breath, she opened the door and walked in.

Micali looked up at her in surprise. Seeing the strange clothing on Heather made her frown. Heather knew she was realizing it was time for her to make a decision. "I was worried about you."

"I am fine, Micali." She smiled at her friend. "The doctors healed me."

"How?"

"Our technology is more advanced than anything you have seen." She opened her gown to show her back. As flawless as before the whip cut into it, there was no evidence of the damage done by Lewmard.

Micali stepped up to touch where the whip marks had been. "There is no sign of the cruelty he did to you. I have never seen anything like this."

"Nothing on my skin, but it is still here." Heather touched her head. "That will take longer to heal."

"What happens now?" Micali looked at her hands, afraid to think about what was coming.

"First, you two need to change." Heather looked at the girl they had rescued. She had been silent since they brought Retorin into the tent. "Giansa, your parents are waiting to take you home, but we need to talk about your boyfriend."

"What will happen to him?" She stood at Heather's words.

"Nothing, but if you two had been successful I would have a different answer. You are the daughter of an ambassador and there are laws in place to keep you safe. It was believed you were kidnapped, which is why they asked me to come and find you. You did scream, didn't you?"

"Well, yes, but I didn't know what was happening then." She touched Heather's arm. "Once he explained what we had to do to be together I understood why he took me the way he did."

"And you two went about it all the wrong way. There are rules to cover people marrying into the society they are working with and if you had listened to what you were taught before you arrived here you would have known that." Heather didn't mean to snap at the girl, but her attitude toward this was a little too flippant.

"But I do know those laws. This planet never signed any sort of treaty to make them liable. It's still too new to the coalition. That was one of the reasons why my family came here. We were one of the planets wanting to have this planet ratified."

"And you didn't think your parents would allow you to bond with him?"

She hung her head. "I didn't think."

"I'd say. What would have happened if he hadn't been the one who bought you? If my mate hadn't been there to keep you safe? You could have been sold into a slavery you would have regretted."

"He told me he spoke to the owner of the sale. That everything would work out."

"Yet Storm was the one who ended up buying you," Heather reminded her. "What you did was dangerous and stupid."

"Does this mean we can't be together?"

"I didn't say that, but you need to explain everything to your parents. Make them understand why you did what you did." Heather walked to a panel and pressed the door. It opened at her touch. Inside was clothing the girl's parents had given her. She handed the girl the outfit. "They have been worried sick about you."

"I will do my best to make them understand."

Heather turned her attention to Micali. Now she had to

confront her friend. "Have you decided what you want to do?"

"No." Unshed tears filled her eyes. "I had hoped, never mind."

"What?" Heather knew what was in her heart but needed to hear Micali say it out loud. "Come now, Micali. You need to speak your mind. You know we won't just assume we know what you want."

She looked at Heather, blinking back the tears. "I had hoped to go with you."

"Why?"

"I only know this world. If I go some place I don't understand, how would I survive?" She brushed at the tear running down her cheek. "I know you'll keep me safe."

"So the only reason you want to come with us is for protection?" Heather crossed her arms over her chest. "You could stay here and be claimed by one of the families we have met. Either one would treat you well."

"That's not what I want." She looked down. "I had hoped Fridon would want me."

"Then you need to tell him that." Heather rested a hand on her shoulder.

"I can't." She shook her head.

"You must. I told you to make the decision on this. It is up to you, not him."

"You ask too much."

"Micali, you need to learn to take control of your life, and that starts right now. What could the worst be?"

"He tells me he found me as a convenience and nothing more."

"Ah." Heather smiled, understanding her fear, and handed her a gown like hers. "If you don't tell him how you feel, you will lose him for sure. Is that what you want?"

Micali shook her head.

"Then get dressed. This is a Vespian gown. It covers a lot more than you're used to, but I think it will show Fridon where your heart is." She handed the dress to Micali. "When I get back, I'll take you to him so you can tell him how you feel."

———

Micali waited in the room for Heather to return to escort her to Fridon. Her stomach was in knots over what she was being forced to do. How could she ask Fridon to take her with him when the men of her world never allowed that?

The gown Heather had given her covered so much of her body, it felt strange. She fidgeted in the outfit. What if Fridon only saw her as a temporary bed partner? He never mentioned he had someone waiting for him on his home planet, but he could. Her fear of him not wanting her had her wanting to run, but then she would be subjected to being sold again. The thought of another man touching her after Fridon frightened her. No one would ever show her the kindness he had.

If only she knew what he wanted before she was forced to confront him.

Heather opened the door and smiled at her. "Ready?"

She wanted to say no and beg Heather to let her go with them no matter what Fridon wanted, but she knew Heather wouldn't stand for that. If only she had the backbone Heather did.

"It will be okay, Micali. Trust your heart."

Her heart was beating so hard she wasn't sure if it was a good idea to listen to it. They walked to a huge set of doors that opened before Heather could touch a handle. She felt a little ill when they walked in.

Storm stepped up to Heather's side and escorted her to

the older couple hugging and crying over the Giansa. The young girl was in the process of trying to explain what happened to her.

Fridon stood near a window, looking out at the grounds.

She could hear the couple thanking Heather for finding their child. Heather didn't like all the attention and leaned into Storm as she tried to make them aware of all the help she had from Storm, Fridon and her. Why Heather wanted to draw her into this, Micali didn't understand. She hadn't done a thing. Heather gestured toward her, which made Fridon turn around and face her.

His eyes widened when he saw the gown she wore. He came to her side and spoke softly. "You look beautiful."

"Really?" She smoothed the material down. "I feel over-dressed."

"Compared to what you normally wear? I guess so." He laughed and ran a finger down her arm. "But sometimes it's what you can't see that can be arousing."

She didn't know what to say. How was she supposed to broach the subject Heather demanded she talk about? Fridon studied her. Did he know how hard this was for her?

"I understand Heather explained things to you?" He clasped his hands behind him.

"She demanded I speak to you." She didn't speak very loud and looked away. Micali found it hard to look at him.

"Demanded?" He shook his head. "She would never do that."

Tears sprang into her eyes.

"Hey." He lifted her chin, so she had to look at him. "You are really upset about this, aren't you?"

She nodded. More than he could understand.

"Perhaps we should find someplace private to speak?"

"That might be better." More tears filled her eyes and spilled down her cheeks.

He looked at Storm who gave him a slight nod. Then he led her to another room and, closing the doors behind them, he turned to face her. "Perhaps I should begin?"

She nodded again as she fought back tears.

"On my planet women have an equal voice. The leader of our ruling council is female. Heather is part of that council. Our religious leader is female." Fridon touched her chin. "You wouldn't be able to let others make decisions for you."

"Women with power?" She shook her head. "How can I stand up to that?"

"That is the question. We have tried to show you that you do have power and a choice. Not every planet treats their women the way they do here. Some might have in the past, but the women fought back and proved they were worthy of the same respect men had."

"I don't know how?"

"Really?" He smiled and took her hands. "You came to ask me a question."

Her stomach rolled. "Heather said I…"

"I don't care what Heather said. I want to know what you want."

She couldn't look at him as she tried to find the bravery to ask what she needed to ask. "I wish to go with you."

"Why?"

She looked up at him to find him watching her intently.

"What kind of questions is that?" She pressed her hand against her stomach. "I can't stay here and you, you showed me kindness no one ever did. If you have a woman at home, I understand, but I had hoped I meant something to you."

"There is no woman at home, but my world will be so different from what you are used to. You will have to make your own decisions. Tell people your wants and desires. Are you sure that is what you want?"

"I want to be with you. I don't care where it is or if I have to share you."

He gave her a beautiful smile. "I want you with me. I have come to care for you very much and can't see my life without you."

She wrapped her arms around him. "Why couldn't you say that first? My stomach is in knots over this."

"I'm sorry." He touched her chin and lifted her face. "But you had to prove to me you would say what was in your heart. If you can't stand up for yourself, then you won't fit into my world."

"I will do my best, but it will be hard for me."

"I know you can do it."

———

Heather sat next to Storm in the large room with the reunited family. Grateful to be in her old clothes again, she smoothed the material as she nodded when the family got up to leave. After thanking her again, she had lost count on how many times they had already thanked her and Storm, they finally left.

She sighed as the door closed.

"Happy that is over?" Storm touched her cheek, using the gentle movement to draw her to her feet. "You know Bear wants to speak to us."

"He wants to have his exit interviews so he can close the file." She brushed her hair back and plastered on a smile. "Let's go."

They walked into his office and took two of the four chairs in front of his desk. A few moments later, Fridon and Micali joined them. Bear came into the room after they settled.

"Thank you for your prompt arrival. Heather has been

through these things many times, but so you understand, we do interviews with each of you separately. Sometimes questions will be asked to anger or frighten you. Just tell the truth. That is all we're after." He stood and the rest followed.

Heather was brought into the first room. She took the seat offered and waited for the security liaison to enter.

"Commander."

"Lieutenant."

"I see you were able to acquire the target."

She hated it when they spoke about people as if they were nothing. "If you mean the ambassador's daughter then yes. I'm happy to say she has been rescued."

"Tell me what happened."

She did her best to give as much detail as possible, but she knew what they wanted. As she was finishing up, she sensed Storm's frustration. "Are we done? I think I need to defuse a situation."

"Yes."

She stood and walked out the door. The moment she exited she touched Storm's mind.

My heart. Are you okay?

I am fine. These questions are annoying, but nothing I wouldn't have asked in their shoes.

Then whose frustration am I feeling?

Mine! Fridon's thoughts entered her mind. *These questions are ridiculous.*

Storm has questioned you the same way. Is this what you feel all the time? She was amazed she could pick up his thoughts so easily. Their contact had been brief before and with other people it took a few times before she could pick up their thoughts without any effort. He had to have a very open mind.

No, but they are asking me about Micali. They want to know things I don't see as being relevant.

This is no different from any report you have to give on Vespia. Just leave out the personal stuff. Earth doesn't want to hear about that. Tell them how she came to be with us and how she helped in stopping Lewmard and Undar. They want to know why we brought her, so she needs to look important to our mission.

Storm stepped out of his interview and headed straight for her. Crowding her backward, he pinned her against the wall. With a smile on his face, he looked down at her. "The hallway is empty."

"And there is a wall right here." She wrapped her arms around his neck. "Too bad there are far too many people here to my liking."

"I can make you forget all about the people passing." He dipped his head to her throat and started nibbling.

"Commander?"

Heather straightened and looked to see who said her name. One of Bear's aids stood there.

"The admiral asked to see you and your mate."

"Of course." She looked up at the glowing eyes of her mate and could see he wasn't happy to be interrupted. "He knows you and is probably keeping us from getting out of hand."

They followed the aid to Bear's office.

"We seem to have a bit of a problem with one of our exit interviews."

"Fridon?"

"The female." He looked at his screen for a moment. "Micali."

"Please tell me you didn't stick her in with a male. You know she can't talk to them." Heather rubbed her hand against her forehead.

"The agent assigned to her is female and she is talking but doesn't seem to understand the language we have on file. We brought in a translator which hasn't helped. We were hoping you would."

Heather nodded. She turned to Storm and touched his face before following the aid to another room. When she walked in Micali was in tears.

"Heather! They make no sense to me. Their words come across jumbled and when I try to answer they tell me they don't understand."

"I'm sorry, Micali." Heather sat beside her and took her hands. "It is easy to forget you don't have a universal translator. That is how most of us can understand other languages. I'm probably the exception. I learned your language and dialects because I had to work within your society. I'm here to help you."

The interviewer started asking questions, which Heather translated. One question caught her off guard. "Why are you asking that?"

"She is here instead of going back to her world. Why?"

"I have never known Earth to be so interested in anyone's personal life when it came to these exit interviews."

Heather turned back to Micali. "They wish to know if you are intimate with anyone."

"I don't understand."

"They want to know if you are sexually active with anyone."

"You know the answer to that." A light blush filled her cheeks.

"They need to hear you say it."

"Yes, Fridon." She glared at the woman asking the question. "He has promised to take me with him when he leaves."

Heather translated.

BARBARA DONLON BRADLEY

"How? He has to have the papers of ownership to take her off-world."

"And he has that. Storm owned Micali and gifted her to Fridon. There should be a record to prove all of this."

"And you have the papers?"

"Check your files. You'll find Storm paid for three women at the auction. Micali was one of them. But she was gifted to Fridon before that and that should be in your records as well."

"Thank you, commander."

Heather stood and gestured for Micali to follow her.

"Will they make me stay here?" Micali asked in a frightened voice.

"If we have to Storm will make you a free woman so you can make the decision yourself." Heather stopped and looked at her. "I promise you won't be forced to stay here even if I have to kidnap you to make sure you have the life you want."

———

Storm turned when the door of their guest room opened. He smiled when his mate walked in. The frown on her face had him worried. "Something wrong?"

"They questioned Micali's ownership." She walked up to where he was standing and wrapped her arms around his waist. "They're making it sound like they don't have any proof."

"But I paid for her." He growled as he wrapped his arms around her as well.

"I know, but there is something going on if they are behaving this way. I thought anyone was allowed to come and go as they pleased, but I could be wrong. Women have left the planet before, but always with their owner. With

250

Fridon as her owner, I didn't think they would be able to do anything, but I could be wrong. We're going to have to research this more."

"And we will." He brushed his fingers across her brow. "But first we need to wipe this frown off your face."

"I'm not frowning." She grabbed his fingers and kissed them.

He brought her hand to his mouth and kissed her palm. "You have a big heart and worry about something you don't need to. Fridon will bring her home, even if we have to kidnap her."

She laughed. "That is exactly what I told her."

"Good. Now I think you are overdressed." His lips were at her mark.

Heather tilted her head so he could have better access. "Have to say it's been a while since you said that."

"That luscious little garment had me wishing for a seal to slide my fingers through." He worked on the seal of her dress. "It had my attention the whole time."

"I noticed that. You always watch me, and I have gotten used to that, but the gleam in your glowing eyes was different while I wore that outfit."

"My heart, you are so beautiful, and that outfit showed your beauty." He eased her dress off her shoulders. "I found I like you showing off your body."

"So you want me running around half naked?"

"If I could have my way? Of course." He smiled as her dress pooled at her feet. "Much better."

Her fingers skimmed over his chest, brushing his mark in the process.

He grinned. "I see you have been as busy as I have been."

"I'd like to see you in skimpy outfits as well." She eased opened the seal to his trousers. "Perhaps next time you could be the one who is my property and I get to tell you your every move."

"Sounds like fun to me." He dropped his pants to the floor. "We could start right now."

"Really?" She said it as a joke.

"Having you tell me what you want? You always let me take control when we're intimate, but you do have your ways to make me do what you want even when I have other plans." He wrapped his arms around her.

"But you're so good at knowing what I want before I have to say anything."

"True." He nibbled on her neck. "But I can smell what your body wants so knowing what you need is easy, and I do enjoy the way you react to my touch. Like right now."

"What about right now?" She felt a little breathless when he worked his way down to her breast. He did things to her that no other man had been able to do.

"You are becoming excited by my touch. If I touch here." He brushed his fingers across the lower part of her stomach. "You send off a particular scent that tells me you enjoy my touch and want more, but if I touch you here." He slipped his hand down to her folds and started to caress her. Her breath caught in her throat. "But if I touch you here your desire spikes and you can't take much before you need to feel me inside you."

"Storm."

"I know, my heart." He picked her up and brought her to the bed. Laying her down, he continued to stroke her as he climbed on the bed with her. Storm centered himself before he thrust into her. A moan greeted him. Her muscles tightened against him. He slid out, then back in again. He knew she wouldn't be able to take much so set a quick pace to bring her to the edge quickly. Each stroke brought her closer. One particular stroke had her quaking in his arms.

"So close," she said, her voice barely a whisper.

He picked up the scent of how close she was. He loved how he could arouse her so quickly. Storm backed off just a little, wanting to prolong her orgasm. He changed his pace, making the strokes longer and as deep as she could take him in. He felt a ripple run through her, warning him no matter what he did she would explode.

Her hips shifted, changing the angle, and caused him to lose control for a moment. She was going to bring him with her. He could feel it racing toward him with every stroke. It filled his blood and pushed him to pick up the pace once again. Each time she accepted him in she sucked in her breath. Her muscles clamped down on him. "My heart."

It started deep inside, a slow spiral that filled his veins with heat. A desire to find that release clawed at him. He pounded into her, bringing her to the edge of her climax just as he reached his. She clutched at him as her body clenched. She arched against him as her mind flew along with her release.

"Wow."

He brushed hair out of her face. "Feeling a little boneless?"

She gave him a beautiful smile and a nod of her head. Speaking was just a little beyond her at the moment.

He found the fact he could take her breath away a wonderful thing and, in a few minutes, she would feel that breathless moment again.

———

Micali found Fridon standing at the window, staring out. The rooms the man Bear had given them were spacious, and well decorated. She felt out of place yet watching Fridon at the moment she realized he fit in a place like this. Could she live up to his expectations?

He turned when he heard the doors shut behind her.

"You were in your interview longer than the rest of us." He closed the distance between them and touched her shoulder. "Was there a problem?"

"They had to bring in Heather to translate for me." Already she was causing problems.

"Ah." He wrapped his arms around her. "You seem unhappy."

"They are questioning who my owner is." She leaned into his strength as she slipped her arms around his waist. "Perhaps this isn't a good idea."

"Are you changing your mind?"

"No. I—" Heather told her to say what was in her heart. "How am I to keep up with this?" She gestured around the room. "Doors that open without you touching them. Carrying on conversations with people you can't see."

"You'll be fine."

"Will I?" She shook her head. "I have seen the way these people act around you. Heather and Storm are powerful people, aren't they? And you are too, just by association."

"Storm is the next leader of my planet, and Heather is his mate."

"He is royalty?" She felt a little lightheaded.

"I guess you could look at it that way."

"And what are you? Some sort of prince?"

"No." He smiled, relaxing her a little. "I am a soldier being trained to be Storm's assistant, and he doesn't see himself as royalty. He'll hate it if you treat him any differently than before."

"I am nothing more than a servant, Fridon. My father had no land to call his own. I'm not worthy to be in the same room as you."

"That is years of conditioning speaking. Once you leave this planet your past will fade away. We don't have servants on my planet. Everyone works, including Heather and Storm."

"And what will I do?"

"What do you want to do?"

She blinked. "No one has ever asked me that before. You mean I can choose what I want to do with my life? Like being a healer?"

"If that is what you want."

"Oh, yes." Hope filled her. "But what if they won't let me go?"

"You have made your wishes known now. They can't keep you."

"They are investigating Storm's purchase of me." She leaned back to look up at him.

"He also bought his mate and the ambassador's daughter. They'd have to keep all of you if there was any question of who you belong to."

"Yes, but Storm bought me, not you. They can fight it because of something that small."

"The only person who had any claim to you is dead."

She sighed as she rested her head on his chest. "I hope you are right."

"Never underestimate the power of a Vespian. Everything will work out. Now, how about you smile for me?"

She tried, but worried about what could happen.

"Oh, come on, you can do better than that." He touched her face. "I know how to put a smile on your face."

"How?" She wasn't quite sure what he meant by what he said. He just smiled at her as his hands brushed the edges of her dress. Warmth filled her when she felt the brush of his fingers. Micali looked down to find her dress opened. "How did you do that?"

BARBARA DONLON BRADLEY

He took her hands and brought them to the edge of his shirt. "It opens like this."

The seal parted easily. She looked up at him and grinned. Slowly, she found all the seals on his clothes and opened them. They pooled at his feet.

Her clothing had gone the same way. Fridon slipped his arms under her knees and around her back and picked her up. Closing the distance between them and the bed, he deposited her on it before he joined her.

"How does my delicate flower feel now?" He brushed his hand against her collarbone.

"I'm still very worried." She touched his face. "No one has ever been so kind to me. I truly feel like your favorite."

"On Vespia we call our partners mates."

"Will I be your mate?" Her voice came out hesitant. It sounded so different than favorite. Favorite meant the female might not be the only woman, just the one who the male would turn to the most. "Do your people have more than one mate?"

"Only one mate, but we can have more than one sex partner." He paused as he eased her back onto the mattress. "We chose one mate for life. Sex, though, is something we believe should be celebrated. Our society allows us to share the joy of sex with others if our mate approves. Heather and Storm are a perfect example. They are mated and haven't taken other partners. They don't want anyone else. Since Heather is from Earth, it proves to our people that even though she isn't Vespian she can keep Storm happy enough to not want other partners."

"Is that important?" She touched his face, which was inches above hers.

"Before this mission, I didn't quite understand, but then I met you." He touched her face before he lowered his head to capture her lips with his for a quick but heated kiss. "When

256

they took you and Heather, I knew how Storm felt. I worried about what Undar would do to you. He still considered you his property. What he would make you do with him had me furious. I was glad when I found out he was dead because if he had harmed you in any way, I would have killed him myself."

"I am nothing."

"That isn't true." His hands slid down her body. "You are precious to me."

She didn't know what to say. No one ever called her precious. "And you are to me as well."

"You are so beautiful." He surged into her. "You have blossomed like the flower I call you. Undar was cruel and sadistic, and it could have ruined everything for you, but your trust in me humbles me. I don't want anyone but you." He started to move inside her, filling her with excitement.

She felt that wonderful feeling zinging through her blood, making her meet him thrust for thrust. It kept building inside, raising her desire higher and higher. Micali couldn't get enough.

Fridon seemed to know that because in one swift move he flipped them over. Letting her be in control. He touched her in all the right places. Everything felt so good. She picked up the pace, riding him faster. Racing with the release that was filling her. Her body clenched when it hit, causing her to lose control.

Fridon grabbed her hips and pumped into her a few more times before he hit his orgasm as well. She lay on top of him, sated and happy. May the rest of her life be this wonderful.

———

Storm narrowed his eyes as Bear drummed his fingers on the desk. "How long are you going to do that?"

"What?" He stopped in mid drum. "Sorry."

"I have a small problem." Bear sat back in his chair. "The planet's government is saying you can't take Micali and Lewmard from the planet. When you dragged Lewmard from the sale, there was an uproar, and the documents weren't entered correctly. There is no proof of your purchase."

"The man in charge of the sale gave me a verbal agreement and I saw him make a note in his pad. Shall I go and correct this?" Storm stood. His voice was calm, but anger boiled inside.

"No. We're already working on that. The money for the purchase was removed from your account so we just have to make them realize their mistake. But I think they are dragging their feet because of Lewmard. Murderer or not, he is a member of this society, and they want him to stand for his trials here."

"They will set him free to hold that grudge longer and it will expand to cover me as well." Storm shook his head. "No. He wanted to harm my mate so he will feel Vespian justice."

"Why can't you try him here?"

"And let these people see what we do to our criminals? They wouldn't understand our way." Storm looked at Bear. "He has hated Heather since the last time she was here. That hate isn't just going to go away because of some trial. I want to be sure he can never harm my mate again."

"It would be nice if I could reassure them, but I don't know what you do to your criminals either, and their biggest fear is that you'll kill him. Doesn't matter that he has killed, or the harm he has caused Heather each time he has tangled with her. They see you as an off-worlder who has threatened one of their own."

"It shouldn't matter what I do to him since he harmed my mate." Storm frowned. "If I was from this planet, it would be within my rights to kill him for damaging my property. I have studied their laws. I don't understand why they are upset because I want to take him from here."

"It doesn't make sense, but it is something we need to deal with. Are you willing to go on record to say you won't kill him, just incarcerate him?"

Storm rubbed the bridge of his nose. "I could give them an ultimatum. Either I kill him here or he gets to leave with me to face our laws."

"They might see that as a threat."

"If they want me to threaten them, then let me bring a battalion of ships here." He'd make sure the soldiers were all women, too. "That would shut them up quickly."

"Storm, we have to be diplomatic."

"So If I promise not to kill him they will let me take my family home? What about him? Do they understand that I am the next ruler of my planet? That any threat to Heather is a threat to me?"

"I have done my best to explain everything, yes."

"Fine." He didn't like it, but they all wanted to get as far away from here as quickly as they could.

———

The Vespian ship stood on the tarmac ready to take off. Storm had done as Bear had asked and released a statement on how Lewmard would be treated, but he hadn't heard back from the planet on how it was received.

Heather was the first to climb on the ship. Happy to go

home. This had been hard on her. Although the scars were gone and she had pushed what happened deep inside her, Storm didn't think the memories would disappear as quickly.

Fridon entered next, escorting Micali. As much as she said this was what she wanted, Storm wasn't sure. Leaving your home forever wasn't easy, and Micali was feeling the effects now.

Storm touched her arm. "Once you step on that ship there is no turning back."

She looked up at him and smiled. "I don't want to look back."

"Then I'll see you in a few minutes." He turned and waited for Bear to see them off. He knew their friend would be honest and let him know if he had convinced the planet.

It didn't take long. He came alone, and Storm knew the answer before Bear said a word. "They fear my style of justice."

"Fear drives people more than justice at times." He looked at the two guards that escorted him. "They want to offer their sincere apologies, but Lewmard escaped."

"What?"

"They aren't sure what happened, but he disappeared when they were switching him from one location to another."

"You know this won't stop me. I could take my ship into orbit and pinpoint his location, and they would never know."

"I know." Bear remained quiet as the two guards dragged a huge bag forward and left it at Storm's feet.

"What is this?"

"Consider it a present." Bear turned and took a few steps. "Take good care of her, Storm. Trouble seems to follow our girl."

"I have noticed that." He had several of his guards pick

up the bag and haul it into the ship. "Since Lewmard has disappeared are they still going to want to search the ship?"

"Yes. They search every ship as they leave. Just go along with what they want, and you'll be fine."

Storm thanked Bear and headed up the gangplank. A shout and a curse stopped him once the guards had the package up the gangplank and the doors closed.

"Open it so I can be sure it is what I think and then throw him in the brig. The one behind my room." Storm grinned when he confirmed what he hoped was in the bag. "Good, now I shall rest easy knowing this has been dealt with."

He went up to the bridge where his mate and his second-in-training waited. Micali stood beside him. Storm wrapped his arms around Heather as he spoke to Fridon. "Bear told me that Lewmard escaped and ran away, so there isn't much we can do about that, but he gave us a nice gift as a thank you for all we did."

"Really?" He smiled at Storm. "Then we can depart? I'll be happy to get back to Vespia."

"All we need is clearance."

"The planet's security is asking permission to board. Why do they wish to search us?" Fridon looked at Storm. "The papers clearing Micali are on file. I made sure."

"Bear said it was part of their protocol." Storm smiled. He took Heather's hand. "Come, let's greet them. The sooner they do their inspection the sooner we can leave."

"Your ship needs to be cleared for takeoff." The official looked up at Storm as he approached the area they were being held in. Sweat broke out on his brow when he realized just how large Storm was. "I am the one to conduct the search to make sure you have no contraband."

"And if I say no?" Storm crossed his arms over his chest.

"My heart. We have nothing to hide. Let them search."

Heather touched his arm, playing her part in keeping these guards distracted. Searching too hard after they got the gift from Bear would cause problems.

"You wish to argue with me in front of strangers?" he growled at her.

"I only wish to keep this from escalating to war." She pressed her hand against his heart. "Vespia would destroy this planet quickly."

"True." He wrapped his arms around her. "We could come in and take over. Defeating them would only take hours and I would send only women to prove a point."

"I like that idea. I hate the way they treat women, and it would show them just what a woman is capable of." Heather touched her mate's face. "I am sorry you think I was trying to argue with you. Guess I'm feeling a little tired."

"Perhaps you should go and lie down for a while." He touched her face as well. "I'll join you when we're done here."

"May we search?" The head guard's voice shook a little as he asked. Watching them interact had him on edge.

Storm stared at the man for a moment before he nodded. "But you will have a Vespian guard with each of you at all times. This is our territory, and I will not give you the chance to plant something then try to incriminate us."

"We would never do that."

"Would you allow my people to search without an escort?" Storm stared him down.

He shook his head, knowing Storm was right. "Lead the way."

Storm waved the security he had picked out personally for this search. He looked at the man who was in charge. "I go with you."

They worked their way through sections assigned to

them. Storm didn't say a word as the man searched through each of the cabins he had been assigned. They approached Fridon's room.

"This the man who owns Micali?"

"I own Micali and gave her to him."

"And the papers are on file?"

"Of course." Anger laced his voice. "Do I need to prove this again and again?"

"No." The man looked around the small cabin, opening doors, looking under the bed or any other place he thought where something could be hiding. Once he was sure there was nothing to find, he moved onto the next set of rooms. He worked his way down until he hit the last room on his list.

"That is my quarters, and my mate is resting."

"I must search the room."

"You disturb her, and I will take your head."

"I promise not to do anything to upset her." He walked in and stopped when he spotted her naked form lying on the bed. She lay on her side, her hair spilling over the pillow. Eyes closed, Heather had the cover draped over her in such a way the guard couldn't see more than a hint of Storm's favorite places, but it allowed most of her to be exposed to his gaze. She had posed in such a provocative position it made him forget why he went into the room for a minute, which was her goal.

Storm wished he could touch that silky smooth skin.

So I did a good job then.

My heart, if we were alone, I'd show you how this image affects me.

Now we need to see if he can be distracted as easily.

Storm agreed. He did his best not to rush the man out of the room. He needed to let him decide he had seen enough. Heather's mind caressed his, keeping him calm when the man crossed a little too close to where she lay. He made like he was going to look under the bed when Storm took one step forward.

"I will not disturb her, but I must look."

Storm knew there was nothing under there. Heather kept their rooms meticulously clean, but Heather exposed herself so the guard wouldn't look too closely at the wall behind the bed where Lewmard was hidden.

Storm frowned but gave the man a curt nod. "One of her lashes flutters and you're done."

He nodded as he dropped to his hands and knees. Heather sighed and shifted her leg. The man stared at the shapely calf so close to his face. Storm cleared his throat and the guard remembered why he was in the room in the first place. Giving the underside of the bed a cursory glance, he stood and opened a few closet doors, finding nothing out of the ordinary.

He headed to the door. Storm followed him out and closed the door behind him. "Are you satisfied?"

"I need to speak to the rest of my men, but I see nothing out of the ordinary."

Storm led him back to the main bay where several of his security stood with several of the planet's guards. They had finished their search as well. Each one looked at their leader and shook their heads. So far, no one found anything, which was what Storm expected.

Fridon joined him. "Are they finished yet? We have finished our preflight checklist."

"We still have two escorts out." Storm pressed a button on his collar. A few moments later, the two pairs missing came into view.

Once the man talked to his last two men, he turned to Storm. "Nothing was found."

"So do we have clearance?"

"I must speak with the minister."

"You are dragging your feet even though you have searched this ship and have found nothing. Shall I come back with five of our fastest ships? It wouldn't take long for my people to subdue your planet." He turned to Fridon, anger rolling off him. "I am done with these people. You are in control. I'm going to spend time with my mate. Let her ease my anger away."

———

Heather remained on the bed, waiting for Storm to return.

"That stupid little man is still keeping us." He stopped and grinned when he saw she was still draped on the bed. "If he hadn't been in the room earlier, you'd be thoroughly satisfied right now."

"So would you." She shifted so she could look up at him.

"Have you been in that same position since I left?"

"Pretty much." She laid her head back down on one arm she had been resting it on when he entered. "Your eyes held too much promise for me to move."

"And what did I promise with my eyes?" He opened the seal of his uniform.

"That you would fill me again and again until I scream." She smiled when he removed his uniform and climbed on the bed.

"Now that sounds like something I can do. The question is where I should start." His hands slid across her stomach. "I know what you want me to do, but I do enjoy surprising you."

"I know." She hadn't moved, still on her side, looking up at her mate with promise. "This whole mission has been you being the dominant one. You could let me be in control."

"I know you don't believe me." He pressed a kiss to her

bare shoulder. "But you're in control a lot more than you realize."

"Uh-huh." She lifted her head and propped it up on a hand. "And who is the one who is always trying to control how long he can play with his playground before it explodes?"

He laughed as he stretched out beside her. He brushed hair off her neck, but the way she was laying had her mark on the other side.

"Sorry. In order to get the right look I had to lie this way. I can move if you wish."

"You look beautiful, and I hate to destroy the image you created, but you know my hands have a mind of their own." He brushed his hands across her hips. "You'll be moving soon enough."

"Those hands of yours do like touching me." One of her hands reached out to trace the plains of the muscles on his chest. "I seem to have a problem with that as well."

"I have corrupted you." He moved until she was lying on her back, and he had himself propped up over her. "Something I'm proud of."

"You should be." She wrapped one leg around his hip, pulling him closer. "Sex wasn't big on my list of things to do before I met you. Now I can't seem to get enough."

"You just needed the right man to unlock the desire you had bottled up inside." He dipped his head to her mark, sucking the delicate tissue into his mouth. His desire for her was so strong he was willing to forgo any foreplay if she was.

"Oh, boy, did I find him." She tilted her head as she shifted under him.

"My heart." He couldn't stop himself as he thrust into her. "I'm afraid your provocative pose had me fantasizing this moment for too long."

"Not going to complain, since I was thinking the same thing." She adjusted herself so she could slip her other leg around his hips. The moment she did that he slipped in deeper. A low moan escaped her. "That feels so good."

"Glad to hear it." Storm set a pace that drew a sigh out of Heather. "Because I love the way you grip me so intimately."

"You talk too much." She arched up against him.

"Sometimes I do."

"Then let's just enjoy this moment." She felt little frissons of heat fill her. Immense joy surrounded her. Shifting her hips, she met each thrust and soon felt the beginnings of her release start to surround her. Everything tingled. She picked up the tempo, finding the orgasm pending so close yet just out of her reach.

Storm continued to move in and out while he worked on the soft tissue of her neck. She felt the beginning of her climax deep in her core. Slowly, like a flame, it licked along her bloodstream until it filled her. An all-encompassing euphoria. Heather held her breath as it finally washed over her. She floated amongst the stars for a moment, before she landed back in her body, looking up at the man who always knew how to make her soar.

"My heart."

———

Storm stood in front of the monitor with Lewmard at his side. In order to do what he wanted, he had to get permission from the Elders. He grinned when his mother appeared on the screen.

"This is the man who whipped your mate?" She studied Lewmard. "He looks too weak to withstand our penal colony. Perhaps it would be better if you killed him."

"Yes, Ma'am, that was my first thought, but I promised his planet I wouldn't kill him. As the next ruler of our planet, I must keep my word."

Lewmard had kept his mouth shut until then. "Ruler?"

"Quiet." Storm growled at him.

"I see he had no idea who you were, Storm, or what power you and Heather wield." She paused for a moment. "We will make a decision and let you know."

The screen went blank.

"You are letting a woman decide my fate?" Lewmard snapped.

"You are a mean, petty, little man." Storm had him by the throat and off the ground again. "That woman is the current leader of my planet and my mother so watch what you say. Not every planet is as backward as yours. She will confer with the rest of the council to decide what to do with you. If they decide you aren't worth the fuel to detour to the planet, I'll have to come up with another way to dispose of you."

"You could always jettison him into the void of space," commented Heather. "He does deserve that."

"True, but I can't push the button." He dropped Lewmard on the deck. "I did promise not to kill him."

"Not sure why you're so worried about that, since they don't know we have him, but I would be happy to push the button." Heather stared at Lewmard. "It would be a pleasure to end his life."

"His people would never know, but I would. My promise stands as long as the council goes along with my request." Storm crossed his arms over his chest. "But it might be a good idea to get Fridon to help you get him ready for the airlock. Just in case."

She smiled and nodded.

"Wait!"

"What? You going to plea for mercy when you never had

that for my mate?" Storm shook his head. "Talk to the woman you whipped twice. She is the only one who can stop this now."

Lewmard hung his head in defeat.

———

The ship orbited the planet where those Vespians who committed crimes were sent. Storm had gotten permission from the Elders as he expected. As aggressive as they were as a race, they never killed those who committed crimes against other Vespians. Not when they could put them here to be rehabilitated.

"I was really looking forward to pushing that button." Heather walked with him to the hanger bay.

Storm laughed. "I know my heart, but this is better. The people here might have broken our laws, but they are still Vespian and know the price for harming the next ruler's mate. He will learn his lesson."

"Can I ask what will happen now?" She looked up at her mate.

"Since he's not a Vespian he doesn't deserve to face the council. The security on this planet is trained to judge those who have committed crimes that the Elders don't sentence." Storm nodded to Fridon when he entered the bay. "Then he'll have to face the people sent here. They won't take kindly to what he did to you. I promise."

"Everything is ready, sir."

"Good. This shouldn't take too long, but I must stay until he gets his sentence, since I am his accuser." He took Heather into his arms and kissed her. "You can relax, knowing he will not be able to harm anyone else ever again."

"I will."

Storm climbed into the shuttle that would take them to the planet. After securing Lewmard, Storm had shoved him back into the bag he had been delivered in and had several guards wrestle it into the cargo hold behind him. He pulled out of the main ship's bay and cruised into the atmosphere of the planet below. Once he landed, he lifted the bag and slung it over his shoulder.

He walked into the main hall and everyone there snapped to attention. They were surprised to see Head of Security. The message he had sent hadn't made it to them yet. He grinned. Someone would hear of this later.

"Sir?" The guard on duty stepped up to him. "Is this an impromptu inspection?"

"No. I have brought a new prisoner. He has violent tendencies and non-Vespian."

"I will pull the proper people together so he can be tried."

Storm nodded as he loaded his grievances against the man into the system. It didn't take long. As he expected, Lewmard was found guilty. Being the next leader of the planet had its perks. They never even let him out of the bag. He carted him down a long hall and out a large set of heavy doors.

They now stood in a wooded area. Storm spoke loudly so he could be heard as he dropped his burden down. "I have some fresh meat for you."

Lewmard struggled to get out of the bag.

Several people came forward. When they saw him, they whispered his name.

"They know you?" He cowered where he stood, noticing that he was so much smaller than any of the people here.

"I put several of them here for their own good." Storm released his restraints, then shoved him forward. He spoke louder so he could be heard. "This man caused physical harm to my mate. Vespian law doesn't allow anyone to harm another. As several of you know."

One stepped forward. Storm recognized him. He had been sent there for harming a fellow officer. His violent tendencies had been reprimanded several times before he was sentenced and had actually already paid his time, but when offered the opportunity to return to Vespia he declined, liking it on the penal colony better. There were several people who had done that over the years. "We will teach him how to show proper respect to the next leader of Vespia."

Storm nodded and turned.

"We have a woman here." The same man spoke.

He turned back, wondering why they brought this up. There were lots of females here.

"She is pregnant."

"How far along?"

"I just found out." The young woman stepped out so Storm could see her.

"You sure?" He grinned, realizing he sounded like Heather.

"Pretty sure."

"I will send my personal physician." A child? No child could survive here on the colony. "I will make the council aware so we can make accommodations to move you."

"I don't wish to be moved. My mate is here, and we want to stay, but my child needs to go to family on Vespia." She stepped close to the man who had told him of the pregnancy.

"Giving your child up will be hard." He needed to speak to the council. In the past, women from this post would be moved to a safe place until the birth of their child. Then the decision to send her back here or allow her to stay on Vespia would be decided. But the other women never demanded to stay because of their mate. Did she know that he had already fulfilled his sentence? Perhaps she was the reason he stayed.

"I know, but the safety of our child is more important."

Storm agreed. He nodded. They could isolate her until she gave birth, but he would let Kuarto examine her and decide what should be done. Storm turned from the small crowd gathering around Lewmard and walked back into the security center. He spoke to the security guard on duty. "When was the last time you did scans of the inmates?"

"Two days ago."

"I need the scans and files of the people I just spoke to." He didn't know their names, but he knew the camera watching would identify them quickly.

"Of course, sir. I shall have it uploaded to the ship."

"Good." Storm signed the forms he needed to make Lewmard's sentence legal, then headed to his ship. By the time he boarded the main ship the inmates' files were waiting for him. He went to his room to read.

Heather entered right after him. She wrapped her arms around him as he pulled up the files.

"Where have you been hiding?"

"On the bridge. Waiting for you to come back. I headed here the moment you started to dock." She leaned back to look up at him. "How did you beat me here?"

"Long legs?" He pulled her into his lap. "I have a few files to work through before I can give you all my focus."

Heather looked at the picture of the young woman on the screen. "New girlfriend?"

"Ha! You would be far too jealous. She is an inmate who is pregnant. It is rare, but when it happens, we do our best to reintegrate them back into society. Unless they want to stay."

"Does that happen?" she wrapped her arms around his neck.

"It is a life they get used to. Some find Vespian society too mundane once they have been here. As a race, we love a challenge." He nuzzled her neck. "I think I have proved that with you."

"You consider me a challenge?"

He laughed. "Let me finish what I need to do, and I'll prove to you how much I enjoy that challenge."

———

Heather sighed as the ship landed on Vespia. "It's good to be home."

"It is." Storm pulled her against him. "Ready, Fridon?"

"Yes, sir." He turned to the frightened woman beside him. "Are you ready to meet your new home?"

She nodded and clutched his hand like it was a lifeline.

"Micali, you will love Vespia. I promise."

Storm stepped off the ship first, followed by his mate, then Fridon stepped off and waited for Micali to join him. She looked around in wide-eyed wonder. People in the area looked at her with curiosity. She stuck close to him.

"So what do we have here?" asked one of his friends.

"This is Micali. I have asked her to be my mate." Fridon looked down at Micali as she clung to him.

"Another off-worlder? I believe our commander has rubbed off on you."

"Dare you to say that to his face." He looked at Storm, who was talking to his mother at the moment.

"Never! You know I have the greatest respect for Heather and am only teasing." His friend slapped him on the back. "You have been spending a lot of time with Storm. Then you

BARBARA DONLON BRADLEY

bring home a pretty little stranger just like he did. You know we're going to say something."

"And you're not happy unless you are causing trouble."

"Exactly." He turned to Micali. "Welcome to Vespia. Hope you like it here."

She nodded.

Fridon smiled as he shifted his hold on her. "If you'll excuse me?" He didn't give his friend a chance to stop him. Pulling Micali along with him, he walked toward a small transport that he had requested.

"Where are we going?"

"I want to show you my world. Let you see firsthand why we love it here so much." He entered first, heading toward the pilot seat.

"Micali, come and strap in while I get this airborne."

She sat in the chair he pointed to and snapped on her restraints. "These are different from the ones on the big ship."

"The spaceship has special ones because of the space travel. Leaving and entering an atmosphere can harm you if you're not properly protected. We won't be leaving the atmosphere this time. These restraints are designed to keep you from rolling on the floor during takeoff."

"And why is there a bed in here?"

"Special request." He grinned at her. "It could take some time for you to see the whole planet and I wouldn't want you to get bored."

"I don't think I could ever get bored with you."

"Then let's go."

Heather played with her daughter on the floor while their son followed his father around their rooms. "Will they allow him to take her as a mate?"

"I have spoken to the council, and they agree she could stay. As far as being his mate, only time will tell. Mating outside our race is rare, but it does happen. She'll be checked out by the medical staff. If they find she can get pregnant easily, they will approve the match immediately." Storm picked up their son and sat down next to his mate. "We try to bring people in who will contribute to our society. I'm sure Earth does the same thing. Micali has no training we can use to accept her."

"She did show signs of being able to heal. I think she'd be good in the medical field and would make her more valuable to Vespia. I fear if they don't allow this, Fridon will go where he can be with her."

"And I made the council aware of that. Don't worry, my heart, they will make the right decision. They always do."

Their son walked to his mother and climbed into her lap. He curled around his sister, and they fell asleep.

"They have missed you." Storm brushed a kiss against his son, then his daughter's head.

"My little hearts. I missed them too." She looked up at her mate. "Help me move them?"

He picked up their son then took their daughter when Heather handed her to him. Once she was standing, she took their daughter back. With Storm's arm around her, she walked to the children's room and placed their daughter in her bed. Storm took their son and did the same thing.

"So now they are sleeping what do you wish to do?" asked Storm as he focused on Heather.

"We need to work on the naming ceremony." She knew what he was hinting at but sometimes it was fun to act like she had no clue to what he wanted.

"It can wait until dinner with the family." He took her hand and drew her out of the children's room.

"So we have a little time then." She grinned as she pressed her hand against his chest. "May I have a few moments? I have a surprise for you."

"Really?" He grinned back. "What do you have planned for me?"

"You'll see." She disappeared into their room, which he always took as a good sign. When she came back in, she had a robe on.

"What is this?"

"Think of it as a present to unwrap."

He came within inches and touched her face. "A present? I have enjoyed the other gifts you have given me."

"I think you're going to enjoy this one too." She placed the ties of her robe into his hands. He undid the cinch she had put in the belt and let it drop to the ground.

The demicup top she wore was made out of a see-through lavender lace instead of the bejeweled top she had worn while on Aruka. The skirt was close to the one she wore on the planet as well. It was made of a light purple lace at the top and a see-through material made up the rest of the skirt except for the very bottom, which also had the lace.

"I thought you hated what that outfit represented." Seeing it brought the glow to his eyes.

"It did, until I saw what it did to you. Constantly. It made me realize that it wasn't the outfit that I hated but the way I was treated. You made me feel sexy and special in this. I enjoyed the way it affected you. How you would watch me as I moved."

"You are beautiful and my heart." He stepped up to her and cupped her cheek. "I don't care what you wear as long as you are happy, although I do like what I'm looking at right now."

She stood proud as his eyes skimmed over her, taking in the way the lace hugged her form. He drew her to him, capturing her lips with his as he pulled her into his embrace, lifting her so her feet couldn't touch the floor anymore. He intensified the kiss, his tongue begging for entrance, which she gave. His tongue swept into her mouth, dancing with hers. Heather melted against him as she got caught up in the desire filling her. His clothing blocked her hands from touching his warm skin.

She searched for the seal of his uniform, slipping her hands inside to feel the rapid beat of his heart. Storm broke the kiss and sat her down long enough to pull his uniform off before taking her back in his arms. He lifted her and carried her to the bed, depositing her first then climbing on the bed. The glow in his eyes and the smile on his face made Heather's insides flutter.

He kissed her exposed stomach, then the valley between her breasts before he worked his way up to her mark. He used one hand to slide up her body, starting at mid-thigh, he caressed her skin to her hip then her waist until he reached the lacy top she wore. Storm palmed her breast through the material, brushing the tip as his fingers moved to the center. The closure opened and his hand went back to her breast.

Storm kissed his way down to her collarbone then to the other breast, drawing the pebbled peak into his mouth. His tongue swirled around the tip of her breast, before sucking on the rosy tissue and drawing a moan from her.

"Storm." Her voice was soft, but her need great.

His other hand slid down her stomach, under the lace and to her core. She arched up against his hand as he massaged her, drawing her closer to her orgasm. The wonderfully soft caresses sent her spiraling out of control.

He shifted his attention back to her throat as he centered himself and entered her. Her body vibrated at the sweet invasion. Storm gave her a few moments to regain control before he started to drive into her. Each time he filled her she felt little tremors. Her need for release licked at her insides. Wanting more, she met him thrust for thrust, knowing what she desired was just beyond her reach.

Storm changed the tempo much to her frustration then delight. She could feel him rub against the sensitive spot where the most powerful orgasms came from, just the right amount of friction to push her to the edge, but not over. Whenever she got close, he would shift to back off a little just to bring her to the edge again.

"Please." It was all she could say.

"My heart." He drove into her once more and her world shattered. Their minds entwined and made their climaxes twice as powerful. Heather's muscles tighten against him, pushing him to pound into her, hitting his orgasm when she hit hers.

A tear escaped her eye.

"Why are you crying, my heart?"

"That was so beautiful and helped me release the last of the hate I had inside." She touched his face. "I shall never fear this outfit again. Thank you."

———

Toki wore her formal robes. The twins stood between their parents, looking so cute in their formal Vespian outfits. She had the joy of naming them. Heather and Storm had tried so hard to find out what she had chosen, but true to her position, she kept it to herself. Choosing names had to be done right. Uncle had gone into great detail on how to do this, but he knew the first names she had to choose would be for her niece and nephew.

She made a small gesture and Storm stepped forward

with his son. Once he stood in front of Toki Storm stepped back to stand with Heather and their daughter. Kneeling down to speak to her nephew, she whispered his name into his ear.

"'Terrik?" he tried to whisper, but the volume of his voice was so loud everyone could hear.

She said it again.

He turned to his parents. "Moma! My name is Pruter-rik." He raced to his father with a big grin on his face.

"Do you know what the name means?" asked his father.

"Protector."

Storm smiled at his mate as he kissed the top of his son's head.

Her niece was next. The tiny girl bounced over to her aunt, so full of joy and happiness. She knelt in front of her as well and whispered her name in her ear. She nodded and turned to leave.

"You need to say your name." Toki stopped her niece and spoke softly to her.

"I do? Why?" Big violet eyes looked up at her in confusion.

"There is power in being the first one to say it to the crowd." She touched the cherub's little face.

"Oh." She turned to her parents. "I am to say my name out loud?"

She questioned things the way her mother did. Toki smiled. She was a lot like her mother and her brother was a lot like his father. Her brother and his mate had their hands full. Heather nodded.

"It is very pretty, Mommy. My name is Zunarka."

"It is very pretty." Heather walked to her daughter and scooped her up. "But I will still call you Bubbles from time to time."

"I don't mind. I like bubbles. They are pretty, too."

"Just like you, sweetheart."

Storm came to her side and kissed his daughter on the head before drawing Heather to him for a heated kiss. "My heart."

Their son followed Storm, who picked him up and held him in his arms.

"Mama?"

"Yes. Terrik?"

"You stay now? Missed you."

"I missed you too. Very much. Although we have to travel from time to time, I promise to take you with us when we can. When we can't, I will work on creating a link that will keep us together so we'll always be close. You three and your father are my universe, and I always want to be close."

THE END

———

Don't miss out on your next favorite book!

Join the Satin Romance mailing list
www.satinromance.com/mail.html

THANK YOU FOR READING

———

Did you enjoy this book?

We invite you to leave a review at your favorite book site, such as Goodreads, Amazon, Barnes & Noble, etc.

DID YOU KNOW THAT LEAVING A REVIEW...

- Helps other readers find books they may enjoy.
- Gives you a chance to let your voice be heard.
- Gives authors recognition for their hard work.
- Doesn't have to be long. A sentence or two about why you liked the book will do.

ABOUT THE AUTHOR

Writing for Barbara Donlon Bradley started innocently enough, like most she kept diaries, journals, and wrote an occasional letter but she also had a vivid imagination and wrote scenes and short stories adding characters to her favorite shows and comic books.

As time went on, she found the passion for writing to be a strong drive for her. Humor is also very strong in her life. No matter how hard she tries to write something deep and dark, it will never happen. That humor bleeds into her writing. Since she can't beat it, she has learned to use it to her advantage.

Now she lives in Tidewater Virginia with a cat who thinks he owns everything, her husband and daughter.

www.barbaradonlonbradley.com

ALSO BY BARBARA DONLON BRADLEY

Novels

Love Is…

A Portrait in Time

Love on the Run

Love's Quest Series

A Quest For Love

Magical Quest

Desire Series

Dominated by Desire

Passionate Desire

Animal Desire

Unwanted Desire

Hesitant Desire

www.ingramcontent.com/pod-product-compliance
Lightning Source LLC
Chambersburg PA
CBHW030958260626
47169CB00002B/602